"Grant, wake up," Brigid said, shaking the man by his shoulder

Please be alive, she thought. Please be alive.

Grant shifted a little with the force of Brigid's shaking, then his eyes flickered open and he smiled. "What? Did I miss something?" he asked. His voice sounded weak and quiet, like he had just woken up, and his eyes were bloodshot.

"I thought you were zoning out on me," Brigid said, smiling briefly. "Don't do that again."

Grant began to reply, but the words were lost as he began coughing. He rolled on his side and covered his mouth with his hand. When he drew his hand away it was spattered in black spittle. "Wh-what is this?" he asked, bewildered. He didn't sound like an ex-Magistrate to Brigid anymore—he sounded like a lost child, frightened by something he didn't understand.

"I think you may have become infected," Brigid said, hating the words as they left her mouth, as if saying them had somehow made it happen, made it real. "That one who jumped you, he…spat at you."

Other titles in this series:

Outer Darkness
Armageddon Axis
Wreath of Fire
Shadow Scourge
Hell Rising
Doom Dynasty
Tigers of Heaven
Purgatory Road
Sargasso Plunder
Tomb of Time
Prodigal Chalice
Devil in the Moon
Dragoneye
Far Empire
Equinox Zero
Talon and Fang
Sea of Plague
Awakening
Mad God's Wrath
Sun Lord
Mask of the Sphinx
Uluru Destiny
Evil Abyss
Children of the Serpent
Successors
Cerberus Storm
Refuge
Rim of the World
Lords of the Deep
Hydra's Ring

Closing the Cosmic Eye
Skull Throne
Satan's Seed
Dark Goddess
Grailstone Gambit
Ghostwalk
Pantheon of Vengeance
Death Cry
Serpent's Tooth
Shadow Box
Janus Trap
Warlord of the Pit
Reality Echo
Infinity Breach
Oblivion Stone
Distortion Offensive
Cradle of Destiny
Scarlet Dream
Truth Engine
Infestation Cubed
Planet Hate
Dragon City
God War
Genesis Sinister
Savage Dawn
Sorrow Space
Immortal Twilight
Cosmic Rift
Necropolis
Shadow Born

James Axler
Outlanders®

JUDGMENT PLAGUE

A GOLD EAGLE BOOK FROM
WORLDWIDE®

TORONTO • NEW YORK • LONDON
AMSTERDAM • PARIS • SYDNEY • HAMBURG
STOCKHOLM • ATHENS • TOKYO • MILAN
MADRID • WARSAW • BUDAPEST • AUCKLAND

Recycling programs
for this product may
not exist in your area.

First edition November 2014

ISBN-13: 978-0-373-63884-0

JUDGMENT PLAGUE

Copyright © 2014 by Worldwide Library

Special thanks to Rik Hoskin for his contribution to this work.

Printed in U.S.A.

It is better to murder during time of plague.
                    —English Proverb

What, will these hands ne'er be clean?
                    —William Shakespeare,
                      Macbeth

The Road to Outlands—
From Secret Government Files to the Future

Almost two hundred years after the global holocaust, Kane, a former Magistrate of Cobaltville, often thought the world had been lucky to survive at all after a nuclear device detonated in the Russian embassy in Washington, D.C. The aftermath—forever known as skydark—reshaped continents and turned civilization into ashes.

Nearly depopulated, America became the Deathlands—poisoned by radiation, home to chaos and mutated life forms. Feudal rule reappeared in the form of baronies, while remote outposts clung to a brutish existence.

What eventually helped shape this wasteland were the redoubts, the secret preholocaust military installations with stores of weapons, and the home of gateways, the locational matter-transfer facilities. Some of the redoubts hid clues that had once fed wild theories of government cover-ups and alien visitations.

Rearmed from redoubt stockpiles, the barons consolidated their power and reclaimed technology for the villes. Their power, supported by some invisible authority, extended beyond their fortified walls to what was now called the Outlands. It was here that the rootstock of humanity survived, living with hellzones and chemical storms, hounded by Magistrates.

In the villes, rigid laws were enforced—to atone for the sins of the past and prepare the way for a better future. That was the barons' public credo and their right-to-rule.

Kane, along with friend and fellow Magistrate Grant, had upheld that claim until a fateful Outlands expedition. A displaced piece of technology...a question to a keeper of the archives...a vague clue about alien masters—and their world shifted radically. Suddenly, Brigid Baptiste, the archivist, faced summary execution, and Grant a quick termination. For Kane there was forgiveness if he pledged his unquestioning allegiance to Baron Cobalt and his unknown masters and abandoned his friends.

But that allegiance would make him support a mysterious and alien power and deny loyalty and friends. Then what else was there?

Kane had been brought up solely to serve the ville. Brigid's only link with her family was her mother's red-gold hair, green eyes and supple form. Grant's clues to his lineage were his ebony skin and powerful physique. But Domi, she of the white hair, was an Outlander pressed into sexual servitude in Cobaltville. She at least knew her roots and was a reminder to the exiles that the outcasts belonged in the human family.

Parents, friends, community—the very rootedness of humanity was denied. With no continuity, there was no forward momentum to the future. And that was the crux—when Kane began to wonder if there was a future.

For Kane, it wouldn't do. So the only way was out—way, way out.

After their escape, they found shelter at the forgotten Cerberus redoubt headed by Lakesh, a scientist, Cobaltville's head archivist, and secret opponent of the barons.

With their past turned into a lie, their future threatened, only one thing was left to give meaning to the outcasts. The hunger for freedom, the will to resist the hostile influences. And perhaps, by opposing, end them.

Chapter 1

The Geiger counter on the dashboard flashed red, ticking over into the danger zone. For a moment, DePaul's fixed expression slipped, his eyes widening as he saw the telltale flicker that meant they had entered a patch of radioactivity.

"Chin up, rookie," Irons said from the seat beside him. "Nothing out there I ain't seen a hundred times."

Irons was a magistrate in the barony of Cobaltville. He was in his mid-forties, with thick hair that had turned steel-gray, lines around his eyes and mouth, and a scar on his chin where some deviant had taken a potshot at him a dozen years before. He wore the uniform of a magistrate—black molded armor that sheathed his body like an insect's shell, a bright red shield painted across the left breast to show his rank of office. His helmet was poised on the seat behind him, within easy reach. It was Irons's job to monitor DePaul—a rookie magistrate in his final year of training, following in the footsteps of his father.

Irons sat next to DePaul, flashing him that fatherly smile that spoke of how he was indulging the lad, not teaching him.

Up front, Bellevue was driving the SandCat, navigating the dirt roads that reached out from Cobaltville like spokes, unpaved and unmarked. Bellevue was a tall man with skin so dark it looked like licorice, picking up the highlights of any illumination so that it seemed to have a sheen. Bellevue was twenty-five and had been active in the field for almost a decade. Like DePaul, like Irons, he had followed in his father's footsteps, born solely for the task of being a magistrate, drilled from a young age in the ways of Cobaltville law.

"Coming up on Mesa Verde," Bellevue said from his place at the steering wheel.

DePaul peered out the windshield at the towering sandstone structures that dominated the horizon. Brown-orange in color, the colossal rocks had been carved with windows and doors by human hands, hundreds of years before.

"Pretty different to home, ain't it?" Irons said.

DePaul shook his head in wonder. "I've never seen anything like this." It was true. He had never had cause to leave the walled confines of Cobaltville in all his seventeen years. This was his first trip beyond ville limits and out into the wild.

DePaul was a young man with jet-black hair and a narrow face. His hair was cut magistrate short and slicked back from his forehead, revealing his widow's peak. He had dark eyes, a darker brown than his father's, and those eyes seemed to take in every detail, every nuance of whatever was placed before them. He had been small for his age, but the late blossoming of puberty had given him taut muscles and long legs, and now he regularly outmatched his strongest classmates in any test of physical strength. He remained slender, however, giving him the appearance of a spectre when he dressed in the dark armor of a magistrate.

DePaul was well on the way to becoming a full-fledged one. He had excelled in exams, scoring top marks in knowledge and interpretation of the law. That had not come as a surprise to his father; the boy's memory had been prodigious even at the age of ten. DePaul showed a steady hand in stress tests, was a crack shot and had survived to become last man standing in five of the six simulations he had been placed in with his classmates this year. In the remaining simulation he had come second only when one of his own team betrayed him at the finishing task.

DePaul was quick-thinking and quick to adapt, and he had displayed endurance that belied his slender frame.

Irons liked the kid, had warmed to him over the last few weeks that they had been stationed together. He had taken DePaul on a few regular patrols of the ville and down in the Tartarus Pits. The lad was all right—quiet maybe, but all right. He certainly had a memory on him; his attention to detail was up there with the best of the magistrates. He reminded Irons a lot of his father, a good mag who had taken a knock to the head during a routine pit patrol and never recovered. His son would go far, further even than the old man—Magistrate Irons was certain of that. But his recommendation would come another day, once they had completed a circuit of the Outlands and investigated rumors of a mutie farm located close to the Mesa Verde structures.

Bellevue had had less interaction with DePaul, but he remembered his father and could see the old man's looks in the kid's face, and his mannerisms. The youth came from good stock, and that counted for a lot.

The SandCat bumped over a patch of rough ground, its engine emitting a low rumble as it navigated the uneven terrain. Exclusive to the Magistrate Division, the SandCat was an armored vehicle with a low-slung, blocky chassis supported by a pair of flat, retractable tracks. Its exterior was a ceramic armaglass compound that could shrug off small arms fire, and it featured a swiveling gun turret up top armed with twin USMG-73 heavy machine guns.

They were moving out away from Cobaltville on a routine patrol of the surrounding areas. Forays like this were a necessary chore, to ensure there was nothing brewing in the lands near the ville that might challenge the baron's rule. Baron Cobalt was very shrewd and protective concerning the retention of his power.

Bellevue turned the wheel and the SandCat's engine growled with a low purr as it bumped over a patch of loose shingle and began to ascend a slope behind the Mesa. Some of this land had been used for research by the barons; some of it might even now be in use, for all the magistrates in the SandCat knew. Bellevue just stuck to the path and followed the target beacon that his onboard software had set before him.

A moment later, the armored vehicle nudged over the incline and began to descend toward a ragtag sprawl of tents surrounding a cattle pen.

"Well, lookee here," Bellevue muttered as he pumped gas to the engine.

The pen was populated not by cattle but by muties. There were at least fifty of them, and they each wore a see-through plastic, one-piece suit as they sat or lay sprawled out in the scorching midday sun like sunbathers. The muties were humanoid, and looked human enough, except that beneath their transparent coverings they were utterly hairless and their skin was red

and cracked, with blisters and sores all over. That may
have been the effect of the sun, though some of it was
a natural defense for these types. Called sweaties, they
oozed a poisonous compound from their sweat glands
that, when imbibed, had a hallucinogenic effect on humans. People farmed them sometimes, distilling their
sweat and selling it. The plastic jumpsuits they wore
had a greenhouse effect, Magistrate Irons knew, and
there would be a collection rig set in the rear that gathered the sweat they generated. The poor bastards were
so ill-treated and so hot that they could hardly move. It
was all they could do to lie there in the dust as the sun
beat down on their roasting bodies, cooking them alive.

It was more than the magistrates had expected from
the Deathbird's fly-past report. Bellevue eased off the
accelerator and the SandCat crept slowly toward the
half-dozen tents that were set out beside the pen.

"What is this?" DePaul asked.

"Sweat farm," Irons told him, reaching for his helmet. "We're going out there, rookie. You're going to
need your helmet."

Obediently, DePaul reached for his head gear.
"They're muties, right?"

Irons nodded.

DePaul had never seen a mutie before, not in the
flesh, anyway. "Then what are they doing here? What
are they doing to them?"

"It's a drugs op," Irons explained, checking that his sin
eater pistol was loaded. "They make the muties sweat, then
the farmers here take that sweat and refine it, sell it on."

"Why?" DePaul asked, pushing his helmet down
over his face. The Magistrate casque was black and
covered the wearer's skull all the way down the back.

The front covered the top half of the user's head, before meeting with a dark-tinted visor that protected and hid the eyes, leaving only the mouth on display. The result was intimidating, turning the mags into near-faceless upholders of the law.

"People want to get away from what they are," Irons explained, "especially here in the Outlands. Trust me, kid, it ain't much of a life that these people have."

"But they're breaking the law," DePaul stated, "which means we stop them."

"Be glad of it, too," Irons said, "if any of that stuff is destined for Cobaltville streets. Which it probably is."

Beyond the SandCat, the illegal ranchers were exiting their tents, watching the familiar mag vehicle pull up. They were a motley crew, six in all, dressed in undershirts and shorts, one woman among them with her hair—blond dreadlocks—tied back with a rainbow-patterned bandana. They all wore breath masks over their mouth and nose, and several openly wore blasters holstered at their hips.

"You got this?" Bellevue asked, as he pulled the SandCat to a halt.

"Sure, me and the rookie can handle these mooks," Irons assured him. Then he gestured to the turret gun, above and behind where he and DePaul sat. "Keep your trigger finger handy, though."

"Always do," Bellevue confirmed, flipping open the secondary control panel on the dashboard that operated the twin USMG machine guns.

Irons swung back the gull-wing door of the SandCat and stepped out onto the dirt, with DePaul following a moment later. DePaul glanced behind them as he did, imagining he might still be able to see the golden towers of Cobaltville waiting like an oasis in the distance. He couldn't; they were too far from its protective hub.

A rancher from the group spoke up, his voice sounding artificial through the plastic of the breath mask, his thumbs hooked in his belt loops, a smug grin on his mustached face. "You lost, Magistrate?"

"No, sir," Irons replied, eyeing the group. Six people wasn't enough for a farm like this; given the number of tents, he'd expect at least eight, maybe more if they employed extra muscle. He made a subtle gesture with the fingers of his left hand, enough that DePaul knew he needed to stay alert.

Behind Irons, the rookie looked around, scanning the tents and the plains, the high ridges of the mesa that loomed close by. Plenty of places to hide.

"Then you maybe come to see me," the farm spokesman said, "but I not remember inviting you. Did I invite you?"

Irons disliked the man already. He was cocky—too cocky, even for a bandit. He thought he had the upper hand here and he wasn't afraid to let the magistrates know that.

"This here is illegal incarceration," Magistrate Irons said, gesturing to the pen where the muties agonised in their sweatsuits. "And you are on barony land. Now, we could do this easy or we could do it hard. I'm a little long in the tooth for hard, so what say you let these poor wretched creatures go, and close up this stinking operation, and I won't cause you any more aggravation."

"You think you're going to cause me aggravation?" the cocky rancher challenged, taking a step toward Irons and the SandCat.

DePaul saw a movement over to his left in the distance. Someone was crouching there, behind a cluster of sand-beige rocks as tall as a man.

Irons stepped forward, too, pacing toward the edge of the cattle pen, with DePaul following.

"I've made you the offer," Irons explained. "It's non-negotiable. Pack up your tents, close your farm and move on. Otherwise, I won't hesitate to bring the full force of the law down on you."

The rancher laughed. "Hah, full force o' the law? What's that mean—you and the kid here?"

"Yeah," Irons said, turning to the rancher. "Me and the kid." His eyes were hidden by the visor, and yet the rancher could make no mistake that he was being stared at.

"Bored," the man said. Then he shrugged and made as if to turn his back on the two mags. The shrug was a practiced move, intended to disguise the way his right hand was reaching down for the blaster holstered at his hip. But he never got the chance to unleather it— DePaul saw it and moved quicker, his right arm coming up, hand pointing at the rancher over the shoulder of his instructor. With a practiced flinch of his wrist tendons, DePaul brought the sin eater pistol into his hand from its hidden sheath in his sleeve, propelled by the mechanism he wore strapped there.

A compact 9 mm automatic, the sin eater was the official sidearm of the Magistrate Division, and was recognized even way out in the Outlands. The weapon retracted from sight while not in use, its butt folding over the top of the barrel to reduce its stored length to just ten inches. The holster operated by a specific flinch of the wrist tendon, powering the blaster straight into the user's hand. The weapon's trigger had no guard;

the necessity for one had never been foreseen, since the magistrates were believed to be infallible. Which meant that as the gun touched DePaul's hand, the trigger was depressed and a burst of 9 mm titanium-shelled bullets spit from the muzzle, cutting down the rancher even as he grabbed the butt of his own pistol.

The man toppled to the dirt with an agonized cry, his hand still locked on the pistol he had not had the chance to draw. His breath mask was shattered, blood gushing over his jaw.

All around, the other ranch hands were reaching for their own weapons, some worn proudly on their hips, others stuffed in hidden places in their waistbands or tucked into the pockets of their pants.

Irons had his blaster in his hand a moment later, reeling off shots at the nearest of the illegal farmhands as they reached for their guns. Above and behind him, the twin USMG-73s came to life on the roof of the SandCat, sending a relentless stream of bullets into the ranchers as they ran for cover. The woman with the blond dreads went down in a hail of fire, and so did another of the farmhands, his chest erupting with blood as the SandCat's bullets drilled through him. Everyone else ran for cover, including the two magistrates, as bullets flew back and forth between the two groups.

Irons and DePaul were behind the armored side of the SandCat in seconds, a trail of bullets cutting the ground all around them.

"Quick thinking," the older man said as his partner reloaded his pistol.

"Saw him reach," DePaul said. "Made the decision without hesitation, the way they taught me in the academy."

Irons nodded, satisfied with the rookie's reasoning.

The turret of the SandCat continued to send bullets at the retreating farmers, the sound brutally loud as it echoed from the distant mesa walls. Another of the farmers went down when he poked his head out from behind a pressured canister used to collect the mutie sweat. A moment later a bullet clipped the container and it went up in a burst of expelled gas, hissing like some colossal snake as it spewed its contents into the air.

Without warning, a line of bullets rattled against the side of the Sandcat, inches from the magistrates' heads. Both mags turned, searching for the sniper.

"Spotted someone hiding in the shadows of the rocks," DePaul commented.

"I saw him, too," Irons agreed. "We need to pick him off if—"

DePaul was on his feet and running toward the rock face immediately. "Cover me!" he called back.

Irons ducked as more bullets slapped against the ceramic armaglass side of the SandCat. Then he was around its front edge, blasting his sin eater again as another of the farmhands tried to sneak up on him. His play was backed by Bellevue on the turret, whose bullets cut another of the ranchers down before he could take two steps out from cover.

DePaul ran, the sin eater thrust before him as he ascended the incline toward where the sniper was hiding in the long shadow of the mesa. A bullet whizzed past him, while two more flicked against the ground just a few feet behind. DePaul weaved, shifting his body left and right as more bullets cut the air. He was taking a heck of a chance here, he knew, but sometimes a chance was all you had.

The sniper kept firing, three more bullets burning the air just feet from the sprinting magistrate rookie. Then there came a lull; he guessed the gunner was reloading.

DePaul scrambled up the dry and dusty incline, his rubber-soled boots dislodging loose soil and small stones as he hurried toward the sniper's hiding place. He saw a head appear between two boulders to his left, a flicker of silhouette glimpsed only for a moment. He ran at the nearest one, keeping his balance as he clambered up its side. The rock was fifteen feet in height and the faded orange color of sand.

DePaul reached the top in seconds, the sound of his footsteps lost in the continued reports of blasterfire coming from the ranch. He crouched down, peering over the side. The sniper was down there, kneeling behind the rock, eye to the scope of his rifle. He had dusty blond hair and wore a kerchief over his mouth and nose to stop him from breathing in the dirt that was being kicked up by the wind. He had obviously lost his target in that brief moment when he had reloaded and the rookie magistrate had clambered out of sight.

Steadying himself, DePaul leaned forward with his Sin Eater and squeezed the trigger, sending a swift burst of fire at his would-be killer. The sniper gave a startled cry as bullets rained down on him from above, but before he could react, one drilled into his skull and he sank down like a wet sheet of paper.

Still crouching atop the rock, DePaul turned, scanning the area all the way back to the ranch. The gunfire was easing now, the constant blasts replaced by occasional bursts of sound as Irons and Bellevue mopped up the last of the farmhands. There was no one else about.

Whatever other security the farm had employed had been drawn into the firefight and killed.

DePaul scrambled back down the rock, marching around to its far side and checking on his target. The man was dead, eyes open but unfocused, blood pooling beneath his head. DePaul took the man's rifle and checked him over, swiftly and professionally, for other weapons, finding a hand pistol and a knife. He stripped him of these before making his way back down to the farm compound, by which time the senior magistrates had finished containing the farmers.

"You did good today, rookie," Irons told DePaul as he saw him approach. He was disarming the dead ranchers, tossing their guns behind him into the open door of the Sandcat. Bellevue sat on the lip of the seat, taking stock of the illegal weapons.

"Thanks," DePaul said. "Sorry I missed the main action."

"You got the main action," Irons corrected. "Nailed it. That sniper woulda had both our heads if you hadn't moved so quickly. You did yourself proud."

"What happens now?" he asked, gazing around at the farm and the dead bodies left in the wake of the firefight. There was a scent in the air this close to the pen, sweet like refined sugar. It was mutie sweat, buckets of it, waiting to be processed and sold.

"We'll free the muties," Irons told him, "and leave for the birds and wolves these poor saps who thought they could take on magistrates."

DePaul nodded. His first patrol of the Outlands had been a success.

Chapter 2

Ten years later

"Well, this royally stinks," Kane said as he pulled the re-breather mask from his face. Barely covering his mouth and nostrils, the mask fed oxygen in the same way a diver's breath mask does.

Kane waded through the murky, knee-deep water that covered the floor outside the mat-trans chamber, a scowl on his face as he looked around. He had expected trouble, hence the rebreather, but it was still grim seeing the place in person. He lit the way with a compact but powerful xenon flashlight that bathed the mold-scarred walls of the control room in stark brilliance.

Kane was a tall, broad-shouldered man in his early thirties, with long, rangy limbs and a sleek, muscular torso hidden beneath the second skin of his shadow suit. He was handsome, with a square jaw, and had dark, cropped hair and gray-blue eyes that seemed to take in every detail and could look right through you.

There was something of the wolf about Kane, both in his alertness and the way he held himself, and personal-itywise, too, for he could be both loner and pack leader.

The shadow suit's dark weave clung to his taut body, made from an incredible fabric that acted like armor and was capable of deflecting a blade and redistributing blunt trauma. The shadow suit had other capabilities, too, providing a regulated environment for its wearer, allowing Kane to survive in extremes of temperature without breaking a sweat or catching a chill. He had augmented his shadow suit with a denim jacket with enough pockets to hide crucial supplies for a scouting mission like this one, dark pants and scuffed leather boots with age-old creases in them. The boots were a legacy from his days as a Cobaltville Magistrate, copies of the boots he had worn on shift before he had crossed Baron Cobalt and fled from the ville along with his partner and best friend, Grant, and a remarkable woman called Brigid Baptiste.

Both Grant and Brigid accompanied Kane now. They were also wearing rebreathers and were wading along behind him as he exited the mat-trans chamber and made his way through the flooded control room of the redoubt. The trio was the exploration team for an outlawed group called Cerberus, based in the Bitterroot Mountains of Montana and dedicated to the protection of humankind.

Brigid pocketed her rebreather. "Everyone be careful. That water smells stagnant," she said, wrinkling her nose.

"Don't drink it," Kane said. "Gotcha."

Brigid shook her head in despair at his flippant attitude. Typical Kane.

Brigid was a beautiful woman in her late twenties, with pale skin, emerald eyes and long red hair the color of sunset, tied back for the mission today. Her high forehead suggested intelligence, while her full lips spoke of a more passionate side. In reality she exhibited both these facets and many more besides. Like Kane, Brigid wore a shadow suit. In her case, she had augmented it with a short dark jacket that did nothing to disguise the swell of her breasts, and she wore a low-slung holster at her hip holding her trusted TP-9 semiautomatic pistol.

Where Kane had been a magistrate, Brigid was once an archivist, and while she could hold her own in a fight, she was equally at home poring over books and data. She had one particular quality that made this a weapon in its own right—an eidetic memory that meant she could retain information in the manner of a photograph in her mind's eye. Her incredible bank of knowledge had helped herself and her companions out of more than one tight corner.

The final member of the team was Grant, an ominous, hulking figure with skin dark as mahogany. Like Kane, he was an ex-magistrate who had been caught up in the same conspiracy and forced to flee from Cobaltville to roam the Outlands. In his mid-thirties, Grant had recently taken to shaving his head, and sported a gunslinger's mustache. Like his companions, he wore a shadow suit, over which he had added his favored duster coat. The garment appeared to be made of black leather, though in truth the fabric was a fireproof Kevlar-Nomex weave capable of deflecting bullets. Neither he nor Kane appeared armed, but they were; their blasters were hidden in quick-release holsters strapped to their wrists, the same sin eater weapons they had worn as magistrates years before.

Grant sniffed the air but could not really detect the stagnant, musty smell the others spoke of. His nose had been broken multiple times, which had affected its sensitivity. "Shouldn't be wet like this," he grumbled in a voice like rumbling thunder. "Something must've sprung a leak."

"Great deduction, Detective," Kane deadpanned as he led the way through the room and out to the twin aisles of monitoring desks that faced the mat-trans chamber.

Together, the trio scouted the control room, assuring themselves that they were alone and not being observed. The room was large, roughly thirty feet square, with rows of computers that dominated the space and had once been used, two hundred years ago, to monitor and program the comings and goings via the mat-trans unit. There were other desks here, too, one housing a half dozen telephone receivers, each one a different color. A couch and two easy chairs were set around a low coffee table in the farthest corner. Ancient magazines rested atop the table, while the water lapped just inches below.

There were also several large computer banks lining one of the walls, a massive CPU held in a metal cabinet with armaglass front, and a whole row of printers with paper still spooling from them as if the site had been abandoned two minutes ago and not two centuries. The paper in the bottom-most printer had come free, however, and its slowly disintegrating remains floated on the dirty water that had filled the room. Beside the farthest bank of printers was a reinforced steel door rolled back on its tracks. Water sloshed in the corridor beyond, level with that in the control room.

Everything here had been dedicated to one thing: the operation of the mat-trans, a system of transport dating back to the late twentieth century, where it had been the sole province of the United States military. Similar projects existed worldwide, but the U.S. system had been retained solely for the military in a series of hidden redoubts, protected bases that could withstand a nuclear assault. The redoubts had been devised as backup should the worst happen, and when it had, on that fateful January day in 2001, and nuclear missiles had rained down on the United States and across the world, the redoubts had stood firm as safe havens for anyone who could gain access to them. However, hidden and secret as they were, plus being locked, and heavily protected with military codes, they had by and large proved to be impregnable and often impossible to find. Which was why so many of them survived two centuries on, like the buried tombs of ancient Pharaohs.

This redoubt, however, had highlighted a problem less than twenty-four hours ago, which had been picked up by the powerful monitoring equipment of the Cerberus facility.

Grant made his way through the doors and into the corridor beyond. "I'll check out the local amenities," he joked, though his face was deadly serious. The team had done these kinds of missions before, and knew it didn't pay to be anything less than careful when entering unknown territory.

Wading back through the murky water that swished almost to her knees, Brigid engaged her commtact and reported in. "Cerberus, we're in. Mat-trans is clear. Automatic lights have failed, and the control room is waterlogged."

The commtacts were small implanted communications devices worn by all Cerberus field personnel. Each subdermal device was a top-of-the-line communication unit, the designs for which had been discovered among the artifacts in Redoubt Yankee several years before by the Cerberus exiles. Commtacts featured sensor circuitry incorporating an analog-to-digital voice encoder that was embedded in a subject's mastoid bone. Once the pintles made contact, transmissions were funneled directly to the wearer's auditory canals through the skull casing, vibrating the ear canal to create sound, which had the effect that they could pick up and enhance any subvocalisation. In theory, even if a user went deaf, he or she would still be able to hear, after a fashion, courtesy of the commtact device.

A voice came back over Brigid's commtact a moment later, broadcast from the Cerberus redoubt many miles away in Montana. It was Brewster Philboyd, one of the operators who helped run the base, including its communications desk. "Any signs of damage?" he asked.

"Negative," Brigid confirmed. She was already eyeing the mat-trans using the powerful illumination of her xenon beam. The octagonal chamber took up fully one-third of the control room, featuring a sealed door like an airlock, and armaglass walls that could repel a bullet. The glass was tinted a muddy shade of brown, much like the water that had seeped into the redoubt. There were some scuff marks here and there, and the base was hidden beneath the murky water, but nothing looked broken, and the monitoring desks that served the mat-trans were undamaged.

"Remote reports flagged a reengaging of the power cores," Philboyd reminded Brigid, as if she of all people would ever need reminding.

"Well, I can't see any signs of…" She paused as Kane indicated something with the toe of his boot. It was hard to see with the swirl of dirty water masking it, but several panels at the base of the mat-trans chamber's exterior had been pulled away, bent back with considerable force. The affected panels were located in line with the lone door. "What is that?" Brigid muttered.

"Please repeat," Philboyd responded.

She ignored him, ducking down to get a closer look.

"Seems like someone took a crowbar to it," Kane said, tapping one of the bent grilles with his toe. "Went at it pretty hard, too—these things are built sturdy."

Brigid examined the submerged, damaged plate, reaching in and wiggling it a little this way and that. The water was ice-cold, smarting like a bite. The panel was a covering for the circuitry that controlled the functionality of the mat-trans, with a slatted section to allow for excess heat to be expelled in times of high traffic. The plate was made of burnished steel and was still connected—in a fashion—to the mat-trans chamber itself, albeit by just one rivet that was barely clinging to its drill hole. "Looks like someone's tried to gain access," Brigid summarized over the commtact link.

"'Nother one here." Kane indicated another panel around the side of the chamber's base. This one had been removed entirely. "Got some marks here, too," he added, shining the fierce beam of his flashlight on the armaglass beside the door.

When Brigid looked she saw triple scrapes marking the surface, running quite low down—hip and knee level—both left and right of the door. The gashes looked like…

"Claws," she said, relaying the observation to Philboyd back at home base. "Someone's definitely been trying to get inside."

"Or some*thing*," Kane remarked poignantly.

Cerberus was at the center of the mat-trans network,

and its personnel monitored the system for any potential problems or threats. With the instantaneous nature of travel via its system, the mat-trans was, potentially, a very powerful resource to any group. However, it was largely unknown to the general public—and Cerberus intended to keep it that way. When a standard monitoring query had resulted in an error code response from this particular mat-trans unit, the CAT Alpha exploration team, made up of Kane, Grant and Brigid, had been sent to investigate. This unit was located about eighty miles east of Cobaltville, the old stomping ground of Kane and his partners. A mile underground and taking water from who knew where, it felt a long way from home.

A new voice spoke over the linked commtacts as Brigid examined the indentations in the mat-trans wall. "Can you elaborate on that, dear Brigid?" It was Mohandas Lakesh Singh, popularly known as Lakesh, the leader of the Cerberus operation and a man with an incredible history with the mat-trans project. A theoretical physicist and cyberneticist, Lakesh had been born in the twentieth century, where his expertise had been applied to the original development of the mat-trans process. A combination of cryogenic hibernation and organ replacement had seen him emerge in the twenty-third century as the leader of what had begun as a covert rebellion against Baron Cobalt, but had ultimately developed into something even more noble—the Cerberus organization.

Brigid ran her fingers along the indentations in the armaglass. "Regular relative placement, three score marks each time," she said, thoughtfully. "These are claw marks."

Kane looked at her and nodded grimly. "Same thing I was thinking, Baptiste."

Lakesh sounded thoughtful as he spoke over their commtacts. "A wild animal would not have the intelligence to break into a redoubt, nor the motivation to try to access the mat-trans."

"Maybe no one broke in," Kane said. "The place is waterlogged—could be a wall breach somewhere."

"But look, Kane," Brigid interrupted. "The claw marks around the door, the removed panels—this is a deliberate attempt to gain entry into the mat-trans. And Lakesh is right—no wild animal would do that."

"Then it's one that's not so wild," Kane retorted defiantly. "I swear, you brain-boxes and your logic—"

Before he could finish the insult, Grant came stomping in from the corridor where he had been scouting, a worried look on his face. "Wake up, guys—there's something alive out there."

"Something—?" Kane began, jogging across the room to the open door.

Brigid activated her commtact and signed off. "Lakesh, Brewster, we'll have to get back to you shortly. Looks like we may have a situation here." She cut the communication before either man could reply.

Kane and she followed Grant through the open door.

OUTSIDE, THE corridor was knee deep in water and its walls were streaked with mold. Its proportions were large, wide enough to drive a SandCat through without touching.

"Down there," Grant said, pointing to his left.

Kane followed him, both men sloshing through the dark water, while Brigid followed more slowly.

"What did you see?" Kane asked, keeping his voice low.

"Can't be sure," Grant replied. "Looked big, though—either a leg or a tail moving just beneath the water. When it crossed into the circle of light it turned real fast and scooted back the way it came."

"So it's not blind, then," Kane reasoned. "Just shy."

"It could be whatever's been tampering with the mat-trans," Brigid proposed in a whisper.

"Could be," Kane agreed as the group continued making slow progress along the corridor.

There was nothing there, just that knee-deep water and the mold, the sense of cold palpable all around them despite the environmental stability granted by their shadow suits.

The Cerberus crew trudged onward, sloshing slowly through the murky waters. The light of their xenon beams lit the dark walls and cloudy depths.

"I don't like this," Kane muttered, his nose twitching as he took the lead. Back in his days as a hard-contact magistrate, he had been known for his point-man sense, an indefinable ability to detect danger in what seemed to be the most harmless of situations. The gift seemed uncanny, but was in fact a combination of the same five senses anyone else had, but so acute it seemed incredible.

"What do you sense?" Brigid asked.

"Not sure," Kane said, running the beam of his flash-light over the tunnel-like walls before them. He cocked his head, listening. "There's something moving out that way," he murmured, taking another step.

Without warning, he disappeared, sinking beneath the waters in a rush of movement.

Chapter 3

"What th—!" Grant spit as he waded through the water after Kane's disappearing form.

"Grant, wait!" Brigid called, reaching for the big man's arm.

Although her strength was nothing compared to his own, he stopped when he felt her hand touch him. "Kane's in there…." he began.

"I saw," Brigid confirmed, "but we have to be logical about this or we'll all get dragged under."

Grant knew she was right.

"Kane, do you copy?" she called, activating the subdermal commtact. "Kane, I repeat—do you copy?"

Grant frowned as he looked at her.

"Nothing," she admitted. She looked at the dark water in the harsh beam of her xenon flashlight. "I'd estimate this is less than two feet deep," she reasoned.

"Maybe eighteen inches," Grant agreed.

"Where we stand," Brigid continued. "But Kane dropped, which means it's deeper ahead."

Grant nodded, passing her his flashlight. "Here, hold this," he said. Then, following her logic, he sank down on his knees and crawled forward, hands sluicing through the water as he felt his way. "Hard floor," he reported, "with a little give, like carpet maybe." He reached forward, moving slowly. "Still floor, still floor…*there!*" He turned back to Brigid, smiling. "There's a drop here, stairs maybe."

She watched as he dipped lower, still reaching forward, testing the terrain. "Careful," she said, when his face came close to the water.

"It's all right," Grant assured her. "I think I feel somethi—"

At that moment, Grant felt something wrap around his arm, and in an instant he, too, was dragged under.

Brigid splashed forward, playing the beam of the flashlight over the dark surface. "Didn't I just say to be careful?" she muttered, gazing into the murk.

GRANT WAS SINKING. There was something dragging on his right arm, using its weight to pull him down in the water, deep down into the gloom. He had at least had foresight enough to take a breath as he'd felt the thing grab him, wrap around him, pull him down. Now he circulated that breath in his lungs as he was dragged ever onward.

He couldn't see a thing, it was so dark. The only light was back up at the surface: Brigid using the xenon flashlight.

He would drown. That's what was going to happen.

Forget about finding Kane for a moment, just save yourself, Grant told himself. You ain't no good to Kane dead.

The thing held tightly to his right wrist like a manacle, a dark shape dragging him down and down and down. For a moment Grant saw something flash in the darkness, a row of teeth wide as his forearm.

As the creature opened its mouth for a better grip, Grant pulled his arm away, then kicked as hard as he could, simultaneously stunning whatever it was and propelling himself away, back toward the surface.

TOPSIDE, BRIGID Baptiste was standing at the edge of the deep well beneath the redoubt floor. It should not be there, she knew—redoubts were designed to be impregnable, and the mat-trans located at the base.

She wondered how big the gap was. Could she step over it, if she managed to locate the far rim? And how deep was it? A few feet, or a quarter mile or more? Most importantly, where did it lead?

She tried her commtact again, desperately hoping for an answer from Kane or from Grant, wishing that one of them could hear her and respond.

"Come on, Kane, come on, Grant—one of you say something already," she hissed into the hidden mic.

Then she spotted a dark shape materializing beneath her in the depths, and a moment later the waters surged and Grant came lunging to the surface, gasping for air.

"Grant, you're okay," she called, wading over to him.

He winced as she shone the light over his face, one thousand candles of wattage blasting into his eyes like a nuclear explosion.

"Sorry...sorry," Brigid began, turning the beam away. As she did so, she saw the figure looming behind her, also emerging from the water, twin rows of teeth gleaming as they caught the flashlight's ray. The creature's skin looked dark and rippled in the harsh glare of the xenon light, almost like armor, and for a moment Brigid's mind whirled, fearing that this was another Annunaki overlord, reemerged on Earth to enslave mankind. But it wasn't Annunaki; it seemed more animal than human, a wild thing.

The creature pulled itself out of the water into a position that Brigid guessed was a close approximation of standing upright. It was unclothed and taller than a man, about seven feet at full extension, with a long snout like a dog and lips pulled back from vicious pointed teeth. The teeth followed the jaw around from sides to front, each one the length of Brigid's pinkie finger. The being had a thick, muscular tail, as long again as its height, curling across the floor, just visible in the water. Brigid figured it had been a crocodile once, a few iterations of DNA ago. It was a mutie now.

"Brigid," Grant gasped from behind her, "get down."

She responded automatically, ducking low as Grant began firing on the emerging creature. Two bullets flew, racing to the target, drilling against the chest of the croc-like mutie. The sin eater sounded loud in the confines of the corridor, echoes reverberating with the swish of the water. In the aftermath, the croc staggered back a step, then plunged back down, disappearing with a splash of its enormous tail.

Brigid spoke angrily, still watching the location where the creature had disappeared. "What are you thinking? We don't know if that thing's a friend or foe."

"Yeah, we do. One of them just pulled me down under the surface," Grant declared. "I'm calling it."

Brigid flashed him a look before scanning the vicinity. "Any sign of Kane?" she asked.

"I couldn't see shit down there," Grant told her. "But I can tell you this much—it's a bastard long drop."

"What is it?" Brigid asked. "A well? Sinkhole?"

He glared at her. "I was too busy fighting for my life to check."

"Humph. It happens," she retorted, playing the xenon beam about once more.

Suddenly there was movement all around the two Cerberus warriors. They sensed it as much as saw it, and then five more of the croc-like creatures emerged from the water—two from the corridor leading back to the mat-trans, three more from the deeper space behind Grant.

"We could be in trouble," he muttered, raising his blaster again.

AIR. THAT CAME first. Everything else came in a rush afterward, filling in with memory and logic and guesswork, but the air came first. Kane breathed it, grateful, feeling that slosh of liquid inside him where he had sampled a mouthful of the filthy water when he had been dragged beneath the surface.

How long had he been held under? A minute? More? He had blacked out, the cold ache of the water pressing against him even through the protection of his shadow suit. His face still felt like ice.

Kane heard something: a voice. It sounded awfully close, and for a moment he wondered if he was awake or asleep, because he couldn't recall where the heck he was.

His eyes snapped open, only to find pitch darkness, a black so absolute the thought that he could be inside a box or a sack crossed his mind. But no, there was no material pressed against his face, and he couldn't feel that telltale bounce of air as he breathed out, so he wasn't close to a wall or box lid.

He was soaking wet, his clothes heavy, as if they would drag him down where he lay. He was stretched out on his back. Wet, lying on his back. On cold stone.

He could feel the cool hardness scrape against the back of his head when he tried to move.

He felt dizzy, off balance, and realized that the floor beneath him tilted at an angle, leaving his feet lower than his head.

Automatically he felt for the weight at his wrist, the familiar bulk of the sin eater in its hidden sheath under his sleeve. It was still there. Good. Someone was going to get it, pretty soon, too, unless he got some answers.

What had happened? Thinking back, he could see the water, clouded black with pollutant. He had been checking the redoubt corridor and then the floor had dropped away and he had found himself sinking into the liquid. No, not sinking—he had been dragged, weights on his legs, something guiding his passage. No air to breathe, of course—the descent had been too sudden for that—so he had held his breath, mouth tasting of the dark water that had carpeted the deck, and then he was here. Somewhere between "there" and "here," Kane figured, he had blacked out.

The voice in his head had been Brigid's, calling him and Grant. The commtact.

"Baptiste?" Kane subvocalised, not saying the word but just breathing it. The commtact's pickup would enhance the word into speech, relay it to Brigid, wherever she was.

He waited a moment. No reply.

All the while, Kane was listening. Listening intensely to the space around him, the way the echoes resounded, the ambient sounds of the room. There was water here; he could hear its telltale blup as something dripped into a larger body of water, like a melting stalactite over a pool.

There was also the rhythmic sound of ripples, of water being brushed lightly by a breeze.

There was something else, too—*breathing*. Soft, hardly discernible over the dripping and the rippling, but there just the same when Kane filtered out all the other sounds and put them into categories. The breathing seemed close in the darkness; not loud, but close.

Kane stirred slightly, testing to see what reaction he would get. The thing beside him stirred, too. It was maybe ten feet away, moving around his three o'clock.

Okay, Kane thought. Shoot or make friends? Decisions, decisions. What would Baptiste do?

It was a tough one. Kane knew that Brigid would make friends, or at least she would try to, but whatever had happened to get him here—and he was still struggling to recall all of it—seemed to involve drowning or kidnapping or a little bit of both. At least he had air to breathe now, even if it smelled like the back end of a burned-out SandCat.

The thing shuffled, rough skin running over the stones of the floor. Kane heard it sniff twice, scenting the air. Then he heard another noise, a quiet rumble, not from the thing's throat but from its belly. It was hungry.

"WHAT THE HECK are they?" Grant asked as he trained his sin eater on the first of the emerging croc creatures.

"Beats me," Brigid admitted. "They look like muties—maybe an offshoot of the scalies that were prevalent in this area a hundred years ago." As she spoke, she was checking the ammunition in her TP-9 semiautomatic pistol. The TP-9 was a bulky hand pistol with a covered targeting scope across the top finished in molded matte black. The grip was set just off center beneath the barrel, creating a lopsided square in the user's hand, hand and wrist making the final side and corner.

And then the crocs moved, lips pulling back to show their impressive teeth, hissing deep in their throats as they began to attack. There was no time for negotiation now—it was do or die.

The crocs swished their tails to propel themselves from the water, hurtling toward the intruders like rockets.

Grant sent a triple burst of fire from his sin eater, three bullets whipping across the space between himself and his attackers in quick succession. As he did so, he was dropping back toward the nearest wall, using it for cover as the closest of the croc-like creatures came at him with snapping jaws. Grant brought his left arm up in defense, groaned as he felt those vicious jaws chomp down on the Kevlar armor of his coat.

Beside him, Brigid's pistol flashed in the darkness, sending a score of 9 mm bullets at the first of her attackers as it leaped at her, stagnant water pouring from its ridged, naked frame. The bullets scored a direct hit, cutting a line across the creature's thick skin in pockmarks—one, two, three, four—from its waist to its meaty pectoral. Their impact did not seem to even slow the creature; it moved like lightning toward Brigid, and its hands—eerily human despite their coating of thick scales—grabbed for her blaster.

In a moment, the mutant had a hold on the muzzle of her TP-9, sweeping it aside as it came toward her with widening jaws.

THE SIN EATER appeared in Kane's hand instantly, commanded there by a practiced flinch of his wrist tendons as he lay on his back on the cold stone. He could hear the creature's feet thumping over the rock floor as his finger met the pistol's trigger, and suddenly the quiet, regular sounds of water dripping and wind across water were broken by the noise of gunfire.

Kane located his foe by sound alone, holding the trigger down for an extended burst of fire. He heard the other stagger, its movements interrupted, and then a cry like a hiss of steam, followed by the thump of the body dropping to the floor.

Kane eased his finger from the trigger, still holding the blaster poised in the direction of his unseen foe. Hope I'm right about this, he thought as he reached into a utility pocket in his jacket with his free hand. An instant later, Kane had pulled free what appeared to be a pair of sunglasses, which he slipped over the bridge of his nose. They had specially coated polymer lenses and were designed to draw every available iota of light to create an image of whatever was around the viewer, acting as a kind of proxy night vision. Kane pushed himself into a crouch and examined the scene.

He was in an artificial cavern with an arched ceiling and strip of floor, all constructed of regular, carved stone. The floor beneath was tilted, leaving half the room submerged beneath a stretch of dark water. It all smelled rank, bitter, like rainwater on manure.

The creature lay before him, sprawled half in and half out of the water. It looked kind of like a crocodile, only larger and with powerful legs like a man's, and a tail that disappeared into the water as it curled. The tail twitched, sending ripples across the water.

Kane eyed the creature, making sure it was down. The tail twitched once more, then stopped. He figured it was dead.

Kane paced across to the croc-thing, looking around the cavern. They were in a sewer, maybe; it was hard to tell for sure, but it looked a lot like one. He figured it had served the redoubt two hundred years before, when it had been built. The redoubts were self-sufficient and could be closed off entirely from the outside world, but some had been served by networks of sewers and service tunnels when they were being constructed. Most of those service tunnels had been shut off, blocked up, concreted over. This one, it seemed, had survived.

The creature on the floor was naked and must have stood nine feet tall, with the muscular tail to propel it through the water. It looked like a croc, with a long muzzle featuring rows of teeth as long as Kane's index finger. But it also had a human quality, despite its coarse, armorlike skin. A chill went down Kane's spine as he wondered if it was an offshoot of the Annunaki or the Naga, two lizardlike races that had reached for power in the post-nukecaust Earth—the former a race of alien would-be world conquerors, the latter a genetic offshoot of the Annunaki seeded on Earth. But Kane checked himself, recalling stories of the mutie races that used to walk the so-called Deathlands that grew up in the wake of the nukecaust. Some of those creatures had been lizardlike in appearance, the radiation turning them into twisted genetic dumping grounds for weird combinations of mismatched DNA. It was a chill-or-be-chilled world in those days, or that's what the old-timers used to say.

Kane stepped past the dead lizard, scanned his surroundings through the polymer lenses.

Behind the creature were sacs of organic matter, attached to the walls with what appeared to be a kind of gluclike webbing. There were eight in all, each one oval and almost as long as a man's torso. *Eggs.* Kane studied them for a few seconds, peering closely at their translucent shells. There were things waiting inside, half-formed creatures no longer than his forearm. "Baby crocs," he muttered.

Beyond that, a large bore hole lay in the far wall. The hole was circular and wide enough to grant access to a man or even a small vehicle, and certainly large enough to let these croc things come and go as they pleased. "Now then, where do *you* lead to?" Kane wondered aloud.

Whatever he and his companions had stumbled on here, it looked like a mutie breeding ground, the kind of place those put-upon mutie races had gone to hide when man had reasserted himself as the dominant life-form in the post-apocalypse world. Kane almost felt sorry for the muties, but he knew that their nesting this close to an operating mat-trans unit spelled trouble. Muties weren't dumb, even the ones more animal than man. If they could figure a way to get the mat-trans working, they might spread like an infection, settling new colonies right across the North American continent. And if they should meet with humans, as was inevitable, it wasn't much of a leap to assume that unrest would follow— the kind of unrest that brings a body count in its wake.

Kane looked at the lizard corpse again, sneering. "Poor bastard," he muttered, shaking his head, "you've got no idea what they'd do to you up there. If you knew, you'd think what I did here was a show of mercy."

GRANT YOWLED IN pain, his scream echoing in the waterlogged corridor. The croc mutie had clamped its jaws around his left arm and was endeavouring to close them. The Kevlar weave of Grant's coat was strong, acting like plate armor, and beneath it he wore the shadow suit, with its own armorlike quality. But he could still feel those two-inch-long teeth driving into his flesh.

"Get the hell offa me," he snarled, twisting his body around and swinging the beast with him despite its bulk. Grant was strong—it had occasionally been commented that his strength verged on the superhuman, in fact. With all his strength, he shoved the croc, still clamped to his arm, against the closest mold-dark wall, fixing it in place. Then, with his other hand, he rammed the muzzle of the sin eater point-blank against the thing's round eye and blasted.

The first bullet destroyed the creature's eye and Grant felt the pressure on his arm ease for an instant. He kept firing, delivering bullets into the creature's skull and brain. The sin eater bucked in his hand and he felt the impact of the bullets reverberate through his arm where the mutie gripped him.

JUST A FEW steps away, Brigid was struggling with her own foe. It lunged at her, the seven-foot-long tail swishing behind as it darted across the watery floor of the corridor. The bullets from the TP-9 were having next to no effect. They just rebounded from the monstrous thing's thick hide.

Brigid skipped back, the heels of her boots splashing in the dark water that carpeted the redoubt floor. She thought fast, struggling to find a way to keep this creature—and its brethren—from devouring her and Grant. There had to be a way—and there was, if she could just create enough space to make it work!

Brigid turned her back to the monsters. "Come and get me!" she shouted, scrambling down the corridor, back toward the control room and its mat-trans chamber.

Three of the mutie crocs followed, issuing a discordant hiss from their throats as they chased after their prey. Is that how they speak? Brigid wondered. Despite their appearance they were clearly intelligent, and those marks around the mat-trans showed where some of them had tried to work the device to jump to a different location.

She was in the control room now, the mat-trans chamber waiting before her, the muddy brown armaglass looking like a coffee spill as it caught the beam of her xenon flashlight. She reached for the chamber door, rapidly typing in the code to unlock it.

The crocs slowed as they reached the doorway to the control room, stalking warily inside.

"Just a little closer," Brigid murmured to herself, stepping back through the open door of the mat-trans. As she did, she pulled the rebreather mask from her pocket. It was small, not much larger than a marker pen, and rested neatly in her left palm.

Brigid watched the humanlike crocs approach on hind legs, using their tails to balance. They were intrigued to see the mat-trans finally open, a door they had perhaps spent days trying to unlock, without success. "That's right, boys," she taunted. "Store's open. Come on in."

Whether they could understand her words or not— and Brigid was inclined to guess that they couldn't—the crocs moved in response, charging the last few feet between the control desks and the open door, one of them leaping over a desk in his haste. For a moment, all Brigid

seemed to see in the dancing flicker of her xenon beam
were three mouths the size of mantraps, opening wider
to reveal thick, muscular tongues as long as her forearm,
surrounded by twin rows of dagger-sharp teeth.

Brigid threw the thing in her hand then, flipping it
into the open mouth of the middle croc, just three feet
from her extended arm. As the rebreather sailed into
the creature's mouth, she blasted a single bullet from
her TP-9 and fell back, all in one gesture.

Brigid was still sailing toward the floor as the bullet struck the rebreather, and in an instant the device's
pressurised supply of oxygen caught light in a cruel
explosion, obliterating the head of the lead croc and
catching the other two in its wake.

Brigid hit the floor with a slap, the armaglass walls
of the mat-trans chamber protecting her from the worst
of the explosion.

MEANWHILE, AS the first croc slipped back from Grant,
its long face splattered with chunks of its own flesh
and ruined eyeball, a second one was moving more
warily toward the powerfully built ex-magistrate. With
a flinch of his wrist tendons, Grant sent his sin eater
pistol back into its hidden holster and reached into a
sheathlike pocket in his duster. A moment later his hand
reappeared wielding a Copperhead assault subgun. The
Copperhead was a favorite field weapon of Grant's, and
it featured a two-foot-long barrel, with grip and trigger
in front of the breech in the bullpup design, allowing
the gun to be used single-handed. It also featured an
optical, image-intensified scope coupled with a laser
autotargeter mounted on top of the frame. The Copperhead possessed a 700-round-per-minute rate of fire

and was equipped with an extended magazine holding thirty-five 4.85 mm steel-jacketed rounds. Grant preferred the Copperhead thanks to its ease of use and the sheer level of destruction it could create.

As the muscular mutie leaped at him, he depressed the trigger, unleashing a storm of 4.85 mm death at his foe. The Copperhead's reports sounded deafening in the enclosed space of the corridor, and the bullets cut through the charging beast like a hot knife through butter. The croc slowed, stumbled, then finally sank to the waterlogged deck two feet from Grant, landing with a great splash of dirty water.

Grant stared down, saw green-tinted blood mixing with the filthy water, lost instants later amid the swill.

"Dumb animal didn't know what it was up against," he muttered as he stalked down the corridor to where Brigid had disappeared.

Grant was halfway there when he heard the explosion of her destroyed rebreather. He didn't just hear it, he felt it, too, the concussive force thudding against his chest like a physical blow.

"Brigid?" he called, running as best he could through the waterlogged tunnel.

He stopped at the open door to the control room, the Copperhead held ready as he glanced inside the door. The place was a scene of devastation. Several consoles at the center had been reduced to slag, and the headless body of one of the croc-men lay sprawled amid their debris. Besides that, over to the sides of the room, two more croc muties were lying in pools of their own blood, spasms running through their sprawled bodies. One was on fire, flames licking up toward the ceiling in a vibrant plume.

"Brigid?" Grant called again, stepping carefully into the room.

"I'm here," she called back, working the latch of the mat-trans chamber. Grant looked at her.

"You okay?" he asked.

She nodded. "Armaglass saved me," she explained, glancing around the room to see the result of her action for the first time.

"What did you do? Explosive?"

"Rebreather," Brigid told him. "Just took a spark from a bullet. Oxygen and fire don't play nice together."

Grant nodded. "Yeah, I can see that. The mat-trans okay?"

"Should be," Brigid assured him. "Where's Kane?"

Grant made a face, then turned and hurried back down the corridor, with Brigid following, toward where they had last seen their partner.

KANE WORKED THROUGH the egg sacs, delivering a single bullet from his sin eater into each forming creature inside, aborting them before they could be born.

Then he slipped the rebreather over his mouth and paced to where the floor sank beneath the water. He needed to find Grant and Brigid and show them the entrance he had discovered. Could be a lot more trouble yet before they had this pest-hole cleaned up.

Chapter 4

They regrouped, then followed Kane back into the water, using the waterproof xenon flashlights to light their way. Grant and Kane still had their rebreathers, but Brigid had sacrificed hers in the struggle with the crocs, so she shared with Grant, taking a breath every fifty seconds while they explored the submerged structure of the redoubt. Brigid was a superb swimmer, and she was adept at holding her breath, using circular breathing techniques to keep from drowning.

They came across no further living muties, although there was a rotting corpse deep below, on the bottom, weighted down with some kind of air-conditioning unit that had been pulled out or broken away from a wall. Brigid speculated that the unit may have fallen on the croc, killing it.

There was something else under there, too: ancient boring machinery, powerful caterpillar tracks and a pointed drill extended before them like a nose. Brigid pointed it out as they swam past. She guessed it dated back to the early days of the Deathlands, when uncontaminated water had been scarce, but technology was still functioning. In that period, people had done anything they could to obtain clean water.

Before long they were back at the place where Kane

had awoken after the first attack, the area he had identified as an old sewer pipe.

"Looks like this isn't the end of it," he reiterated, pointing to the hole in the wall.

Brigid eyed the ruined egg sacs for a heartfelt moment, wondering at what Kane had done. "They were children," she said. "You shouldn't have—"

"They tried to kill me, Baptiste," Kane snapped back. "Me and you and Grant. No discussion, no explanation. They just dragged me under—"

"Me, too," Grant added, "or they tried to."

Brigid shook her head regretfully. "They were probably hungry, living down here like this."

"Then I sympathize," Kane said hotly, "but that won't stop me putting up a fight when something starts chomping down on my leg."

They left it at that, the atmosphere between the trio strained. Brigid knew Kane was right in one sense. They had come here without any intention to hurt anything, but had been forced to defend themselves. She herself had been cornered and forced to kill three of the strange mutated creatures. Even so, it wouldn't sit easy with her, especially killing unborn things like the ones Kane had dispatched.

"I wonder what they are," she said, crouching down to examine the body of the adult that Kane had shot.

"Some kind of mutie," he replied dismissively.

"This one's a female," she told him, and then she indicated the eggs. "Their mother, probably, trying to feed her brood.

"But they're not a strain of mutie I recognize," Brigid continued. "They share superficial similarities to scalies, but they're more animal than that."

"A new strain?" Grant proposed.

"Could be," she mused, "but they shouldn't be appearing like this."

Kane stepped over to the wide hole and peeked inside. "You think maybe we should go check out the source?" It was obvious he wanted to. That was the reason he had brought them back here.

"Yes, we should," Brigid agreed, checking and reloading her pistol before she slipped it back into its holster.

With his head still in the hole, Kane called a hearty "Hello-o-o!" and listened for a response. The only thing to come back was the distant echo of his own voice.

"Smart," Brigid muttered to herself with a shake of her head.

"So," Kane asked, "you want me to go first?"

"You're point man," Grant said.

"Why not," Brigid added. "Look how much it helped us last time."

THE THREE CERBERUS warriors clambered through the rough gap in the wall. They were in a long, roughly carved tunnel that stretched through a thick layer of poured concrete. The space was unlit, and way longer than their xenon beams could reach, leaving a whole swathe of the hole in darkness.

The concrete walls felt rough where they had been drilled into and broken up, and were scuffed and dark with mold. There was a little water on the floor here, not a stream but just a shallow trickle a couple inches across at its widest point.

"Water's coming in from somewhere," Brigid observed, running her beam on the glistening flow.

"Clean water," Grant pointed out, noting its clearness.

The water was flowing steadily toward them, coming from the direction they were headed.

Kane marched on. The tunnel was on a gradual slope, and a few stretches had rugged, uneven steps carved in the floor. "Someone certainly wanted to get down here," he said grimly.

"Or they wanted to get away from whatever is up there," Grant suggested solemnly.

"You saw the borer," Brigid pointed out. "Could be this tunnel's been here for a long time."

There was a sense of foreboding as they climbed the gentle slope to whatever waited above. Nothing came to block their path and there was no sign of life, not even insects feasting on the mold. The trickling of water was the only movement they could detect.

It took six minutes until the powerful xenon beams reached the end of the rough-hewn tunnel, seven until the Cerberus teammates had finished their ascent to its egress. The exit, like the rest of the tunnel, was roughly carved, an almost circular hole leading to whatever lay beyond.

Kane dowsed his flashlight and the others did the same, replacing the polymer-coated lenses over their eyes to see in the darkness rather than warn anyone of their approach. Looking back, he estimated that they had climbed at least a quarter mile up from the underground redoubt, and he guessed that they must be close to ground level.

Kane went ahead, crouch-walking toward the gap in the wall, anxiously manipulating his fingers as he itched to draw his sin eater once again. Behind him, Grant had

drawn the Copperhead assault subgun and held it close
to his body, pointed at the floor. If they met any more
of those croc muties he would be ready. Brigid brought
up the rear, her eyes fixed on the space behind them,
making sure they didn't get snared in a classic ambush
with no way back.

Kane let his point-man sense attune to the new environment, stilling his mind and listening, smelling,
feeling the way the wind currents moved. Whatever lay
beyond the hole smelled old and dusty, but otherwise
didn't smell much at all. He was pretty sure there was
no one around, and certainly no more of the croc things,
unless they'd taken to using mouthwash.

Through the gap and into the next space. It was huge,
momentarily dwarfing Kane with its proportions after
the claustrophobic tunnel. He was in a room a little larger
than a tennis court, containing a sunken space in the
floor. The sunken area was rectangular and filled most
of the room, with broad steps leading down into it and
a metal ladder running up one side. It took a moment
for Kane to recognize what it was—a swimming pool.

Grant followed a moment later, with Brigid just behind him, both of them glancing around warily.

"So," Grant whispered, "where are we?"

"Pool," Kane said, indicating the sunken space. He
paced around the rim, scanning the room.

The pool was empty of water, but contained several
boxes or crates, stacked one on top of the other. There
were similar crates dotted around the sides, as well as
a pile of material—probably clothes or towels, Kane
guessed—near one wall. Up close, the material smelled
musty. The room had no windows, but it featured two
sets of double doors, set off center on the shorter walls.

Kane paced swiftly to the nearest doors, indicating Grant should do likewise for the far set. Moments later the two ex-mags were standing at the doors, listening for signs of life beyond them.

"On three?" Kane called across the room.

Grant nodded, running his index finger down the side of his nose as he caught his teammate's eye. They called the gesture the one percent salute, a ritual between them that averred that no matter how much you plan for, there's always that rogue element—that one percent—that can throw a wrench in the works. The salute was meant to be ironic, but the two men saw it almost as a lucky charm when they found themselves entering an unknown situation.

Kane did a silent count on his fingers and then the two ex-magistrates pushed at the doors they stood before. None of them opened.

"Locked."

"Locked," Grant agreed.

The top halves of each door featured a glass panel, but all of them seemed to have been obscured on the far side. Certain now that they were alone, Kane flipped his xenon flashlight back on and ran it over the windows and down the sliver of space between the doors to see if he could find a lock.

"Looks like someone's put something against the other side of this one," he stated, trotting back and keeping his voice at conversational level. "Looks like wood—maybe a dresser or cabinet."

Grant tried his own doors again, pushing at them with his prodigious strength. "There's some give here," he told the others. "Might be able to force it."

Kane looked from the empty pool to the doors, and

finally settled his gaze on Brigid. "What do you figure this place is? Some kind of public baths?"

"Could be, but could just as easily be one person's private pool," she said.

"Looks kind of old," Kane said to her.

"Reclaimed from prenukecaust stock maybe," Brigid suggested. "Rebuilt or built to old specs. A lot of the materials we've come to use every day date back to those predark designs, remember." She didn't need to add that even her own blaster was of prenukecaust design, first fashioned in the late twentieth century.

CONCLUDING THAT THE only alternative exits in the room were narrow ventilation ducts, which had been sealed for years, the Cerberus crew agreed to try the doors that Grant had felt give. Kane and Brigid waited behind him while he put all his weight into moving them. The twin doors bulged outward, and the team could hear the rattle of chains. For a moment nothing happened, then came a splintering of wood as Grant applied more force, pushing his shoulder against the narrow gap between the panels.

There was a loud cracking and then the doors shuddered backward as they split from their frames, crashing to the floor with a metallic clatter of chain links, followed by an eerie silence.

Grant stepped back, pulling his Copperhead from its hidden sheath.

"Well, I guess that's one way of opening a door," Brigid said quietly.

Grant waited by the doorway, scanning the space beyond. It was dark out there, just as it had been inside. He saw a corridor lined with windows on one side and a rash of peeling paint on the other. The panes were so grimy they let in almost no light, a wash of mud caking their exterior. Apart from furniture, which included a pewlike bench and a trophy cabinet, the corridor was empty.

"What happened here?" Brigid whispered as she stepped forward to examine the scene.

"Maybe the crocs ate everyone," Kane suggested. Though his tone was light, he was only half joking.

She shook her head, her usually vibrant hair almost purple in the semidarkness. "No, they locked the crocs in here, with the pool," she reasoned. "Then they probably drained it in hopes of killing them."

"How do you figure that?" Kane asked.

Brigid pointed to the fallen doors, the length of chain still wrapped tightly around their handles. "It's been locked from outside," she said. "The crocs couldn't get out even if they wanted to."

"Unless they had a bruiser like Grant on their team," Kane added, but he accepted Brigid's point.

THEY PACED AHEAD, more confident now, using the xenon beams to light their way.

There were rooms bleeding off the corridor, some with closed doors, others with just open doorways. The Cerberus trio were used to that. They had grown up in Cobaltville under the Program of Unification, which stated that no individual should have a lock to bar the entry of another.

There were several communal dressing rooms, showers and a large space that Brigid speculated had been used for social events. There were also several smaller rooms, including an office and a number of toilet stalls.

All the rooms were unoccupied and in a run-down state, although they were mostly clean. It was as if the whole building had been deserted and forgotten, left as a frozen moment in time.

There were a few pictures here and there, posters on the walls, photographs on desks and in drawers. The Cerberus team examined these, looking for signs of something going wrong. But they found nothing untoward; the people in the pictures looked normal.

Behind one door was a staircase, with more crates of belongings on the steps, along with several heaps of towels. The others waited in the doorway while Kane trotted up the steps, checking where they led. He found himself in an upper room with a low ceiling and naked support beams, an attic filled with cold and damp.

As in much of the building, a large chunk of the space was given over to storage, but sunlight painted a square on one small section of the floor. Kane paced across to it, glancing around until he located its source. There was a small gap between two support beams of the sloping roof, a ventilation hole where the wall met the eaves. Kane squeezed past the struts and peered through it.

Beyond lay a ville, a small community of a couple dozen buildings, most of them single story, lit by the midmorning sun. There was a paved street running from this building into the ville, with a few benches dotted along its length and a statue at a corner. The place seemed lifeless and empty. Empty except for one thing: a SandCat waiting at the far end, its markings familiar to Kane even after all this time. Cobaltville magistrates.

Chapter 5

"Mags," Kane muttered, looking at the SandCat through the gap.

Kane had been a Cobaltville magistrate once, as had Grant, his partner on the beat until they fell afoul of a conspiracy orchestrated by Cobaltville's leader. Baron Cobalt had turned out to be something other than human, a hybrid of alien DNA, holding the genetic key to a race far older than humankind. That race, the Annunaki, had caused Kane and his Cerberus teammates no end of trouble over the past few years, but it had all started with Baron Cobalt and his cruel desire to manipulate humanity for his own ends.

Kane watched through the gap below the eaves for over a minute, waiting to see if anything moved out there by the SandCat. The squat vehicle was parked, he realized, and nothing entered or exited its sealed doors. The gun turret atop its roof was silent, the guns bowed as if in defeat.

Maybe the SandCat had been left here during a routine patrol; maybe it had broken down. Or maybe the magistrates were here right now, searching the seemingly deserted ville, maybe even rounding up and chilling the locals for some imagined infraction to the baronial world order. Kane listened at the gap a moment longer, but could hear nothing, just the wind whistling through the streets.

Eventually, he backed away from the spy hole and made his way back through the attic and down the stairs to where his partners were waiting.

"You find something up there?" Grant asked. He and Brigid had been waiting five minutes, but it didn't matter to them. They knew some things took time and that Kane would have called them via commtact had he got into any difficulty.

He nodded. "Spy hole up there. Can see the whole ville," he said.

"What's it look like?" Brigid asked.

"Dead," Kane said, "but there are mags here, I think, or maybe just one. Can see a SandCat, anyway."

"Marked?" Grant asked.

"With the familiar red shield," Kane replied, nodding grimly. "One of us, or what we used to be."

Brigid had tensed as the discussion progressed, and she looked now from Kane to Grant. "Either of you guys want to tackle a magistrate? Because I sure don't."

"Nothing we can't handle," Kane said, though he sounded less certain than his words suggested. "If there's mags skulking around a little out-of-the-way community like this, I want to know why, and I want to know where the heck everyone's gone to."

Together, the Cerberus exiles made their way through the building's corridors, which followed a large, rectangular pattern roughly outlining the pool in the center. The three were searching for an exit, but the doors they tried were locked, just like the ones to the pool. These were external doors, however, heavier than the ones Grant had broken through, and would take tools or explosives to breach.

"We'll break a window on the far side and sneak out that way," Kane finally suggested.

"The noise could bring someone," Brigid warned.

"Then we'd best stay on our toes," he replied, eyeing the windows and mentally weighing their proportions. He needed one that would be large enough to allow him and Grant to slip through safely. Brigid, too, though there was a lot less of her to slip. Several of the windows had large, square frames with no cross struts holding them in place, which made them ideal for what Kane had in mind. "There we are," he muttered.

Having selected a window, Kane searched around for something to smash it with.

"Need me to do this?" Grant asked, brandishing his Copperhead subgun.

Kane raised his eyebrows, figuring that his teammate was planning to blast the window clean out of its frame. But Grant reversed the subgun, turning the butt toward the glass.

"Wait here," Brigid instructed, before Grant could smash the window. "And don't do anything till I get back."

She was gone less than a minute, and when she returned she was carrying one of the towels that littered several rooms and the stairwell. "Use this," she instructed, waving the terry cloth toward the window that Grant was about to break. "It'll muffle the noise."

So doing, Grant smashed through the window, and a few moments later the three Cerberus teammates were stepping outside the abandoned swimming pool complex for the first time.

It was warm out there, the sun trundling slowly toward its midday zenith. Brigid gasped as she trod on something just beyond the window. It was a bone, and when she looked she saw many more partly buried in the ground they walked on, scattered there as if on display.

"Bones," Kane said, emotionless. His old magistrate training had kicked in once more, that ability to divorce himself from the potential horrors of a situation and simply deal with it like a machine.

Crouching down, Brigid examined a few of the bones without touching them. They were white, but dirty where the soil had marked them. "Human," she said after just a few seconds' consideration.

Kane looked around, taking in the area around them with its smattering of loose bones. "How many? People, I mean," he asked.

Brigid looked in turn, narrowing her eyes for a moment in thought. "Fifteen, maybe twenty. Hard to say."

Grant shook his head grimly. "What happened to them?" he asked, though he knew he couldn't expect an answer.

"Fed to the crocs maybe," Kane proposed, "before they locked them in the pool and forgot all about them."

Brigid nodded, pulling herself erect. "Could be."

Together, the band of Cerberus warriors made their way across the patch of bones to what would be the front of the building, the direction where Kane had spotted the SandCat. There were more bones all about, some broken, some just shards now, glinting sharply in the overturned soil. Whatever had happened here had killed a lot of people in a very short time.

The side of the building was decorated with stone chips, making the wall rough to the touch. Kane went ahead, pressing himself lightly against it as he moved warily toward the front. He peered around the corner, darted back, then scanned more carefully once he was confident no one was in the immediate vicinity.

"How's it look?" Grant asked. He kept his voice to a whisper.

"Quiet," Kane said, "and empty."

In front of the pool building was a little courtyard with a line of apple trees in blossom, tufts of white flowers like cotton wool on their branches. The courtyard featured two benches and a path leading to the main street that Kane had watched from the hole in the roof space.

Out there, the street was wide enough for two Sand-Cats to pass, and the stone paving looked to be in good working order, albeit a little weatherworn. The buildings fit that description, too—well-built, a little weatherworn, but all of them well-kept. It looked for all the world like a nice place to live. The only thing that broke that illusion was the absolute lifelessness of the whole ville. Nothing moved, no sound carried from workshops or distant conversations. It was like a museum piece.

Kane watched for a moment longer, his eyes fixed on the SandCat that waited at the end of the street. The bulky vehicle sat low to the ground, like a jungle cat waiting to pounce.

Kane turned back to the others, his expression pensive. "The coast is clear—in fact, it's all too clear. Let's be careful."

With that, he stalked ahead into the courtyard, keeping to the shadows and using the trees as cover. He moved swiftly and his companions followed, spreading out a little to ensure that if they were spotted they would not make an easy, single target.

Kane hurried ahead in a crouching run, leaving the others in the courtyard amid the apple trees. He crossed the street, ducking close to the side of a two-story building that would cover the SandCat driver's view of him. The tinted windshield of the vehicle gave nothing away; all Kane could do was move quickly and hope he wasn't spotted. He pressed his back against the wall, glanced around the corner to ensure no one had materialized from the SandCat, then encouraged Grant and Brigid to join him with a swift hand gesture.

Like Kane, the two ran swiftly across the street, keeping their movements as quiet as they could. They met up at the building's edge.

"You think mags did this?" Grant asked.

"Did what?" Kane challenged. "We don't know what happened here or why."

As he finished speaking, there came a groaning sound from behind them. It was coming from inside the building the Cerberus teammates were pressed against, and it sounded like a human voice. All three of them turned, to try to locate and identify the sound.

"Sounded human." Brigid confirmed what the others were thinking.

The wall to the building was solid brick, with just one slit window very high up, and it ended in a wooden fence that surrounded a yard or storage area of some kind. The fence was a little over six feet tall.

"No door," Kane stated. He didn't want to walk around and risk being seen. "We'll use the fence." With that, he trotted along to where the fence began and reached up to the top.

"You just plan to go in there?" Brigid asked, a note of warning in her voice.

"Some people would say that was reckless," Kane said, "but those are the same people who get shot in the back 'cause they never checked what the noise was."

Brigid nodded once, accepting his point. Then she watched as Kane lifted himself up and scrambled swiftly over the wall, all taut muscles and smooth movements. When he'd dropped down, disappearing behind the high fence, she turned back to Grant. "One of these days he's going to be wrong," she said. "Then he'll get killed."

"Not Kane," Grant said. "He's lucky, the kind of luck you hone into an instinct. That instinct has saved my ass on more than one occasion."

"Yeah," Brigid sighed resignedly. "Mine, too."

A YARD LAY behind the building, a gate in the fence to Kane's right, which he saw led to some kind of service alley. The two-story building was made of gray stone, discolored here and there where the elements had worked at it. There was a single window, and a wooden door that had been painted blue some time ago, long enough that the paint was scratched and flaking around the edges.

Above this were two more windows, looking into rooms on the second story.

Kane checked above him, but spotted no one at the windows. He glanced into the lower window—kitchen—then tried the handle of the door. Unlocked, the door opened with a creak of hinges that hadn't been oiled in a long time.

Kane stepped into the kitchen and stopped. There was a dog bowl on the floor, licked clean. Beside it lay the rotting corpse of a dog, flies buzzing around it. It was a large breed, a German shepherd maybe, but it was hard to be sure because so much had decomposed.

Kane moved past the corpse, doing his best to ignore the stench, and continued through the kitchen doorway. It led directly into a living room, which contained two chairs big enough to hold two or three people each, and a sideboard housing trinkets of indeterminate value. Besides the peeling wallpaper, there was something else, too—a figure sitting in one of the chairs with its back to Kane.

"Hello?" he began as he stepped into the room. "I mean you no harm—"

Kane stopped as he saw the figure's face. Its eyes were hollow and there were trails of thick black liquid running down its cheeks from those empty eyes. More liquid oozed from its nostrils and mouth.

Chapter 6

Kane blanched, stepping back from the man in the chair. He looked to be in his forties, though it was hard to tell. He was dead—that much was certain—and the liquid trails that ran over his face had dried there, congealing into something that looked sticky.

Kane flicked his gaze to the ceiling, searching for the source of the liquid—thinking it had maybe dripped from above. But no, there was nothing up there, just the paint, yellowed from tobacco.

The smell of the room struck him, an odor of meat turned bad.

Kane looked back at the dead man in the chair. He wore a dressing gown, beneath which were bedclothes, and thick socks on his feet. It was as though the man had got out of bed and sat down, and then died right then and there. Which meant he had probably felt sick, maybe even for a while. The drapes were closed, but they weren't thick and so the sunlight still came in, turned a warm ochre color as it struck the material.

Belatedly, Kane pulled the rebreather mask from his jacket and slipped it over his mouth and nostrils. He had been breathing the air here for maybe a minute, long enough, possibly, to catch whatever it was that had killed the man. There was a lot of disease out there, and baseline radioactivity was still high in places, high enough that magistrates had been regularly dosed with immunity shots to combat its possible side effects if they had to leave the security of the ville.

Kane's commtact snapped to life then, surprising him in the silence of the old house. "Kane? You okay? Found a way in yet?" Grant asked.

"I'm in," he confirmed. "Found a dead body. Still searching."

He trekked through the living room toward the far door, moving to the front of the house. He stopped momentarily at the window, inching back the edge of the drapes until he could see down the street. The SandCat was still there, silent, waiting.

Kane moved on to the entry, and a staircase lined with wooden banisters.

OUTSIDE, GRANT relayed Kane's response to Brigid while she crouched at the edge of the wall, watching the street.

"Seems like we walked into deadville," Grant finished, shaking his head grimly.

Brigid looked up at him for a moment, and her emerald eyes seemed to bore into his. "The trouble with deadville is that it used to be aliveville, which means we need to find out what happened here before it kills us, too."

"Agreed."

They returned to silence, watching the empty streets and the unmoving SandCat, waiting for Kane's next report.

AS HE REACHED the top of the stairs, Kane heard the groan again, louder now that he was inside the building. There were three doors up here, plus a loft ladder hanging down from above.

Kane moved toward the closed door of the nearest room, resisting the urge to call his sin eater back into his hand. The weapon could be called instantaneously—he had to trust that, or he could end up spooking whoever was here if he went in with a blaster already in his hand.

The door gave after a gentle push. It was a bedroom, Kane saw, with a figure lying in the bed, propped up in a sitting position, pillows against the wall. It was a woman and, like the man downstairs, she was dead. Her face appeared to have caved in, and the eyes were just dark shadows now, that same dark liquid congealed in thick lines.

Kane closed the door, stepped out into the corridor. He couldn't help the dead.

He moved to the next room, another closed door, tried it. The door opened a few inches, then stopped as it struck something. The groan came again, loud now, from just inside.

Kane pressed against the door and wedged his head into the gap, trying to look in. "Hey, is someone there?" he asked.

The room was in pitch darkness, the response another groan. Kane stood there, narrowing his eyes, waiting for them to adjust to the lack of light. It was a bathroom, he saw after a moment: shower cubicle, sink, toilet stall. Someone was sitting crouched in the shower, arms wrapped around knees, head down so that their long hair fell in front of their face. Like the lights, the shower was off.

Kane reached for the xenon flashlight and switched on its beam, angling it away, at the floor behind him. "I'm turning on a light," he explained. "It's going to be bright. Close your eyes."

He raised the flashlight, playing the beam through the gap in the door. It gleamed off the shiny surfaces of the glass and tiles and faucets, flashes of chrome as metal caught the light. The figure in the shower flinched just a little, snuffling like an animal but not moving.

"Hey," Kane called. "You all right? You need help?"

The figure didn't speak, just issued a pained howl from deep in its chest. It was dressed in soiled clothes, matted hair over its face.

Something was behind the door, stopping it from opening. Kane stepped back, pressed against the panel and shoved harder, forcing whatever was there to move back. The door moved a foot and a half, accompanied by a scraping noise, then there was a thud and it wouldn't swing any wider. It was enough for him to pass through, and he went shoulder first.

Kane stepped into the bathroom, checked immediately behind the door. A figure was sprawled there, flat on its back, dead eyes open and turned black, the already-familiar trace of black liquid smeared across its face. The figure was naked, but it had wasted away so much that it was hard to tell if it was male or female; it looked like a skeleton protruding from a bag of skin. Kane glanced at the corpse's groin: male, black smeared genitals and the floor beneath where something had leaked out. The assessment had taken two seconds.

Kane moved across the room, angling the xenon beam at the ceiling so as not to dazzle the groaning figure. It was still bright enough to light the space.

"You okay?" he asked again. "You hurt?"

The figure still did not respond, but just sat there, barely moving.

Kane padded forward, suddenly on high alert, his senses scanning for any danger, any attack. His eyes flicked to the toilet stall, couldn't help but notice the mess that festered there. Black slime was spread up the sides of the basin, over the seat and across the back and the wall behind it. More black splattered the floor, as if someone had spilled paint there.

Kane turned back to the figure crouched in the shower, saw now that it was a woman, long dark hair obscuring her face, her frame wasting away like the corpses he had found in the house. He guessed she was young, a teenager maybe, but it was hard to tell—she was little more than skin and bones. "It's okay," he said gently. "I can help you."

Kane crouched down before her. She didn't move, didn't respond, just issued another of those painful, agonized groans from somewhere behind her curtain of hair.

Kane reached forward, warning the woman what he was about to do, then pushed her hair back until he could see her face. Her head was tilted down, with black streaks running from her eyes and nose and mouth like a river that had burst its banks.

Kane resisted the urge to jump away.

"SOMEONE'S OUT THERE," Brigid hissed. She was still at the building's edge, watching the street, her back to Grant.

"What?" he asked, glancing behind him, back to where Kane had slipped over the fence.

"Dressed in black," Brigid explained in a low voice. "It's a mag…I think."

She could see the figure in the distance, but only from behind. He was dressed in a long black coat that almost touched the ground, like the coats magistrates wore in storm conditions, along with a helmet covering his head. Brigid watched as he stopped at the driver's side of the waiting SandCat. The gull-wing door whirred open and the figure ducked inside. A moment later, the engine roared to life.

"He's moving," Brigid whispered to Grant as he joined her at the corner of the building. "SandCat's turning."

Standing over Brigid, Grant poked his head around the corner, eyes focusing on the SandCat at the far end of the street. As she had stated, it had pulled away from the curb and was performing a three-point turn, reversing its direction. He was barely able to hear the engine from this far away; even in the silent ville the purr of the engine was lost to the wind.

"Lone mag," he mused, "or maybe there's a partner inside, operating the guns. What were they doing here, I wonder?"

Brigid glanced up at him. "Maybe gathering data by remote," she said.

"Yeah, maybe," Grant stated. "We need to investigate while the coast is clear. Who knows how soon they'll return."

"Grant, no—that's inviting trouble," Brigid told him.

"Then what?" he asked. "It's the only sign of life we've seen so far, which makes it our only lead."

Brigid's mind raced. "Satellite," she said, thinking aloud. "Cerberus can track it."

Grant watched the SandCat slowly pull away. Its rear fender was toward them now, which meant the driver wouldn't spot them easily. "I don't like it," Grant said. "I'm going to go check where they're going." He stepped away from the wall. "You and Kane follow when you're ready." With that, he turned and began sprinting up the street, sticking close to the buildings, using their shadows and his own dark clothing to mask his movements.

Brigid muttered a curse about impulsive partners and their knack for getting into trouble, then activated her commtact.

"Cerberus, this is Brigid," she said to the empty air.

Brewster Philboyd's cheerful voice responded immediately. "Brigid, do you have an update for us?"

"Major update," she replied, "but we're still putting the pieces together. Can you get a spy-eye trained on a magistrate SandCat that's just left our location?"

"A what?" Lakesh cut in over the shared comm frequency.

"Just put the eye on it," Brigid said. "You can triangulate from my transponder, right?"

"On it," Brewster confirmed.

The transponder device was surgically fitted for all Cerberus field personnel, designed to broadcast their location, as well as details on their health, such as heart rate and brain activity, to the home base in real time. Back in the Cerberus operations room, Lakesh and his team could access such details about Grant, Kane and Brigid even as they went about their mission, relayed over the satellite links and interpreted via a sophisticated computer program.

As Grant sprinted away down the street, Brigid followed at a more leisurely pace, checking the side doors and watching for snipers or other would-be threats. "Kane?" she said into her hidden commtact. "We're splitting up. SandCat has departed. Grant's checking out where it's heading."

KANE HEARD BRIGID'S words softly over his commtact, but he sensed it wasn't the time to respond. He didn't want to spook the girl in the shower.

"Tell me your name," Kane said, holding his other hand out as he brushed the woman's dark hair away from her face. The black tears glistened on her cheeks, pooling in the hollows beneath her sunken eyes.

The woman shook, clearly agitated as he met her gaze.

"I'm Kane," he said, trying to reassure her. "I only want to help."

The woman unleashed an agonized shriek, then suddenly moved, head tilting rapidly toward Kane's face as if to butt him. He pulled back, but she grabbed him, both hands reaching for his face.

"Wh—?" he began, as the woman was dragged back with him, her face rushing at his.

Then she struck him, her nose against his, mouth pressed on his, lips parted.

Chapter 7

The woman crashed down on Kane, her face pressed against his. She was trying to kiss him.

With a little effort, he pushed her away. Though she was skeletal, she still had strength in her limbs, strength enough to cling to him as he tried to lift her.

"Get off me," Kane snarled, shoving the woman aside.

He had seen this before, the sudden wave of adoration for a rescuer; in magistrate training they had called it shining knight syndrome. At least, that's what he thought this was.

The corpselike woman lay there on the floor at the base of the open shower cubicle, not moving. Kane could see the floor of the shower now; it was smeared with black, congealed liquid, thick as oil. The blackness circled the drain in a spiral, like a child's drawing of a firework.

Kane stood up, watching the woman as she lay there, perfectly still. "I'm sorry," he said. "I didn't mean to hurt you. You just…it's just that you took me by surprise, is all." As he spoke, he wiped at his face where she had struck him, her mouth on his in that desperate kiss. The rebreather was still in place, but it was smeared with liquid, and when he pulled his hand away, Kane saw the tacky black ooze glistening on his fingers.

"What is this stuff?" he muttered, studying it closely.

On the bathroom floor, the woman watched through the strands of her hair, realized her mistake. A moment later she leaped away, moving with unbelievable speed, issuing a groaning scream from deep in her throat.

GRANT RAN, hugging the shadows, his eyes tracking the retreating SandCat, then flicking left and right to check for any sign of threat from the buildings to either side of him. They were almost silent, but he could hear low voices as he ran past them, mumbled pleas and agonized groans like the one Kane had gone to investigate.

Grant was two-thirds of the way down the street when something stepped from a shadowy alleyway between houses and stood in his path. The figure was tall and thin, head bowed so that its chin touched its throat. It was dressed in street clothes—not a magistrate. Grant's eyes flicked ahead, watching the SandCat continue to roar away as he slowed his pace. Should he ignore the stranger, run past him? Or should he stop and interrogate him, see if he knew anything about the bones and the strained voices?

The figure opened its mouth as Grant approached, issuing a terrible groan, followed by something else: vomit, black as midnight, running from its mouth like tar.

Grant stopped, bringing himself up short before the vomiting man. "You okay, man?" he asked. "You need…something?"

The man doubled over, vomiting more forcefully, and a gush of black ooze spattered across the street between his feet. There was more ooze coming from his eyes, Grant saw now, and a dark trickle ran down from his left ear and both nostrils.

"What happened to you?" Grant asked, keeping a wary distance. "Did...did someone do this to you?"

BRIGID, MEANWHILE, proceeded more slowly down the empty street, peering in the windows of buildings for signs of life. Three doors down she found what looked to be a meeting room or a saloon, shades drawn halfway down. She had to crouch to peer inside, and when she did she saw chairs arranged in a circle, with a dozen pairs of legs sitting in them. There were people in there, a ville meeting, maybe. Could that explain the sense of the place being abandoned?

Brigid rose and tried the door, then stepped into the building.

THE MAN STAGGERED unsteadily toward Grant, black drool dribbling from his lips.

"Can you speak?" Grant asked.

Three lurching steps. Four. Five. Six.

The man was two feet away from Grant now. His head moved slowly, as if it weighed too much for his neck, and he peered up through squinted eyes turned black with the gunk inside him. Dark spittle lined the man's mouth.

He reached for Grant, grabbing the left lapel of his coat and using him for balance as he drew closer.

"It's okay, man," Grant said, trying to calm him. "I'm not here to hurt you, just to talk."

The man groaned again, then hacked up a gob of blackness onto Grant's coat.

"Hey, whoa!" Grant ordered. He had been spit at before; it was an occupational hazard back when he was a magistrate doing pedestrian pit patrol in the Tartarus Pits.

The man's grip tightened on Grant's lapel and he raised his head, staring at him through those dark orbs. Spittle glistened around his lips and he began to hack again.

As THE GIRL leaped at him, Kane brought his arms up, swatting at her even as she reached for his face.

The rebreather, he realized. She was trying to remove the rebreather.

Kane shoved the woman away as she grabbed the device, and she staggered back, her grip freed. Kane's left hand went to the mask to make sure it was still secure over his mouth and nostrils. It was.

The woman lay against the wall in a tangle of limbs, a low moaning issuing from her throat as she watched Kane through her unwashed bangs. Her head sagged back and she slumped, as if the life had gone out of her.

She had tried to kiss him, Kane realized—twice. Contact—that had to be the key. Transmission through the mixing of bodily fluids, passing the black tears between victims.

"Grant, Baptiste!" Kane commanded, after activating his commtact. "Put your rebreathers on, right now. Got a…plague carrier here along with three dead victims. I think it may be passed by saliva."

OUT IN THE street, the dark-eyed figure who had clutched Grant's lapel aimed a gob of spit into his face. Grant shoved him back, wiping the spittle from his cheek. As he did so, Kane's warning came through over the commtact. Grant reached into his pocket for his rebreather unit—and stopped. It wasn't there! He had shared the rebreather with Brigid when they had been forced to swim through the submerged levels of the redoubt, he recalled. She must have been the last one using it, and had pocketed it without thinking.

The figure in the ragged clothes had stumbled back, and stood like a puppet with a string cut, barely retaining balance.

"Do that again and I'll shoot you," Grant warned, bringing up his right hand and commanding the sin eater to appear from its hiding place in the wrist holster.

The dead-eyed man swayed uncomfortably, watching Grant through those empty orbs. It was like watching a stalk of corn swaying back and forth in the breeze, barely keeping upright.

Grant stepped away from the man, eyed the distance where the SandCat had been heading. It had disappeared from view, obscured by the rolling landscape beyond the ville limits. *Dammit*.

HEEDING KANE'S WARNING, Brigid slipped the rebreather over her face as she entered the building, stepping straight into the room with the circle of chairs. An eerie silence greeted her.

It was a drinking establishment of some kind, or at least it had been, with a bar taking up the majority of one wall, bottles lined up behind it. Most of the bottles were empty, some missing, some smashed.

At first glance she thought the floor had been painted black. But when she looked more carefully, Brigid saw that the blackness was glistening, and it felt tacky underfoot, a congealing liquid ooze.

The tables had been pushed back to the sides of the room, allowing space for the large circle of chairs that had been set out. There were over twenty chairs in all, each one occupied, with even more pushed back near the rear of the room in an abbreviated second row that ran in a quarter circle. No one moved. More people lay on the floor, as if they had fallen there and couldn't get up.

"Anyone alive?" Brigid asked, gazing around the room.

No one answered. Her words merely echoed in the silence for a moment.

Brigid paced across the room to the circle of chairs, peering behind her as she realized more people were propped against the walls there, slumped over, blackness on their faces, trailing down from their eyes and nostrils and mouths.

The people in the chairs were the same, sunken faces smeared in black, pools of it congealed on their clothes, settling in their laps and running down the legs of the chairs to feed the mess that painted the floor. It was a kind of infection, she guessed, eating away at the citizens of this ville. Where it came from and how it had killed so many, she couldn't begin to fathom.

THE TEAM REGROUPED thirty minutes later, discussing their findings over the commtacts before they met up.

Kane had left the woman in the house. He had considered killing her out of mercy, but decided against it. Based on the evidence he had seen, she would die soon enough, ravaged by whatever black assault had taken her family and was eating through her body. Her desire to contact him, to kiss him, preyed on his mind, though, and he wondered if leaving her alive might be creating problems in the longer term. He locked the house up, breaking down a wooden shed he found in the backyard and using it to board up the doors and windows, locking the diseased woman inside.

Grant's would-be dance partner had sagged in the street and just sat there, legs splayed out before him, rocking back and forth with a line of jet-black drool seeping over his bottom lip. He seemed completely unaware of Grant now, lost in the end stage of the mysterious infection.

Brigid told the two men of the saloon with the corpses, and Grant confirmed that the same scene was repeated right across the ville, dead bodies slumped in rooms and doorways, two lying on sun loungers in their overgrown backyard, faces obscured by the black smear.

"You think the mags had something to do with this?" Grant asked as the trio strode past the last buildings of the ville.

"They were here," Kane said. "That's all we know just now. But if it's manmade..."

"Why would they kill the population of a little place like this?" Brigid asked, shaking her head. "It doesn't make sense. It's simply not their style."

"Baptiste's right," Kane confirmed. "Mags come down pretty hard on lawbreakers, and we..." He stopped, corrected himself. "They'll track a perp to the ends of the Earth if they're considered a high enough threat. But poisoning a community—that's not policy."

Grant turned back, eyeing the ville with its single road. A hand-carved sign had been nailed to a post at the edge of the ville: Freeville, a Place Where Barons Can Go to Hell.

Reading the sign, Kane grimaced. "Lotta hate for the barons and what they did to normal folk," he said.

"Lotta hate for the magistrates who enforced their laws, too," Grant reminded him grimly.

They were all thinking the same thing—that maybe what they had found here had been done as punishment, after all, for a community that defied baronial law.

Chapter 8

Sitting at a desk in the Cerberus operations room, Brewster Philboyd worked the computer software with practiced ease, bringing up a live satellite surveillance feed on the monitor before him.

The control room was a large area bubbling with the murmur of people working. The room was made up of twin rows of monitoring desks, twenty in all, each with its own computer terminal. Roughly one-half of the desks were currently manned, the on-call team in the middle of an eight-hour shift. The room was lit by soft overhead lights that complemented the glow of the computer terminals, and desk lamps were switched on here and there as personnel worked at their own designated projects.

One corner of the room led into the mat-trans chamber, its armaglass a tan-brown color. The far wall was dominated by a Mercator map marked with colorful lines that showed the many available pathways of the mat-trans network, in the style of a twenty-first-century map of an airline's flight routes.

Philboyd sat at one of the terminals, operating a trackball to bring the satellite feed where Brigid had indicated in her recent communication. Brewster Philboyd was a tall man with dirty-blond hair, a high forehead and acne-scarred cheeks. He wore black-framed glasses, behind which his eyes were fixed on the screen, searching for details in the Sonoran Desert. Like the other personnel on shift, he wore a white jumpsuit bisected by a blue zipper up the front.

As Philboyd worked, Mohandas Lakesh Singh paced over, a worried frown on his face. Lakesh was of medium height, with an aquiline nose and refined mouth. His glossy black hair was swept back from his face, a sprinkling of white showing at the temples and sides. In contrast to his dusky skin, he had penetrating blue eyes that were alert to every detail. Though he looked to be in his fifties, Lakesh was far older than that—two hundred years older, in fact. Through a combination of cryogenic freezing and organ transplant, he had survived from the middle of the twentieth century all the way through to the twenty-third, where he now functioned as the founder and head of the Cerberus organization. Lakesh was not alone in his strange relationship to the years—the Cerberus redoubt was staffed by a large number of cryogenic "freezies" who had been discovered on the Manitius Moon Base, having been placed in cryogenic stasis by the military at the turn of the twenty-first century.

"How is it looking?" Lakesh asked briskly, sidling up to Philboyd's terminal.

Brewster nodded, using his cursor to indicate the tiny moving shadow on the expanse of red-tinted earth showing on the satellite feed. "Our boy's moving. He's roughly two miles out from the location of CAT Alpha," Philboyd explained, using the official designation that had been assigned to Kane's exploration team. "Making slow progress over the terrain."

Lakesh peered at the screen and nodded. "Keep on him," he directed. "Let me know if there's any change."

Lakesh thrived in his role of desk jockey to the brave explorers dispatched from the safety of the Cerberus headquarters. The redoubt was built into one of the mountains in the Bitterroot Range, well hidden from view. It occupied an ancient military complex that had been forgotten or ignored in the two centuries since the nukecaust. In the years since that nuclear devastation, a peculiar mythology had grown up around the mountains with their dark, foreboding forests and seemingly bottomless ravines. The wilderness surrounding the redoubt was virtually unpopulated; the nearest settlement could be found in the flatlands some miles away and consisted of a small band of Indians, Sioux and Cheyenne, led by a shaman named Sky Dog.

The redoubt was manned by a full complement of staff, over fifty in total, many of whom were experts in their chosen field of scientific study. Lakesh himself was a physics genius, and had been crucial in the development of the mat-trans system two centuries ago—a means of transportation that his team still relied upon all these years later.

Two orbiting satellites provided much of the empirical data for the Cerberus team. Gaining access to the satellites had taken long man-hours of intense trial-and-error work by many of the top scientists on hand at the mountain base. Now the Cerberus staff could access live feeds from the orbiting Vela-class reconnaissance satellite and the Keyhole Comsat, using concealed uplinks that were tucked beneath camouflage netting, hidden away within the rocky clefts of the mountain range. This arrangement offered a near limitless stream of feed data and provided near-instantaneous communication with field teams across the globe.

Just now, Philboyd was using the Vela-class satellite to track the mysterious SandCat that Kane's team had spotted. He watched as it bumped over the scrubland beyond the ville limits, making its way west. Philboyd continued to watch for several minutes, calculating the vehicle's speed using a tracking program. It was making slow progress, as the terrain made for rough going.

Eventually the SandCat stopped, having traveled just four miles from where it had first been spotted. Philboyd tapped his fingers on the side of his desk in anticipation, watching the distant overhead view of the vehicle as it waited in place.

"It's stopped," he announced, peering over his shoulder to Lakesh's desk, which was located at the rear of the large control room.

"I'll be right there," Lakesh said, and made his way across the room between the rows of desks. Once there, he studied the image on-screen. The SandCat—showing as little more than a tiny rectangle of black against the reddish soil—was no longer moving. However, there was nothing noteworthy around it. The shadows of ridges and a few cactuses showed in smears of gray-black, but otherwise the terrain was dead.

"How long has it been stopped like this?" Lakesh questioned.

"A little over two minutes," Philboyd answered, checking the clock that showed in the corner of his computer screen.

"Did you see any movement?" he queried. "Did anyone leave the cab?"

Philboyd shook his head, not taking his eyes from the

screen. "The resolution's not good enough. Weather report shows some clouds in the sky, not enough to block our view entirely, but enough to blot the image. I can't get any tighter in."

Lakesh breathed heavily through his nose as he weighed the problem. "Get a map overlay. Let's see what's around there, past and present."

Philboyd nodded, typing the request into his computer terminal. A moment later, a detailed map of the terrain appeared over the satellite image, although it added little insight into what was, in essence, untouched desert.

Philboyd continued tapping his keys until a second layer of detail was added to the first, and then a third and a fourth. On and on he worked, drawing more information from the historical records stored in the Cerberus database.

"This is interesting," he said as a new layer showed on screen. A blocky compound appeared close to the position of the SandCat, encompassing 120 square feet. "There was a military facility based there in the year 2000."

"What information do you have about it?" Lakesh asked eagerly.

"It was underground, presumably a bomb test site or research center of some sort," Philboyd summarized after reading the scant detail provided by the file he had tapped into.

Lakesh nodded. "Is it still there?"

"I can't see anything to specifically state that it was deconstructed," Philboyd said. "May have been a victim to the nuclear devastation, of course."

Lakesh pondered this for a few seconds. "An underground facility like that would stand a reasonable chance of survival, however, barring a direct strike."

"Do you think it's still there?" Philboyd asked.

"I think it bears investigation, good friend," he replied.

Brewster Philboyd activated his commtact link, relaying the information to Kane and his team.

Chapter 9

The room had been left almost entirely in darkness, lit only by floor lights to guide an individual's way, and by the vast bank of monitors that covered a whole wall. A lone figure sat in the sole chair in the room, gazing at the different monitor displays. He wore a long coat with the red shield of a Cobaltville Magistrate at his breast, gloves and a helmet with a faceplate that hid his features. DePaul was used to the uniform, so he had no desire to remove it while he conducted his studies.

He had returned to the ops room to finish the analysis, and he sat now before the vast bank of monitor screens, six tall and ten across, each screen showing a different aspect of the test.

The test had been an unqualified success. Barely a single lawbreaker had been left alive, and those that had survived this long were close to death now, hardly more than walking shadows, their insides rebelling, the way they had opposed the law in life. Ten days had been enough to kill almost all of them, so this last week was just mop up.

Behind his faceplate, DePaul smiled.

The analysis data ran across the monitor bank, picking out new insights, comparing data with previous results, extrapolating projected outcomes based on sliding time scales for optimum results. DePaul's eyes glazed over as the data flickered past, his mind drifting back to a decade before, when he had been a rookie magistrate in Cobaltville.

Ten years earlier

DePaul LAY IN the bed, his eyes open, gazing out the window that looked into the hospital room. The skin on his arms was itching and his face burned hot as a newly boiled kettle. He ignored the heat, resisting the urge to scratch at it or rub it; as a magistrate-in-training, he must show absolute discipline if he was to graduate.

He was on Cappa Level of the Administrative Monolith, which dominated the ville like a proud sentinel, its single red orb like an eye watching over the citizens who lived there. Beside the admin block were the smaller towers of the four Enclaves, joined by pedestrian bridges and running almost like steps away from that towering center, dropping below the height of the window ledge as they continued on to the bluffs and the sublevels, and from there to the walls of the ville.

DePaul envied them. He, too, wanted to be out there, watching over the streets, able to roam to the edge of the walls where Baron Cobalt's strict rule remained tight and absolute.

Outside of those walls, the real lawlessness began.

Sure, there were perps within Cobaltville—DePaul had collared more than a few in his brief time on active duty, partnered with Irons as the older mag showed him the ropes. But it was nothing like the hell festering beyond the walls, where mutants still walked free, and mutie farms like the one he and Irons and Bellevue had broken up last week sprang up with little fear of recourse.

DePaul reached idly for his right forearm with his left hand, playing the stubs of his nails across the burning skin there, picking at the scabs.

"Now, now, son," a familiar voice said from the doorway, "you want to keep your hands to yourself."

DePaul looked up, willing the embarrassed blush that threatened to rise to his cheeks to dissipate. Standing in the doorway was Salvo, unit commander of the magistrates, with ultimate authority over rookies like DePaul. Salvo was a broad-shouldered man in his early thirties, sallow faced, with dark hair cropped close to his skull and showing threads of gray. He wore the uniform of a magistrate, the flexible black armor with the crimson shield over the left breast, black gloves and boots. He held his helmet under his arm like an astronaut waiting to board a rocket. He wasn't a big man, but he was big enough to instil fear in every rookie who had ever graduated under him.

DePaul gave a brisk salute, straightening up as he lay in the bed. "Sir, yes sir."

Salvo stood just inside the hospital room, his brown-eyed stare fixed on DePaul, almost burrowing into him. "A week away from the job," he said without emotion. "I don't know how I'd handle it, rookie. But we all get hit by a bug sometimes. Even the jabs the baron gives us in his benevolence cannot immunise a body against everything."

DePaul was struggling to meet his superior's gaze and hold it, finally did so only by force of will. "I hope to be back on patrol soon, sir," he said firmly. "If I had my way, I'd be out there right now, enforcing the law."

Salvo flashed him a hint of a smile; it was very brief and slightly unsettling. "I'm sure you would, but these things take time and I can't have a sick man out there on the street, no matter how good he is."

"My test scores are the highest in my year, sir," De-Paul said. He was not bragging, merely stating fact.

"Test scores aren't the same as experience, boy," Salvo said, a note of warning in his voice. "Never make that mistake."

DePaul nodded once, chastised. "I will get well. I will return to the force and I will bring the law to the masses, the deserving and the undeserving alike. To make this a better world. To stop the rot."

Salvo's eyes narrowed as he gazed past DePaul, out through the window of the recuperation room. "Pleased to hear it, son," he said absently. "See that you do."

With that, the commander turned and left the small room with its single bed and lone occupant. DePaul listened for his booted feet as they crossed the tiled floor outside, making their way to the exit of the medical wing. Alone once more, he cursed the disease that had laid him low, some dirty outlander crap that had got mixed up in his system during that bust out west, when they had broken up the illegal mutie sweat farm.

It was the radiation that had weakened him, the docs had said, left him susceptible to some airborne strain of disease that had slipped into his lungs and manifested in the red rash that was dancing around on his skin like a Tartarus slut on payday.

He wanted to be out there, to be catching perps and making Cobaltville safe, but this damned outlander disease had laid him low and left him weak. When he closed his eyes he saw the mutie ranchers, all swag-

ger and poise; felt the sin eater kick in his hand as he
blasted them. Watched them drop as they were hit, just
like shooting the targets in the rifle range. Every bullet was a line from the law book, a passage delivered
straight to the brain, the heart, the gut of those damned
lawbreakers.

He hated them, those lawbreakers. Lying there, in-
capacitated in the recovery bed with nothing to do but
wait, he learned to hate them all.

DEPAUL SNAPPED BACK to the present, watching the
stream of data flicker across his multiple screens. The
top one showed the sunken-cheeked man reach out to
him, then tumble away, groaning in agony and desperation. DePaul had recorded a man in his death throes,
the stain smeared across his face, desperation burning
in his darkened eyes. The outlander was no longer rational, but was running on some basic instinct. He reached
for DePaul, the ragged nails of his dirty hands passing
across the camera lens. He wanted to pass the sentence
on, wanted to gift it to others. But in his confusion he
had mistaken DePaul for another weak lawbreaker, and
DePaul was never weak.

He muted the sound on the screen, watched as the
outlander fell to the ground.

Chapter 10

Up close, the SandCat looked beat-up.

Kane, Grant and Brigid had trekked out from Free-ville into the unforgiving desert of old Colorado, following the coordinates that Brewster Philboyd had given them over the commtacts. The terrain was unremarkable, one dusty ridge much like another with its cacti and scrubby bushes.

"Just keep going, one foot after the other," Grant said as they began putting distance between themselves and the ville of death.

Brigid was less confident. The thought of marching four miles out in the open desert did not fill her with excitement. "Don't you two ever get tired?" she asked as she hurried to keep up.

"Tired doesn't come into it," Kane replied, keeping his steel-gray eyes fixed on the distant horizon. "Like Grant says, you keep going and you keep your mind active until you reach your destination. That's the way Salvo told us, so that's the way it's done."

Salvo. Brigid had heard the name before. The man was a magistrate and Kane's genetic twin. He had been Kane and Grant's superior back when they were magistrates in Cobaltville, had ridden the loose cannon Kane about protocol. The two had even come to blows in an alternative timeline.

Via satellite surveillance, Philboyd continued watching the enclave where the SandCat had parked, and he advised the Cerberus field crew as they neared the site.

Kane and his team could see the vehicle from over a mile out, visible as a black box in the distance once they ascended a sandy ridge. It stood out, sharp lines against the pale landscape. Once they could see it they were aware that whoever was onboard could likely see them, too, but they knew that should not be a problem unless they approached it with blasters in their hands. After all, the Outlands was full of nomads and roamers, people who trekked across the spaces between the villes, surviving and making what little they could of their lives. In all likelihood, the approaching figures of Kane, Grant and Brigid would be mistaken for such.

The SandCat showed no signs of responding as they neared. The twin barrels of the USMG cannon in its bubblelike protrusion remained still.

"I think it's empty," Kane told the others as they came within fifty feet of the vehicle.

"Seems that way," Brigid agreed.

Grant said nothing, just brushed his index finger to his nose once more in the one-percent salute. It was a reminder of the conventions that ruled their lives: odds, ever changing; danger, always lurking.

There was no road here, just red-gold sand, but there were tire tracks going off in different directions. Grant eyed them a moment. "SandCats," he confirmed. "One or many?"

"Two at least," Brigid replied, pointing to a dark shape that was almost hidden behind the SandCat. The second vehicle was covered with camouflage sheeting so that it blended in with the red-brown terrain, so had not shown up on Philboyd's satellite scan. It was beat-up like the first, with a damaged door on the driver's side—bent in with a chunk missing, glass shattered.

Keeping their distance, Kane and Brigid scanned the parked SandCat, while Grant warily checked on the second. The first vehicle was old and dirty with desert dust, and the caterpillar tracks were worn, with a replacement track—brown where it had once been black—visible over the starboard rear wheels. The magistrate shield—Cobaltville red—was scratched and sprayed with the backwash of sand from its passage across the desert. The SandCat had taken a few strikes here and there, scuffs and dents showing on the ceramic arma-glass shell.

"She's taken a few hits," Brigid observed.

"That armor's designed to take small-arms fire," Kane pointed out. "No magistrate would leave it in that state, but those dents don't look recent."

"I agree," she said, nodding.

"Could be stolen," Grant suggested, joining his companions in their assessment, having checked on the second.

Brigid flashed him a look of surprise. "From the magistrates? I thought they were infallible."

"Lot of stuff ends up in the Outlands," Kane told her, "even mag stuff that shouldn't be here. Could be a patrol got jumped."

She raised her eyebrows. "Does that happen much?"

"Not officially," Grant told her, "but there are a lot of people gunning for mags once they leave the ville walls. Sometimes there are incidents."

"'Incidents,'" Brigid repeated, weighing the word. It

was an interesting way to phrase what was most likely a massacre of the vehicle's occupants.

Philboyd had told them about the underground bunker as they journeyed here. Back at Cerberus, Lakesh and his desk team were still trying to find concrete information about the bunker's use, hoping he wasn't sending Kane's crew into a potentially fatal scenario. However, the most they had come up with was that lab animals had been shipped to the location back in the 1990s, suggesting it may have been a research lab specializing in weaponized diseases.

"A plague factory," Brigid had summarised when Lakesh finished reading out from the information he had unearthed.

The use of the word *plague* disturbed Kane, given what they had seen back in Freeville. "You think something could have escaped?" he wondered.

"Two hundred years for a virus to make a jailbreak?" Brigid replied. "That's asking a lot."

But the presence of two SandCats and their users did not bode well, and thoughts were prominent in each of the team's minds that maybe someone had released something that had spent two centuries in incubation, waiting for its chance to strike.

"Two SandCats and a hidden base," Grant summarized. "Could be a magistrate black ops group."

"Could be. We're going to have to go inside," Kane stated, saying what they were all thinking. "That's the only place we'll get to the bottom of this and find out what's really going on out here."

Grant and Brigid agreed, and without more than a few words, the group split up to search for defenses that might be activated if they entered the underground bunker. The entrance was not hidden, but was located close to the SandCat, a few feet from the driver's door. It looked like a buried pipe standing on its side, the oval opening sunk so that it stood above ground level, but low enough to be mistaken for another mound of sand from a distance.

After satisfying himself that the SandCat was empty, Kane surveyed the opening, looking for cameras or the stubby protrusions that marked a gun muzzle. He could see a gap above the pipelike entrance, presumably where a camera had once been located, but the hole was empty now, its protective grille bent. Other than that, it appeared clear.

As Kane examined the door, first Grant, then Brigid returned from their quick recon. "No defenses around," Grant said. "Just dirt."

Brigid nodded in agreement.

Kane looked pensive. "If this is a mag hangout, then there should be more defenses than a door," he mused.

"*If* it's a mag hangout," Brigid said.

"How's the door look?" Grant asked.

"Coded lock." Kane pointed to a recessed panel holding a numeric keypad. The keypad had a metallic sheen and was set deep in the recess to protect it from the elements.

Without any further discussion, Brigid reached into a secure pocket on her pant leg and pulled out a small handheld device roughly the size of a pocket calculator. It was sealed in a plastic bag, and once she opened it, sat snugly in the palm of her hand. This was an electronic skeleton key, designed to fire off a series of high-frequency probes to obtain the correct code for an electronic keypad without disturbing it. Brigid held it near the recessed panel and activated the scanning software. Diodes flickered on the face of the unit as it ran through hundreds of different combinations in a fraction of a second.

"Five-number lock," she said, staring at the key's tiny display. "Got it. One-seven-eight-eight-zero."

"Zero," Kane said with a smirk. "I could have guessed it, except that last number." As he spoke, he tapped the code into the keypad, while the others stepped back. There was always the possibility that the door was booby-trapped, even for someone who knew the code, and that a shutoff would need to be activated within a short period of the door opening. While Brigid and Grant eased away, Kane commanded the sin eater into his hand and pressed the confirm button that would release the lock.

The metal door drew back on silent runners, revealing a dark corridor that led within.

Kane stepped inside first, while his partners waited outside for the all clear. The walls were poured concrete, gray and featureless. It was old, too; he got the sense that nothing much had changed in the two hundred years since this facility had been built.

Kane reached out with his honed senses, trying to locate any possible forms of danger. Nothing came at him. The corridor was just that, strangely quiet after the whistle of the desert wind over the plains.

A moment's hesitation, then he took another step forward, making his way warily down the hallway. It was unlit and ran twelve feet in length to where a second door waited. Kane paced to it, six strides in all, and realized that this short tunnel functioned as an airlock. This door was metal, with a clear, reinforced armaglass panel that acted as a window into the next part of the subterranean facility. No keypad was visible here, but when Kane pulled at the handle, the door held tight. He guessed that it would open only when the other one was closed.

He made his way back up the corridor, explained to his partners waiting there what he was going to do, then shut the exterior door. Overhead lights flickered on as he did so, illuminating the gray-walled corridor.

Kane went back to the second door and pulled at it. This time the lock gave with an audible electronic tone and the portal swung back. He stepped forward, standing on the threshold. Another corridor waited there, peeling away to his left, with a mat on the floor before his feet. The area was unlit, apart from a dull emergency light located above the door itself and a few specks of illumination coming from the diodes on several computer processors in alcoves. The machines whirred quietly as fans kept them cool.

Kane stood there for a moment, listening and watching. Nothing came to challenge him. The place felt strangely deserted, but he wondered about the computers. Were they live because someone was using them, or had they been brought to life when he had unsealed the door and entered the facility?

He turned back, sealed the interior door, then made his way to the outside door, which he opened.

"Looks clear," Kane told the others, before waving them into the subterranean corridor.

A moment later, all three were sealed inside, making their way to the second door, which they entered.

They stood together in a second corridor, this one at an angle to the first and ending in a wall to their right, meaning they could only proceed to the left. There was emergency-style lighting here, a dim bulb over the door through which they had entered, along with several similar lights boxed in at distant intervals along the way. It lent the space a shadowy, twilight feel. Kane estimated that the corridor stretched twenty-five feet, end to end.

He sniffed the air. "Recycled," he said. "Once the door's closed this place is hermetically sealed."

"Makes sense," Brigid agreed. "You'd want the place sealed tighter than a drum if you were investigating chemical weapons here.

"You notice how clean this place is?" she continued, running a gloved fingertip over the edge of the door. When she pulled it away it was clean of any dust or debris. "It's spotless."

"Nothing unusual in that," Kane said. "It's a science facility, right?"

"Yeah, but one that, if our records are correct, was abandoned before the nukecaust," she reminded him. "The SandCat outside implies that someone's using it now."

Kane shrugged and gestured to the floor mat at the door. "Better wipe your feet then," he said as he proceeded down the corridor.

Brigid and Grant followed, the bulky ex-magistrate bringing up the rear. Grant looked around suspiciously, thrusting his sin eater out before him. "I don't like this," he stated in his low, rumbling voice. "You hear something? A cry, maybe?"

The trio stopped. Kane cocked his head, listening, but no further sound came. "Nothing. Baptiste?"

"I didn't hear anything," she admitted, but none of them could be certain if they were just getting jumpy or if Grant had really heard a cry.

They passed the computer banks and reached the end of the corridor, which branched in a T.

"So?" Kane asked the others. "Left or right?"

Before either of his colleagues could reply, they heard a loud animal-like screeching coming from somewhere down the right-hand corridor.

It seemed that the decision had just been made for them.

"Told you," Grant said.

With a curt nod in that direction, Kane led the Cerberus trio to the right, heading deeper into the underground base, toward the sound of screeching. A moment later they reached a large room.

Kane entered first, and was greeted by a cacophony of screams and shrieks from the room's nightmarish residents.

"What th—?" he exclaimed, unable to believe his eyes.

Chapter 11

DePaul peered up from his work at the lab bench where the centrifuge was mixing the latest batch of the final judgment. He thought he'd heard something, his old magistrate senses coming alert like a dog's.

He stepped away from the bench, listening.

It was just the sound of his experiments, screaming as they always did.

He chastised himself for getting twitchy in anticipation. Soon he would pass judgment on Cobaltville as he had on Freeville. Soon three thousand lawbreakers would feel the wrath of his final judgment.

KANE STOPPED SHORT a couple paces inside the open door, staring around. Grant and Brigid waited in the doorway, peering into the room.

It smelled strongly of disinfectant—so strongly it almost overpowered Kane as the shrieking continued all around him, echoing from the gleaming walls and walkway.

The room was large and poorly lit, with just two emergency lights placed at either end of the space, one over each door. The lack of illumination helped mask the horrors inside.

There were thick metal bars arranged vertically along both walls to either side of Kane, leaving a walkway that was only slightly wider than the narrow corridor from which he and his two companions had entered. The bars delineated cages, ten in all, each one little more than seven feet square. The space left just enough room for the people within to lie down on the ragged blankets that had been strewed in each cell.

People, Kane thought, was a generous term for them.

Grant stepped back from the door, held a hand over his mouth. "Should we be breathing in here?" he asked. "I mean, look at them."

Kane's eyes worked slowly around the cells. Their inhabitants were in terrible condition, and the only thing occupying one of the cells seemed to be a fleshy torso surrounded by black ooze. "You're right," he said. "Probably best we take precautions from here on in."

With that, Kane slipped his rebreather back over his face, ensuring that any air he breathed would be filtered before it reached him. Brigid offered the one she still carried to Grant, who shook his head.

"You keep it," he said, "but let's move quick, okay?"

Kane paced forward, gazing into the cells as the figures shrieked like screamer monkeys, and rattled the bars as they tried to reach for him. The inhabitants were mostly naked, and the bars were cleaned to a mirror shine, showing the marks where their hands touched them.

The first three looked disabled, their bodies crooked, their spines bent like a snake's to accommodate new shapes that a human form should never assume. Their flesh was dark, covered in welts and oozing sores, pus glistening on their bare skin. Kane looked at each in turn, wondering if it was male or female. One had matted hair hanging in strands over his? her? face, while the other two were practically hairless, just a few tufts here and there on their scalps, armpits and pubic regions. They looked underfed.

The next cell contained two smaller figures, possibly children, their skin callused like a scalie. The scaleskins sat on the floor with their arms wrapped around their legs, rocking back and forth and weeping. Even in this light, Kane could see that their tears were infected, having a milky quality to them that tears should never have. He realized something as he stood watching them: their scaled flesh was very similar to the croc muties his team had met with in the redoubt just a few hours before. It seemed too great a similarity to be pure coincidence, and he pointed this out to Brigid and Grant.

Brigid's brow furrowed. "What is this place?" she whispered.

Kane looked at her. "Don't you know, Baptiste? It's a lab and these are the rats."

"They're humans…?" Brigid said, sounding uncertain.

"*Were*," Kane corrected, looking back to the cell with the scaled figures within. Around them, the shrieking was dying down, turning back to pained moans and hisses, a symphony of agony as the occupants calmed after the intrusion.

Brigid checked the cells quickly, then stopped before one with an inmate who still looked mostly human. The figure was standing in the far corner, a little hunched, with emaciated limbs, and a rib cage showing through her flesh. She was a woman, but most of her female attributes had wasted away, leaving only red raw skin showing around brown nipples. Her hair had once been blond, but there were only wisps of it left, long dangling threads that started halfway down her scalp and looped over her shoulders.

"Hi, I'm not going to hurt you," Brigid began. "Can you talk?"

The figure stood rocking, moving her weight from foot to foot.

"We plan to help you," Brigid said through the rebreather mask. "Get you out of here. But we need to know—who did this to you?"

"Was it magistrates?" Kane added, standing beside Brigid.

Without looking up, the naked figure in the corner of the cell coughed. As she did, a trickle of black liquid sputtered from her mouth, before running down her chin.

"Please," Brigid pleaded, "we need as much information as we can get. We want to help."

The woman continued to stand there, swaying slightly as she stared at her feet. The people in the cages around the Cerberus warriors were becoming restless again, their moans of agitation getting louder; sharper.

Kane put his hand on Brigid's arm. "Come on, Baptiste," he said, "this isn't getting us anywhere."

She stood for a moment longer, watching the woman in the cell. "I'm so sorry," Brigid finally muttered, not knowing what else she could say.

The woman in the cell looked up at the whispered words, and Brigid saw the way her eyes were—a washed-out black, like the people they had met in the ruined town of Freeville. Tears ran down her cheeks from those dark eyes, black tears mixed with the red of blood. Dead tears, Brigid thought.

Together, the Cerberus warriors trotted through the room of cells, making their way to the distant exit. The cries of anguish followed them. Kane closed his eyes as he left, letting those cries wash over him like waves on a beach. He had heard similar tortured cries of the abused before in his life, too many times to count.

THE ROOM WITH cells opened into another corridor, this one featuring two doors on the left-hand wall and a heavy fire door at the end. Kane and Grant took turns checking the two doors, but when they pushed them open all they discovered were restrooms featuring toilet stalls and sinks, and in the nearest one, two urinals.

"Boys and girls," Grant explained as he exited the second.

The fire door was much heavier, with a swing-back spring so that it would always seal. Kane waited by it, screening out the anguished howls of the prisoners behind them, listening for any sounds coming from beyond. Uncertain, he pushed at the door gently, letting it inch forward. Then he waited warily again, listening once more. He could not be sure what was beyond; the sound of the air conditioning and the cries of the prisoners were making it hard to discern anything.

Grant saw the uncertainty on his teammate's face, raised his sin eater and covered the door. Kane nodded and pushed through.

It took a moment for his eyes to adjust. The room was dark, but there were patches of very bright light—one over a bench or worktop, another coming from what Kane took at first glance to be a wall of brilliance, but was in fact a bank of separate monitor screens, each one showing a different image. There were more lights low to the floor.

He became aware of a low humming the instant he

entered the room. It was a regular sound, the noise of machinery, running beneath the whirring of the air con's extractor fans.

A moment later, Kane's eyes had adjusted and he saw the room properly for the first time. It was some kind of laboratory, high-tech, with no windows, just the monitor screens that lined one wall. The workbench was lit by a brilliant line of lights that ran around its edge, and atop it an industrial-sized centrifuge spun, near a bubbling concoction in glass tubes and beakers.

Standing over the bench was a being straight out of a nightmare. Despite its hunched posture, Kane could see that the figure was tall. He guessed it was human, too. It was dressed in a long black coat with a high collar buttoned up to the throat. The garment looked to be armored, with interlocking plates forming a rigid line of shielding across its whole length, and there were strange tubes and pipes connecting to different parts of it. The hem, which almost brushed the floor, was adorned with a shimmering line of beading through which some kind of dark liquid seemed to bubble, giving the whole scene a spectral quality. But there was something else, too—the figure wore a masked helmet that covered its entire face. The mask contained a wide, ten-inch-long and pointed beaklike protrusion where the nose would be, lending the figure a crowlike quality.

As Kane stood there, still trying to process what he was seeing, the figure at the desk turned its head and stared at him through two perfectly round, glass eyes that reflected the brilliant, blinding white bench lights. Something else caught the light, too: a familiar red shield sewn over the left breast of the coat. That shield was the badge of office for a Cobaltville Magistrate—the same shield Kane and Grant had worn for most of their adult lives.

"Who are you?" the figure barked, in a voice filtered and enhanced by the strange mask, so that it sounded impossibly deep and alien. It seemed like a poorly edited recording, whatever filter that operated it cutting out any suggestion of breathing. "What are you doing in my clean laboratory?"

Before Kane could reply, the dark figure began stomping toward him, flicking something at his face from a voluminous bell sleeve.

Chapter 12

There was no time to react.

Subconsciously, Kane heard the release of a catch hidden within the spectral figure's open sleeve, the same way his sin eater was hidden in its wrist holster; saw the flash as something shot across the room toward his face. That something was a jet of liquid; dark or colorless, he couldn't tell which, because it was lost in shadow; only the highlights glistened like a laser beam as they caught the illumination from the workbench. The liquid had a smell, too, a kind of acrid, chemical stench like an oil refinery or a burning tire, though Kane couldn't tell exactly what through the rebreather mask.

All this he absorbed in a fraction of a second as the hidden nozzle spit its contents across the room toward him.

As it blasted toward his face like water from a fire hose, Kane felt something strike him from behind—hard—and he went toppling to the floor, even as the stream of foul-smelling liquid hurtled past the spot where he had been standing.

Kane slammed into the floor with a bone-jarring crash, his breath huffing out of him, a gush of liquid lashing against the floor behind him like the strike of a whip. Above him, Grant was tumbling over and away, grunting with the effort as he forced Kane aside after a split-second decision.

Thanks to his teammate's quick thinking, the unknown liquid had mostly missed him. However, as Grant got up from the floor, Kane could see a stream of the glistening liquid running down the left breast of his coat, catching the light like silvery strands of webbing.

"You okay?" Kane asked, bringing himself up into a crouch.

Grant swiped at the gunk with a gloved hand and snarled, even as he powered the sin eater into his fist once more. "Sure," he said, targeting the strangely dressed figure who had sent the jet of liquid at Kane.

"Hey, slow down," Kane called. "We just came to talk."

"Trespassers, outlanders, lawbreakers," the shadowy figure hissed, in that strangely modulated voice. "You bring your filth and your lies here at your peril."

Kane held his hands up in a nonhostile gesture, sending his sin eater back to its hidden sleeve. Grant followed his lead, sending his own weapon back to its hidden holster with a flinch of his wrist tendons, aware that he could instantly recall it to his hand if he needed to.

"You're a magistrate, right?" Kane stated.

The black-clad figure gave no response, just stood stock-still, those round lenses of his eyes fixed in Kane's direction, but giving nothing away.

"We spotted the SandCat outside, recognized the shield," Kane lied. "We're not looking for trouble, just answers."

The dark figure continued to watch Kane and Grant. "Who are you?" he asked.

Kane thought the question over for a moment. Technically, he was still a wanted criminal by the Cobaltville Magistrates, as were Grant and Baptiste. But if this mook hadn't recognized him, then maybe he could bluff his way through this without anyone else getting blasted or drenched or whatever. "Name's John. My business partner, Blake," Kane said, indicating Grant. "We saw the 'cat and figured there might be an opportunity here, if we knew what it was you were doing out here."

DEPAUL WATCHED THE two men through the lenses of his protective suit as the man called John told him his story. As he spoke, a vibrantly colored heads-up display raced before DePaul's eyes, guided by the onboard computer processor whose circuitry was woven into the threads of his environmental suit, searching for two things— weapons and faces.

The Caucasian was armed with a sin eater, as well as a line of metal in his boot that registered as a knife. The black had a sin eater, too, as well as a larger assault gun held in a pouch in the lining of his coat. Sin eaters were magistrate weapons, so were these two mags, he wondered, or had they killed mags and taken their weapons?

The man called John was speaking about a business opportunity. He was a fast talker, clearly used to thinking on his feet, and he spoke with a Cobaltville accent. Could he and his partner be Cobaltville Magistrates working undercover? He certainly had the bearing of a magistrate, and he reminded DePaul of Salvo, his old chief. The sin eaters were too obvious, though, weren't they? Why would an undercover mag reveal that weapon unless pressed to do so?

"WE CAME THROUGH a room of experiments back there, I guess you'd call them," Kane continued, getting into his act. "Wonder if maybe you and your mag buddies might be interested in—"

"Your weapons," the dark-clad figure interrupted, his voice filtered through the modulator of the mask. "Are you magistrate killers?"

"No," Kane assured him, "that's not why we're—"

"Kane," the figure stated.

Kane felt his heart sink.

"And Grant," DePaul continued, reading the data from his HUD, heads-up display, where the computer search had finally identified his two intruders. "Ex-magistrates. Wanted men."

"Yeah, look, it's not how it seems," Kane began.

DePaul took a step toward them. "You break in."

Another step. "You lie."

Another step. "How would an ex-magistrate like yourself judge those actions, Kane?"

Kane's eyes flicked left and right, glancing around for any backup that this mysterious figure might have. Brigid had wisely stayed out of sight, and that might now be his only hope in avoiding an ambush by a whole squad of magistrates in freakish masks.

"Well?" DePaul asked, halting a dozen paces from where Kane and Grant stood across the lab.

"I stopped being a magistrate a long time ago," Kane replied. "I don't judge people anymore."

"A shame," DePaul said. "Your statistics are impressive."

"Were," Kane corrected. "Like I said, I quit the job a long time ago."

REAMS OF DATA were running across the heads-up display. DePaul absorbed it with practiced ease, splitting his attention between taking in the most important parts of the data and watching the two intruders.

Kane had served as a Cobaltville mag for almost a decade, his partner Grant for a little longer than that. Both had received multiple plaudits for meritorious service. They had been good.

But something had changed. They had been drummed out of Cobaltville, he saw. Drummed out for some unstated infraction that they could never fix.

"Lawbreakers," DePaul summarized, as the data filtered past his eyes.

"WHAT'S THAT?" GRANT ASKED. "What did you say?"

"You broke the law," DePaul stated in the modulated tones of his all-encompassing helmet. "You were dismissed. You're wanted men."

"All a misunderstanding," Kane bluffed. "But we found something close by that does need a mag—"

But before another word could be exchanged, the dark figure raised both hands toward the Cerberus men and two bursts of liquid came blasting from beneath the bell sleeves like shots from a gun. Each sleeve contained some kind of nozzle hidden within it, Kane realized, fed by a storage pack hidden in the bulky, almost shapeless barrel of a coat that the nightmarish figure wore.

Kane leaped aside as the stream of foul-smelling liquid spilled across the floor. Close by, Grant dived for cover behind a chair. It wasn't much, but it was all there was in the room.

"Judgment is upon you," DePaul advised the two men. "Surrender to it, or be struck down by it regardless."

"Stand down," Kane ordered, leveling his sin eater at the eerie figure in black.

DePaul fired again, sending thick streams of the odiferous stuff across the length of the lab. The streams were so dark they were almost lost in the shadows. Only the highlights caught the glare from the workbench, like streaks of lightning rushing through the air.

Kane rolled, his sin eater blasting as the jet of foul-smelling liquid splashed the floor around him. A 9 mm bullet was propelled from his weapon's muzzle, whipping across the room toward the ominous figure in the beaklike mask.

Kane's aim was true and his bullet struck the mystery man just above the crimson shield he wore over his left breast. Kane cursed in despair as the bullet hit, then rebounded away, ricocheting across the room with an audible ping.

Grant had adopted a kneeling position, with the chair for cover, and he trained his own sin eater on the nightmarish figure of DePaul. He watched the tall form stalk across the room like a long shadow, marching determinedly toward Kane as the dark-haired Cerberus warrior ran for cover behind the wall of monitors. DePaul raised both arms once more and blasted twin streams at Kane as he skipped backward.

"Judgment is here, fugitive," the mag stated over the sound of rushing liquid.

"Judge this," Grant muttered, and his index finger stroked the trigger of his sin eater, sending a single bullet at that beaked mask.

The 9 mm slug struck the fright mask and DePaul reeled in place, the liquid going wild as it spouted from beneath his hands. He recovered in an instant, turned his glass-eyed gaze on Grant. There was a dent in the mask now, above the left jowl. "Fugitives, lawbreakers," he roared. "Your time has come, your sentence is passed."

Grant leaped back as another stream of the rank juice blasted toward him in a torrent. It slapped against his chest, propelled at such force that it knocked him from his feet. Suddenly, he was reeling backward, heels slipping in the pools of hosed liquid that covered the floor of the room, before he crashed to the deck in a heap. He lay there as the dark chemicals splashed over him, washing his coat and legs. The stuff painted the floor now, pools of it catching the flickering light of the bank of monitors, the brilliant illumination of the lab bench.

The nightmare figure of DePaul stood in the center of the room, sending a rushing stream at Grant as he struggled on the floor.

Bullets weren't having any effect, Kane realized, as he watched from his hiding place behind the bank of monitors. "Gonna have to do this personal, then," he muttered, commanding his sin eater back to its hidden holster.

Kane began running then, hurtling across the space like a missile. DePaul saw him and reacted, raising his other arm toward him and sending another blast of the ice-cold liquid at his rushing form. Kane zigzagged, deftly avoiding the blast, before launching himself at his terrifying foe. Kane leaped into the air and kicked, striking him hard in the chest with the sole of his left boot.

DePaul staggered three steps back and the jets of liquid abruptly ceased.

Kane was on him then, drawing his arm backward, right fist balled.

Pow!

Kane struck the sinister figure across the chin, watched as the beaked head went up and back. He drew his fist back again for the follow through. As he did so, DePaul raised his left arm and triggered the hidden hose in his sleeve once more—and suddenly Kane found his feet slip from under him as he was propelled away by the jet of liquid.

He reeled through the air for a moment, his feet inches above the ground. Then he crashed into the workbench, with its network of tubing and beakers, and the sound of breaking glass rang through the room. The next thing Kane knew, he was lying on the floor behind the bench, his clothes drenched with the unknown liquid, his head spinning as he tried to make sense of what had happened.

On the far side of the bench, DePaul was stalking across the room like the grim specter of death, making his way toward where Kane had fallen, ready to strangle the life out of him once and for all.

Chapter 13

Brigid had been waiting in a crouch outside the heavy door leading into DePaul's lab. The door was propped open slightly, just enough that Brigid could see a sliver of the room from her position. It was dark in there, the flicker of the monitor bank casting eerie shadows. She had heard more than seen the altercation that was playing out inside, had watched as Grant came crashing to the floor amid a stream of barely visible liquid.

Then she saw Kane come rushing out from behind the monitor bank and slap against the tall, dark figure with the strange silhouette, only to be knocked away. It was time to reveal herself, before things got any more out of hand.

"Freeze!" Brigid yelled, stepping through the door and into the room. Her TP-9 semiautomatic was raised in a two-handed grip, and targeted the stranger in black. The floor was wet here, where streams of liquid had been sprayed.

The nightmarish figure turned, glass eyes flashing as they caught the light, the long proboscis of his eerie mask pointed at Brigid across the length of the room. He looked like an insect caught in the light.

"You're outnumbered," Brigid called. "You can't take all three of us." She hoped that the man was alone.

The figure in the fright mask began to charge at Brigid, and she fired, sending the first in a stream of

9 mm bullets at his hurtling form. He moved fast, ignoring the bullets as they rang ineffectively against his armored clothes.

Brigid continued to fire her blaster, knowing better than to negotiate with an enraged foe like this. Her bullets sparked as they struck the figure's coat, before zipping away in loud recoils.

Then he was on her, batting her aside with a single sweep of his arm. Brigid crashed to the floor, rolling amid the puddles of evil-smelling liquid.

JUDGMENT WOULD NOT wait.

DePaul knocked the redhead aside with a single blow and paced to the door. He heard the woman splash to the floor as he hurried out of the lab. She was right—he was outnumbered. What's more, he had been caught unawares, and while a magistrate was always prepared, there was only so much he could do against three armed foes in an enclosed space.

Besides, there was the sentence to pass; that was his most important task. This unexpected altercation was nothing more than a distraction. There were other ways to deal with this trio of blunderers who had somehow found his laboratory.

They would be judged soon enough, found guilty for their crimes. It was the magistrate way, everything that had been drummed into him from the moment he could understand.

He hurried on, marching through the corridor and into the holding area.

BRIGID FELT PAIN blast through her side where she had been slammed against the floor. Her head was fuzzy;

she had lost her grasp on consciousness for a moment when she had been struck by that nightmarish figure.

Slowly, she moved, working past the pain and confusion, forcing herself to a sitting position with the pistol raised and ready.

Behind her, the nightmarish figure had just stepped from the room, the clatter of his boot heels echoing as he strode hurriedly down the corridor beyond.

Brigid pushed herself up, watching the retreating form for a moment. "Kane, Grant—he's escaping!" she cried. The words sounded loud even to her own ears, despite being muffled by the rebreather she still wore over her mouth and nose.

Across the room, Kane heard the words in his confused head, and he forced himself to clamber up from where he had been knocked behind the workbench. His chest burned where he had been struck by the force of that jet of liquid, and his clothes were sodden. He pushed himself to his feet, accompanied by the sound of crunching glass underfoot.

"What is this stuff?" he muttered, stepping in a pool of liquid. It was viscous, with the thick, runny quality of oil. He stared at a puddle of it for a moment, hands pressed to the top of his legs as he tried to catch his second wind. The liquid was not black, as he had first thought, but rather a kind of washed-out gray, speckled with tiny spots—meaning that, like oil and water, whatever it contained would not mix. Which meant that one part of the compound—probably the gray liquid—was being used as a carrier for the other, active ingredient.

But active for what?

"Baptiste?" Kane prompted.

Brigid was at the door, weapon trained on the

opening. "Come on," she shouted. "We have to stop him."

Grant nodded, brushing a chair aside to join them. It slid across the room on its casters, the wheels kicking up sprays of liquid as they passed through the puddles. Grant loaded a new clip in the sin eater as he marched across the room. He joined Kane and Brigid at the door, weapons raised and ready, following the nightmarish figure in black.

"You think he's a magistrate?" Grant asked as they hurried down the corridor past the restrooms.

"Wears the badge," Kane replied dourly.

"But the clothes," Brigid said. "The mask. Hardly standard issue, is it?"

"There were other divisions," Kane said. "In all my time on the force, I never got to see all of them. Could be some low-profile department."

They stopped talking as they reached the next door. It was closed, which meant anything could be waiting behind it. Silently, Grant held his arm up to instruct the others to wait. He would take the lead now, in case the magistrate—if that's what he was—had prepared an ambush.

Grant grabbed the door with his free hand, his sin eater held out before him as he stepped forward into the room of cells. The space was still in darkness, lit only by the twin lights located above the doors.

As Grant stepped over the threshold, he heard a ghastly, inhuman shriek, and something heavy and as large as a suitcase slammed into him, barreling out of the darkness like a tossed rock.

Chapter 14

Kane and Brigid leaped back as two figures came collapsing through the open door. The lower of the two was Grant, crashing back in an ungainly tumble, then slamming into the deck with a bone-jarring crunch. Above him, clinging to him like some gigantic insect, was something that looked only semihuman, arms and legs deceptively extended by its emaciation, its face a black and near-featureless smear. Liquid oozed down its face and naked body, pooling in the indentation between shoulder blades.

Two black eyes glistened like the eyes of a crow in that smeared dark face. Its mouth opened, wide like a yawn, and it unleashed another cry that was part snake hiss, part wolf howl.

As the thing spit a spray of black gunk into Grant's face, his teammates watched in horror, even as they brought their weapons around to target it as the two figures struggled. Then, with a growl, Grant shoved the creature from him, flinging it back through the open door in a single, brutal shunt.

Brigid followed the thing's path with the barrel of her pistol, watching as it caromed through the doorway before crashing against the bars of one of the cages.

"Oh no!" she gasped as she saw that all the cages were open. "Grant—he's freed the prisoners."

Grant pulled himself up from the deck, wiping the black gunk from his face with the back of his hand. "They're not prisoners, they're experiments," he snarled, climbing to his feet. "Failed experiments."

He stomped back into the room of cages, steadying the sin eater with his left hand as he shot the creature that had attacked him, delivering a single, merciful bullet to its brainpan.

Brigid followed, sweeping her pistol left and right as she watched the cruelly misshapen figures that loomed in the darkness. She turned to Kane as he tracked her movements. "Go," she said, "find our guy. Grant and I can deal with this."

Nodding once, Kane bolted through the room of whining prisoners.

"Everyone is going to calm the hell down," Grant instructed, jabbing his sin eater threateningly toward the figures in the room. "Otherwise, you're all going to end up like your dead friend there." He spit on the floor as if to emphasise his point.

A swaying figure spoke up, still standing inside its now open cage. "You said you'd help us," the woman accused, weeping black eyes fixing on Brigid. "Said you'd save us."

Brigid looked at the pitiful creature in the cell and lowered her gun. "We will," she promised. "Grant, stand down. No one else here is going to attack you. They're just…scared."

His pistol remained unwavering before him. "You sure?"

"They're victims, Grant," Brigid replied. "Innocent victims."

He remained unmoving, holding his weapon on the

group of experimental victims. Then he spit again, and Brigid saw the darkness in the saliva.

"Grant?" she asked. "Are you—?"

Without warning, he sank to the floor. Grant was a big man and his fall was like that of a weight dropped from a height. His sin eater clattered against the metal grating that lined the floor.

"Grant!" Brigid called, scampering across to him and kneeling at his side, the prisoners forgotten for the moment.

She reached for his sin eater, plucked it up carefully, aware that the weapon had no safety features. Swiftly, she ejected the clip before checking on her colleague.

KANE RAN.

Legs pumping, one foot in front of the other, he sprinted from the aisle between the cells where the victims had been released, and out into the narrow corridor beyond.

The corridor was empty, but he could hear the clatter of running feet as his quarry hurried up the next turn in the warren, back toward the exit. Must have taken the guy a few moments to get those cells open, a few moments wasted when he could have been out of here. Kane was working on instinct now, trusting—hoping— that the complex was empty except for the weird magistrate in the fright mask.

Kane slowed as he reached the blind corner, nosed his sin eater before him. He could hear movement coming from the distant end of the corridor and knew just what it was—his adversary unlocking the airlock door and making his way to the outside.

Kane sprang into action, whipping around the corner and scrambling up the narrow tunnel. Fright mask was at the end, just as he had guessed, pulling open the door with the armaglass portal. The black figure turned, bringing his free hand up even as he opened the door. Kane ducked as a stream of dark liquid spurted from the hidden nozzle in the man's sleeve, barely seen in the dimly lit corridor.

Kane replied with a triple burst of fire, sending three bullets down the corridor even as he felt the rush of ice-cold liquid splash against his face. He turned as the liquid struck, felt it wash over the left-hand side of his face as he sank back.

Kane's bullets, meanwhile, hit his target, two of them striking his foe in the arm and torso, the third pinging off the reinforced metal frame of the door. The man staggered, but then seemed to shrug them off, his armor once again providing protection from the small-arms fire.

The liquid had done nothing. Kane wiped it from his face, brought his weapon up to blast the retreating figure more, only to see the door slam shut before him.

Kane ran, cursing into the rebreather he wore over mouth and nostrils.

He reached the internal door and pulled. It held on first try, but gave on the second, presumably as the external door resealed itself, closing the airlock from that end.

Kane ran, sprinting up the tunnel-like corridor in great strides, his free hand grabbing for the bar that would unlock the exterior door, even as the one behind him sealed shut. He pulled it open, barely slowing as he made his way out into the brilliance of daylight.

His target was there, slipping into the driver's seat

of one of the SandCats, its gull-wing door wide-open as he got inside. Kane blasted, sending a stream of bullets at the figure even as the door sank back down into its housing. Kane's bullets struck it as it closed, creating flashes of sparks as the ceramic armaglass shielding deflected the shots.

Then Kane heard the familiar growl of the SandCat's engine roaring to life, watched helplessly as it pulled away from the site in a rain of dislodged sand, picking up speed as it hurtled past him.

The other SandCat, Kane thought. That was still there, waiting for a driver. He ran, chancing a single glance over his shoulder as the piloted SandCat bumped away over the red-brown sand.

The second vehicle SandCat was waiting just as they had left it, crouched under the camouflage netting, its armor marred by the relentless passage of windblown sand. The driver's door was damaged, a great chunk missing from the leading edge as if a shark had taken a bite out of it. Through the gap he could see that the driver's seat was empty. Kane reached for the door and—

The SandCat started up without warning, the animal-like growl of its engine taking Kane by surprise.

"What th—?!"

Then the beaten-up vehicle began to move, coasting smoothly out from beneath the camouflage netting and bumping over the rough ground, picking up speed as it followed the path that the first had taken.

Kane cursed as he watched the SandCat hurry away after its twin. It was a drone, linked to the first with a rudimentary artificial intelligence program designed to respond to and compensate for whatever it encountered.

Kane stood by the sunken opening to the underground bunker, cursing once more as he watched the SandCats disappear, trailed by a billowing plume of dust like a marker.

"Dammit."

He had lost his target.

Chapter 15

Inside the bunker, Brigid Baptiste was sitting with Grant as he huddled on the floor of the room of cages. Drool clung to the ex-mag's chin, and he struggled to stifle a cough. Around them, the prisoners were watching warily, frightened by what Grant had done to their cellmate, scared that one of these mysterious strangers might put a bullet in them, too.

Brigid looked up, saw the eyes upon her and the way the shambling figures were retreating to the farthest corners and walls of the room. "We're not going to hurt you," she said.

From a cell to her left, something hissed. It was human, or it had been, but what was left had skin like tooled leather, and dull, discolored eyes the gray-black of storm clouds.

"Everybody calm down," Brigid said, echoing the words Grant had used a few minutes before.

Then she turned her attention back to him. Grant's eyes were closed and there was a new line of drool running from the side of his mouth. The drool was black.

KANE STOOD ALONE amid the tire tracks, watching the retreating plumes of sand get farther away.

"Dammit," he muttered again, shaking his head.

Then he activated his commtact. "Cerberus? This is

Kane. I need a spy-eye on two—repeat, two—moving SandCats, launched from my location."

Brewster Philboyd's voice came back over the commtact in response. "On it, Kane."

"You see them?" Kane pressed.

There was a pause while, at the other end of the connection, Philboyd adjusted the surveillance satellite to locate the vehicles Kane had identified. "Got them. Tracking."

Kane watched the two vehicles disappear over the edge of the bleak horizon. He had lost them—but Cerberus hadn't.

"GRANT?" BRIGID CALLED, shaking him by his shoulder. "Grant, wake up." Please be alive, she thought, please be alive.

Grant rolled a little with the force of Brigid's shaking, then his eyes flickered open and he smiled. "What? Did I miss something?" he asked. His voice sounded weak, as if he had just woken up, and his eyes were bloodshot.

"I thought you were zoning out on me," Brigid told him, showing a brief smile of flawless white teeth. "Don't do that again."

Grant began to promise he wouldn't, but the words were lost as he began coughing, rolling himself on his side and covering his mouth with his palm. When he drew his hand away, it was spattered in black spittle. "Wh-what is this?" he asked, bewildered. He didn't sound like an ex-magistrate to Brigid anymore, but like a lost child, frightened by something he didn't understand.

"I think you may have become infected," Brigid said,

hating the words as they exited her mouth; as if saying it somehow made it happen, made it real. "That one who jumped you—he…spit at you."

Grant's head lolled on his shoulders in a heavy kind of shake. "I don't know. It all happened fast." He blinked, a hard blink, scrunching up his eyes. "Whoa, I could just fall asleep right here, I swear."

"Don't," Brigid insisted. "Just don't."

"Miss my company?" Grant said, his voice weaker already.

No, scared that you'll never wake up, Brigid thought, but she simply nodded and lied. "You wouldn't leave me alone with Kane, would you? The jokes'll kill me."

Grant smiled at that, letting out a laugh that was little more than a breath.

Come on, Kane, Brigid thought. Get back here already. She tried the commtact, but the shielding on this subterranean lair played havoc with the functionality— a known limitation of the otherwise miraculous communications device—and she couldn't raise him or anyone else.

THREE MINUTES LATER, Kane returned, his face fixed in an angry scowl.

Brigid had moved Grant from the room of cells, dragging his body as best she could, and she had propped him up against a blank wall of the corridor that led back to the exit. The dwellers of the cells remained where she had found them, adhering to her instructions to wait until she could be certain that the danger had passed. They seemed listless and timid, and Brigid estimated that most of them were barely ten breaths away from death, anyway. She wondered if Grant would end up like them, if he had been infected by whatever was killing them.

"Kane?" Brigid said as she saw the man striding along the corridor toward her. "What happened?"

"Lost him," Kane explained, "but Brewster's trained an eye on him."

"Took the SandCat?" Brigid guessed.

Kane nodded. "Took both of them. One must be a drone, linked to the lead vehicle with some kind of follow-the-leader program. How's my partner?"

"Still alive," Brigid said, pushing herself up from her crouch and intercepting Kane before he could come any closer. "Keep your rebreather on," she instructed in a quieter voice. "I think Grant's been infected."

"Infected? By what?" Kane demanded hotly.

"Whatever we saw in Freeville," Brigid replied. "Maybe a chemical weapon, maybe some kind of virus—I don't know."

"And that guy in the fright mask did this?" It was barely a question the way Kane growled it, more like an accusation.

"Maybe he's trying to cure it," Brigid retorted. "Did you think of that?"

Kane snorted. "Did you hear what he said to us? What he called us? Fugitives. Outlanders."

"I didn't hear all of it," Brigid replied.

"He knew we were ex-magistrates," Kane told her, "called us wanted men. He said he would bring some kind of judgment or something."

"Judgment?" she repeated. "You mean, like a magistrate passing sentence?"

"Yeah," Kane said thoughtfully, "exactly like a mag passing sentence. A death sentence."

Brigid looked at him, knew the man well enough to recognize his body language. "Kane, what are you thinking?"

"I'm thinking we need to find out who this fright mask is and just what the hell he's been doing out here in the middle of nowhere," Kane said. "But before all that, we need to get my partner back to Cerberus."

Brigid looked thoughtfully at Kane. "You only ever call Grant your partner when you think he's in serious danger, you know?"

"Just see what you can find, Baptiste," Kane told her, before crouching down beside Grant's propped-up form. Carefully, he picked him up. "You okay there, pal? You hanging in there?"

Grant groaned, his limbs floppy and his body heavy as a slab of meat in a freezer.

"Yeah, that's what I thought," Kane said, making his slow way back down the corridor with Grant in his arms. "Why don't you tell me again about how you met Shizuka?"

KANE RADIOED FOR backup and waited outside the subterranean facility. It was good to be out in the open. It gave him a chance to remove the rebreather and suck in fresh air once more. The obvious way to return home was how they had come, but given Grant's condition and the simple factor of the distance involved, Kane could not chance that.

Cerberus could provide a variety of fast-moving systems with which to transport Kane and the others back to base.

A little over an hour later, two Deathbird helicopters arrived. The Deathbirds were modified from the

AH-64 Apache helicopter design, and featured a chain gun in the chin turret, as well as a stock of missiles. They swooped toward the location like great black insects cutting a path through the cloudless skies above what had once been Colorado.

By that time, Brigid had joined Kane outside, having swiftly scanned over a batch of printed computer records she found in the small complex. She had also confirmed that the area contained simple sleeping quarters, enough to bunk six people, but there was no evidence that it had been in use, other than a single pallet whose film-wrapped pillow showed a light indentation where a head had rested.

"Why is it film-wrapped?" Kane asked.

"It's just a sterilized covering, like from a cleaners, or when it came out of the factory," Brigid explained, brushing the detail aside. "Maybe whoever slept there was too tired to remove it."

The detail nagged at Kane's mind, arousing some detective instinct that he couldn't yet frame into words. For now, he left it, letting the odd fact sink in.

No one else seemed to work in the underground facility, and the other dwellers—call them prisoners, victims or lab experiments—had slunk back into their cells after a few minutes of freedom, too lethargic and too scared to do anything but sit and wait.

After a brief exchange over the commtacts, the two Deathbirds swooped down and landed close to where the three teammates waited. Once the dust had settled, the door of the nearest vehicle popped open and its pilot called to Kane. Edwards was another of Cerberus's field operatives, an ex-mag like Kane and Grant, who specialized in security and didn't shy away from a fight. He was a tall man, broad shouldered, with his hair shaved so closely in a crew cut that you could see his scalp peeking through. The short hairstyle seemed to draw attention to his mangled right ear, which a bullet had struck some time ago. Edwards was dressed in combat pants and an undershirt, and he wore a pair of mirrored sunglasses, the better to see while flying east.

"I hear you girls need a ride home," he said as Kane approached the Deathbird.

"We have a man down, Edwards," Kane explained. "Grant took a face full of something noxious while we were exploring, and it's laid him out."

"A good man, then," Edwards acknowledged, his bravado giving way to admiration. He and Grant had had their disagreements in the past, finding themselves on different sides when the Cerberus redoubt was infiltrated almost a year before, and coming to blows more than once. Edwards might treat him as a rival, but he had a lot of time for Grant and knew he was a great man to have by his side in the field.

The other chopper disgorged three Cerberus medical personnel, led by physician Reba DeFore, while pilot Sela Sinclair doubled as security. DeFore was a stocky woman with ash-blond hair she wore up in an elaborate French twist. All four were dressed in haz-chem gear, their helmets under their arms.

"There's some nasty shit in there, DeFore," Kane warned her, as Edwards shrugged free of his safety webbing.

"Brigid briefed us on the way over," DeFore said, donning her helmet. "Whatever's happened to those people, we'll do all we can to help them."

Edwards was just disembarking from his Deathbird.

"Meanwhile, I'm your ride home," he told Kane. "Let me give you a hand getting Grant in the chopper. He's a heavy bastard."

"It's all muscle," Kane told him.

"I can believe that," Edwards agreed. "Tussling with Grant is like wrestling a grizzly bear. And believe me, I speak from experience."

"Yeah, I heard," Kane replied, but his mind was still on what Brigid had said about the pillow. It nagged at him and he couldn't figure out why.

Reba DeFore stabilized Grant, giving him a sedative to help him rest, before okaying him for travel. Though obviously in a weakened state, Grant was fit and the Cerberus medic was confident that he was strong enough to be moved. Getting him back to the redoubt, where a full medical team could be assigned, was his best option.

Edwards and Kane secured the big man's semiconscious form in the back of the Deathbird, while Brigid explained what DeFore's team needed to do here at the site. "From what I can gather, our mystery man's been working on a few projects. So we don't know precisely what's incubating in there," she said. "Be careful and keep the facility in lockdown until you can discern what it is."

"Will do," DeFore acknowledged, before ducking her helmeted head and leading the way into the underground compound.

Less than a minute later, Brigid was sitting in Edwards's Deathbird as it took to the air. The chopper turned north and began the frantic rush back to Montana, where the Cerberus redoubt was located, high in the Bitterroot Mountains.

THE JOURNEY HOME took several hours, but felt longer than it should have. Kane divided his time between gazing out one of the windows and watching Grant, secure in the crash webbing, groaning and sweating with fever.

At one point, somewhere over a place that had once been called Wyoming, Kane's attention was distracted by a whimper. When he looked over he saw that Brigid had her head tilted away, to look out the window, but he could see tears glistening on her cheek. To his relief, the tears were clear, not the disturbing black color he had seen from the dying inhabitants of Freeville.

"Something wrong, Baptiste?" Kane asked, the words coming a little harsher than he meant them, so that they could be heard over the whir of the chopper's rotor blades.

"What? No, I'm fine," she insisted, turning from him.

"You're crying."

Brigid pressed her fingers to her cheek and saw that he was right. "It's nothing. Just…nothing."

"Don't try to kid me, Baptiste," Kane told her. "I've known you too long to fall for that.

"Look, Grant's going to be okay," he continued. "We'll get back to Cerberus and get him the medical attention he needs. Lakesh said Shizuka's already dispatched two of her finest doctors to assist, and DeFore will be back to oversee things before you know it."

"Yeah," Brigid said, her voice cracking.

Kane stared at her, and his blue-gray eyes seemed to be penetrating her soul. They were linked, these two— soul friends, *anam-charas*. Their bond was something arcane, something beyond reason. Where Kane went, Brigid would follow, and vice versa—throughout a thousand different lives and a thousand different faces. Always, Kane would be there to watch over Brigid, and she him, ever and eternal.

"You're worrying about something," Kane said gently, his eyes fixed on hers.

It was a little nothing of a sentence, but it was all he needed to say. The floodgates seemed to open and a new burst of tears was given life. "It's my fault," she said, wiping at her cheeks. "Oh heavens, it's my fault."

"What's your fault?" Kane snapped. "That he went first? That's what we do, Baptiste. Someone has to go first and sometimes that's the guy who takes the first shot."

"No," Brigid insisted with a shake of her head. "Not that. *This*." She opened her clenched fist and showed him what it was she had there. It was the rebreather— Grant's rebreather, the one he had left with her after she had lost hers in the redoubt earlier that day. "I've killed him, Kane. I've killed Grant."

Chapter 16

"He's not going to die," Kane said with more conviction than he felt.

Brigid shook her head, her eyes shifting to stare at Grant's prone form where he had been stretched across the bench seat in the rear of the Deathbird helicopter. "Don't say that, because you don't know. Reba was worried."

"Grant's strong," Kane said, but it came out more like a plea than a statement.

"I killed him," Brigid stated, and her words were like icicles jabbing into Kane's gut.

He didn't know what to say to that. Brigid was convinced, so nothing he could say seemed able to alter that. The silence between the two Cerberus colleagues stretched out, a palpable wall between them as they sat in the rear seats of the Deathbird, its thrumming rotor blades whirring above like shifting sands through an hourglass, marking Grant's final hours. Kane sat dumbstruck, staring at the rebreather in Brigid's outstretched hand. He simply could not take his eyes from it.

Eventually, Edwards unknowingly broke the silence, calling out over the internal speakers. "Four minutes out," he said. "Prep yourselves for landing."

Kane looked past Brigid, out through the chopper's windows. Out there, he could see the familiar silhou-

ette of the Bitterroots, like jagged teeth thrust into the
sky, wisps of cloud flickering past his view as the rotor
blades cut through the air. It looked unwelcoming, cold
and harsh, and yet it looked like home, and Kane was
glad of that. His glance flicked for a moment to Brigid,
where she sat clutching the rebreather she had acquired
from Grant, and he wondered what he could possibly
say.

Edwards busied himself talking with Cerberus flight
control over his commtact, confirming who he was and
explaining the nature of their cargo. Kane had already
radioed ahead when they took off, which meant that
a medical team was already in place, waiting for the
chopper to come home.

An ex-magistrate, Edwards could handle the Deathbird as if he was born to fly it, and was trained to handle most air vehicles in the redoubt. He might not be
the best pilot Cerberus had—he lacked the flourish and
quick thinking that both Kane and Grant displayed during combat, for instance—but he was eminently capable. He brought the Deathbird down in a smooth descent
as they made their approach to the Cerberus mountain
base, swept through the opening hangar bay doors and
brought the 'bird to an effortless stop without jarring
the passengers at all.

"Nice landing, Edwards," Kane said, reaching for
the side door and sliding it back.

Outside in the hangar, three medical staff and two
security people were hurrying over with a gurney, while
behind them, a number of other Cerberus personnel
were watching anxiously, including Lakesh, the albino
warrior called Domi, and Grant's girlfriend, Shizuka.

Kane recognized Dr. Kazuko, a man in his early forties, of Japanese ancestry, leading the group with the gurney. Kazuko was on secondment from the Tigers of Heaven. He had a bronze tan to his features and short, black hair swept back from his forehead. As usual, he wore a simple two-piece cotton outfit with slippers, augmented by an ornamental short sword, a *wakizashi,* sheathed at his waist.

Ruling the island of New Edo off America's west coast, the Tigers of Heaven were a band of warriors with very close ties to Cerberus, not least because their leader, a modern-day samurai called Shizuka, was Grant's lover. Shizuka herself watched from a respectable distance, conscious that she should not get in the way of the medical people as they checked over him. Not even the worry on her face could distract one from her beauty. She was a petite athletic figure, with long, luxuriant, straight black hair and a pale gold complexion, her lips like rose petals. Her delicately tilted eyes met Kane's gaze, her unspoken question clear.

He nodded to her in acknowledgment, then he and Brigid accompanied the medical personnel as they rushed Grant from the hangar to the medical bay, briefing them along the way.

"Do you have any idea what has infected him, Kane-san?" Dr. Kazuko asked, taking the lead as they rolled the gurney into a waiting elevator.

"Not sure," Kane admitted as the automatic doors slid closed. "We ran into a small ville of people who'd succumbed to some kind of…I dunno…plague, maybe. Lot of dead, only a few still living. Could be the same thing, but it's hard to say for certain."

Kazuko monitored Grant's vital signs as Kane spoke, using a portable computer to run a check on his transponder signal. He tapped the touch screen to bring up more detail. "When you say you're not certain, am I to understand that Grant did not exhibit signs of this alteration until well after you had left said location?"

"That's right," Kane said. "Something attacked him in a secret base about four miles out. Baptiste was—" He stopped, suddenly realizing that Brigid had not come with them when they entered the elevator. "Huh."

Sensing Kane's worry, Kazuko peered up from his touch screen, where he was running over Grant's transponder feed. "Is there something bothering you, Kane-san?"

Kane shook his head in disbelief. "I'm surprised Baptiste didn't come with us. I thought…"

One of the medical assistants—Marguerite Palmer, whose light brown hair was tied back in a long braid—spoke up. "I think maybe Lakesh nobbled her to discuss what happened out there. He was pretty worried. We all were."

Kazuko nodded. "Brigid's insights would no doubt be beneficial," he agreed. "We shall run some tests here, but if you could request that she speak with me as soon as she is free, that would be greatly appreciated."

"Will do," Kane confirmed solemnly. But he was worried about Brigid. After what she had said in the Deathbird, he knew she was carrying a lot of guilt.

There had been a time, months before, when Brigid had been brainwashed, and had lost herself to a new personality, one fueled only by hate. When she recovered she had been barely able to function, caught up as she was by the evil she had perpetrated as that other self. Kane feared she might slip into that same depression spiral again, especially if Grant were to die from this.

Kane needed to step in, speak to her, find the words, the argument, the logic to make her realize that what she had done had not caused this.

The elevator halted and the doors slid back, opening onto a broad corridor within the mountain base. The corridor had been cut straight into the rock, with lights hanging from rigs set up along its vast length. It had the coldness of stone, too, and sometimes being inside the mountain redoubt could feel more like spelunking than working in a fully functioning military base.

The floor was polished tile, and doors were arrayed along it at regular intervals. Familiar personnel, many dressed in the white jumpsuits of Cerberus on-duty staff, populated the corridor as they hurried from place to place, going about their daily routines.

"Medical emergency, coming through," Marguerite barked as they rushed the gurney along the hallway.

Personnel stepped aside and a few stopped and saluted Kane respectfully as he and his out-of-commission partner went hurrying past. Yeah, Kane thought bitterly, it's great to be home.

DR. KAZUKO INSISTED on no visitors while he worked on the sedated Grant, checking his metabolic levels and pumping his stomach of its contents. Kane waited just outside the examination room, sitting on the floor with his back to the wall. He knew this room well, had been here time and again when he or one of his teammates got hurt during a field mission. It was the province of Cerberus physician Reba DeFore, but she was still out in the field now, checking on the subterranean lair that he and his team had left.

Kane was flat-out exhausted. It would not take him

five minutes to go to sleep, but he kept himself awake, determined to know about Grant's condition as soon as Dr. Kazuko could tell him. Grant had been his field partner for a lot of years, dating all the way back to their time together as magistrates in Cobaltville.

Cobaltville. It seemed a different life to him now, Kane thought, and he a different man.

AN HOUR PASSED.

Shizuka was waiting solemnly outside the medical wing, arms folded, staring through the observation window as Dr. Kazuko worked on her best friend and lover. She was dressed in supple leather armor, artfully tooled and decorated to accentuate the slender curves of her body. With the twin swords at her waist, *katana* and *wakizashi*, she could have been Grant's personal guard as much as his concerned lover.

Domi joined the woman on catlike, near silent feet. The two warriors acknowledged one another with a curt, silent nod before Domi turned her attention to the window, through which she could see Kazuko's team working on Grant.

Domi cut a strange figure. An albino woman with a petite frame, she wore her hair in a ragged pixie cut that accentuated her sharp cheekbones and slender neck. Her skin and hair were chalk-white, while her eyes were a vivid ruby red. She was wild; some even thought her feral. While the other personnel of the Cerberus redoubt mostly dressed in regulation jumpsuits, or smart-casual when off duty, Domi preferred to wear as few clothes as possible. Right now, she was dressed in an abbreviated crop top that left her belly exposed, and a pair of cutoffs that left her legs bare. She wore no shoes, but had a large hunting knife in a leather sheath strapped to her ankle. She had history with Grant, had become infatuated with him after he had saved her life, and that infatuation had made her relationship with Shizuka tempestuous. Domi had ultimately made her peace with the situation and with the samurai woman, and had finally found love with Lakesh, a man far older than her and far different, but who somehow understood her needs.

"I'm sorry," Domi said at last, watching the medical staff buzzing around Grant's supine frame.

Shizuka inclined her head and looked at her. "Why? Why are you sorry?" she asked, an edge to her voice. "You played no hand in this, Domi. You have no place to be regretful. No place at all."

Domi looked at Shizuka, tears in her eyes. "I'm sorry because I know how you feel about Grant," she said, "and I know how much it must hurt to see him like this." Then she turned back to the glass and continued to watch as Dr. Kazuko and his people added saline feeds and nutrient drips to Grant's unconscious form.

Shizuka had been hard on Domi, for no reason other than her own fear manifesting inappropriately as anger, a feeling that her space was being intruded upon, perhaps. For Domi to say what she had—the wild child, the semiferal outlander who had grown up in the wastes outside of any ville—that must have been difficult.

"I'm sorry," Shizuka said, reaching out and touching Domi's bare arm.

"Why?" she asked, sniffling.

"Because I know how much he means to you, too."

KANE FOUND BRIGID over an hour later. She was sitting alone on the rock-lined plateau outside the redoubt's double doors, her back toward them and legs stretched out before her, watching the last of the afternoon sun sink low in the blue sky. It surprised him that it was only afternoon. It had been a bastard long day already.

"Figured I'd find you out here, Baptiste," he said as he strode toward her.

Brigid turned her head slightly, but not enough to face him, just so that she could see him from the corner of her eye. "Excellent detective work, Magistrate," she said with a note of sarcasm.

"Not that excellent," Kane admitted. "I checked your quarters, the mess hall, the data banks and the gym—including the pool—twice before I thought to look outside."

Brigid said nothing for a moment as Kane walked over and joined her on the sun-warmed outcropping of rock where she was sitting. "How is he?" she asked at last.

"Stable," Kane said. "DeFore will be back soon and she'll have more insight once she's tested the inhabitants in the cells."

"And in the meantime?" Brigid asked, turning to face Kane, fear in her emerald eyes.

"Doc Kazuko's monitoring him," Kane reassured her, "under pain of death from Shizuka. Well, I say death—you never know with Shizuka. Could be something worse than—"

"How can you joke at a time like this?!" Brigid spit angrily, cutting him off in midspeech.

"Sorry," Kane replied. "I'm sorry. Bad joke. Bad taste. But, you know—he's my friend, too. Lying there infected with who knows what, health deteriorating at a rapid pace. So, how can I not joke? Because the other thing—well, that would be too serious and make it all feel too real."

"It is real, Kane," Brigid snapped, tears welling in her eyes. They were already red-rimmed from crying, Kane saw now.

"He's not going to die," he told her. "Not Grant. Not today."

"This…plague got into him," Brigid said, "because he didn't have…because I had his rebreather."

Kane shook his head. "No, it got into him because that subhuman thing attacked him, and it got into *him* because someone—probably that lunatic in the fright mask—has been testing viruses in that lab.

"Besides, Grant doesn't die like this," Kane assured her.

"What, you think he goes down in a blaze of gunfire, saving a wagload of children from some Annunaki death god?" Brigid retorted hotly.

"No, that's how *I* go," Kane told her with a smirk. "Grant lives to a ripe old age, settles down with Shizuka and they have lots of samurai children—like, ten at least—who finally see what a soft side Grant has when he's not fighting those Annunaki death gods."

Brigid smiled despite herself. "You really think he'll make it?"

"Grant's strong," Kane told her. "Strongest man I know. And you're not responsible. You know that, Baptiste."

"I had his rebreather," she said.

"You offered it back to him," Kane reminded her. "You casting yourself as the villain doesn't make Grant any more of a hero, you know? He's already got 'hero' enough in spades. You didn't do anything wrong."

Brigid looked away for a moment, considering the sunset as it played out its last orange rays across the mountain peaks.

Kane wrapped an arm around her, drawing her close. "He'll pull through," he assured her. "Now, come inside and let's start figuring out a strategy for nailing this nutball in the fright mask."

Brigid nodded wearily. "Sure," she said. "Just let me freshen up first."

Then she stood and made her way back to the open redoubt doors, leaving Kane sitting on the rock, watching her go. When she reached the doors, she turned back to him and smiled tentatively. "Catch," she said, and she threw something to Kane that was not much larger than a marker pen. He grabbed it from the air and held it in his hand, smiling to himself. It was Grant's rebreather.

Chapter 17

"What do you mean, you lost 'em?" Kane demanded hotly. He was straddling a chair in the Cerberus ops room, talking to Brewster Philboyd at the comms station, while Lakesh went over the data. Brigid Baptiste was perched on the edge of the desk beside Kane.

The other operatives in the room turned when they heard his raised voice, ducked back to their work when they saw him angrily glaring at them.

"I mean I lost them," Philboyd said. He was not a fighter like Kane, but he was anything but timid and was not given to backing down—from a problem or an argument. "I tracked your SandCats for forty miles, but then cloud cover interrupted the satellite view for too long, and wherever they emerged, I'd lost them. It's not an infallible system, Kane."

He began to reply, but stopped himself, biting down on his anger.

"You scanned, of course," Brigid interjected.

"Of course," Philboyd confirmed. "The vehicles were heading in a rough northeasterly direction, barring a few diversions in the road. Which is to say, the untilled dirt."

"Northeast," Brigid repeated thoughtfully. "That's not back to Freeville—"

"Where?" Brewster asked.

"The rogue settlement where CAT Alpha first discovered evidence of this person we assume to be driving the vehicles," Lakesh said, putting the report data back on Brewster's desk. "Good work, incidentally, Mr. Philboyd."

"Good work?" Kane snapped. "He lost our targets."

"But not their direction," Brigid said.

Kane looked at her uncertainly. "What does that mean?"

"Kane, what's closest to the underground bunker we found?" she asked.

Kane thought for a moment, then the light of recognition flashed across his face. "Cobaltville. Makes sense, as the guy was wearing a Cobaltville Magistrate badge, and so were the SandCats."

"There's just one problem," Brigid said. "I don't think he's a magistrate."

Kane looked at her in astonishment. "What?"

"I looked around his laboratory while you were waiting for Edwards to pick us up, remember," she stated. "I went through what computer records I could access—not all of them, but enough."

"You broke the encryption?" Kane asked. "We weren't there that long."

Brigid shook her head. "He hadn't encrypted everything. I guess he didn't feel much need to, what with being out in the middle of nowhere in a locked bunker. He was using that bunker we found as a research lab, I think, which is why there were those wretched things in the cages. It looked like he was experimenting with some old diseases, stuff that should have been extinct centuries ago."

"Prenukecaust?" Kane mused.

"It makes a certain degree of sense.," Lakesh chimed in. "That base you discovered was a medical research facility used by the military."

"Germ warfare?" Kane asked.

"Nothing so sinister," Lakesh said. "It took us a while to get to the bottom of the information we had on it, but it seemed to be developing vaccines to help soldiers in the Gulf conflict, not hurt people.

"Of course, every vaccine begins with a tiny droplet of the disease that one hopes to cure."

Kane tamped down his irritation as he spoke to Brigid. "You kept all this quiet on the ride back," he said.

"I had some other things on my mind," she retorted, and Kane suddenly felt like a louse for bringing it up.

"Sorry," he said.

"This guy's had magistrate training, though," Kane continued after a moment. "Could see that in the way he fought. He was using those hoses like twin sin eaters. The stances, the movements—it was all there."

"Could be an ex-mag like you," Philboyd pointed out.

"He knew who we were," Kane said, thinking of the way the man had identified him and Grant. "Didn't have any sympathy for our situation. Spoke about passing sentence and bringing judgment."

"Do you think he could be a magistrate who somehow got left out in the cold?" Brigid asked.

"No, he'd be welcomed back in without any problem," Kane said. "But the way he spoke, that mask he wore—the guy's not… I dunno. He wouldn't be let back on the force like that. A psych report would have picked that up and…"

"And?" Lakesh prompted.

Kane looked from Brigid to Lakesh to Philboyd, wondering how much he should tell them about the inner workings of the magistrate system. These were his friends now, and he trusted them—more than he could ever trust the magistrates and their ways. Though the secrecy had been drummed into him, it was misplaced loyalty to keep that old trust after all this time. "Back when I was a mag," Kane began, "they would compile psychometric reports on every serving magistrate at regular intervals. If you were involved on a big operation, especially outside the walls or on triple P—"

"Triple P?" Philboyd queried.

"PPP—pedestrian pit patrol," Brigid clarified. "Checking on the inhabitants of the Tartarus Pits."

"—you would be subject to a full psych evaluation," Kane continued. "These tests were to see how mentally stable you were. Being a magistrate is a demanding job. It can be mentally exhausting, and the things you see while wearing the uniform can change a man. I've seen good men reduced to desk jockeys—no offense, Brewster—and others just quietly let go, never to be heard from again. Those were the ones who ended up in the psych ward, well away from public eyes. Of all the nasty rumors about what happened there; the nicest I heard was that crazy mags got executed, so make of that what you will."

"Conjecture," Brigid began. "Our man is an ex-magistrate who failed a psychometric report and was moved off duty. What would likely have happened?"

"Psych ward, desk job." Kane ticked them off on his fingers., "Demoted to civilian, expelled from the ville. There were a lot of options, some I probably never even heard about."

"He's not happy about this," Brigid said. "He still thinks he's a mag. So when he ends up outside the ville, he starts making a plan."

"What's the plan?" Kane asked.

The next thing that Brigid said sent chills down everyone's spine: "Freeville. That's the plan."

Chapter 18

Two near-identical vehicles roared across the bleak land-scape of the Sonoran Desert, kicking up a dust plume in their wake that could be seen for miles. The follower, a beat-up SandCat with a patched side window and a chunk missing from the driver's door, perfectly mim-icked the lead vehicle, compensating for every turn and bump that its leader negotiated.

Inside the first machine, his face hidden behind the beaked mask of his sterile suit, DePaul grimaced. The drone SandCat was responding perfectly, clinging six feet from his rear fender with its cargo intact, following him toward Cobaltville. But he could not put the thought of the intruders to his laboratory out of his mind. They were guilty, he reminded himself, recalling the words his mentor, Magistrate Irons, had recited again and again: *Everyone's got a crime to hide if you look deep enough, rookie. Everyone's a criminal at heart—you just have to know how to look.*

Recalling Irons, DePaul's mind drifted back to his younger years, when he had still been a rookie magis-trate in Cobaltville.

Ten years earlier

DePaul had spent a total of nine days out of action, recovering from the infection he had picked up at that mutie farm in the Outlands. He had been given a course of strong antibiotics, and the magistrate doctors had insisted on bed rest for the first five of those days of recuperation, but by the sixth they could no longer stop him as he went down to the gym to keep his body in shape. His muscle tone was looking less pronounced, and he wanted it back. He couldn't go out on the streets at anything less than 100 percent perfect.

Ten days later and he was back in uniform, accompanying Irons on a so-called pedestrian pit patrol, a survey of the Tartarus Pits that underpinned Cobaltville, conducted on foot.

Like all villes, Cobaltville was organized in layers, with administration conducted in the highest, or Alpha Level, above which the baron dwelled, alone and unapproachable. Beneath this was Beta Level, where the Historical Division was located, then Cappa Level, which housed the Magistrate Division, including their training and medical facilities. Beneath Cappa was Delta Level, which was dedicated to the preservation, preparation and distribution of food, then Epsilon, where the construction and manufacturing facilities operated.

The Tartarus Pits were located beneath everything, and made up of narrow, twisting streets lit by the lurid light of neon signs. These sectors of the villes were melting pots where the poorest of Cobaltville's citizens lived, and though crime was not rife, there was a certain lawlessness among the inhabitants that was tolerated or stamped on, depending on what message the authorities wanted to send out. The pits provided a cheap source of labor, and movement between the enclaves of the ville and the pits was tightly controlled and restricted.

The Tartarus Pits were accessed by monitored pedway or sealed elevator. Only a magistrate on official business was allowed to enter them.

"Own the streets or the streets will own you," Irons reminded DePaul as they exited the elevator that accessed the Tartarus Pits.

DePaul nodded, holding back a smile. He was glad to be in uniform again, glad to be back at Irons's side while the older man mentored him, taught him everything he would ever need to be a magistrate like his father.

Then the elevator door silently slid back on its hidden housing, and the two men strode out into the pits.

The overcrowded Tartarus Pits stank of human exertion. It was an eye-opener just being down here, DePaul thought, where the worst of humankind festered, a literal underbelly to the glorious ville. What kind of culture needed this? he wondered. It seemed absolute folly to him, to have a whole society, with all its riches and achievements, willfully keep a substantial section of their people in abject poverty, forcing them to fend for themselves where it was not necessary. It reeked of poor planning, and the place felt like a powder keg just waiting for someone to light the fuse.

Irons set the pace, marching down routes he had been down dozens of times before, proud in his uniform and helmet. To his left, DePaul kept up with him, eyeing the market traders and their customers from the tinted plastic of his visor, mouth set in an emotionless line. Foods sizzled and spit on open griddles, smelling of grease and spices so pungent that DePaul could taste them in the back of his throat each time he breathed in. There were sticky scuffs marking the street, and they caught at the soles of his boots, pulling at them for an instant as he and Irons continued to march down the narrow, winding lane of market stalls.

People backed away from the menacing, black-clad figures, and as they got farther down the street, a ripple effect seemed to pass through the crowd, and a space was made for them like the biblical parting of the Red Sea.

It felt good to be back on patrol, DePaul thought. Not just good—it felt *right*. It was right to be here, to bring order to the masses, to instill fear in them so that they knew to behave, that they were being watched, that there was no escape from the eyes of the law.

But he felt something else, too. The smells, the taste of the air, the unwashed people—it felt unclean. *He* felt unclean.

DePaul stopped, feeling his heart pound against his chest.

Irons was three strides ahead of him when he realized that the rookie was no longer at his side. He paused and turned. "You spot something?" he asked.

Irons was already looking around the immediate area, searching for the source of potential danger—DePaul could tell that, even though the man's eyes were hidden by the visor.

"Nothing," DePaul said, but his voice wavered uncertainly.

Irons stepped closer to him, pitching his voice low so that they would not be overheard. Around them, some of the unwashed crowd seemed to have stopped as people noticed the magistrates talking. They assumed that someone was about to get booked, and some of the crowd made to leave the immediate area with as much subtlety as their haste would allow.

"Then what?" Irons said quietly.

"I…" DePaul stopped, unable to say it.

Irons looked at him, visor to visor, trying to read the rookie's body language. DePaul had been trained since birth to assume this role as magistrate, and his body language gave nothing away. Still, Irons detected something, or maybe he guessed it—that old mag instinct doing double duty as it checked on his partner and remained alert to potential threats. "You feel okay? Is it that bug you picked up?"

"No," DePaul said. "That is to say, yes. I'm okay. It's not the bug."

"Then what?"

How could DePaul tell him? He looked at his sleeves, looked at his gloved hands. But what he saw there—how could he say? He could see germs on him, could feel them multiplying even through the protective leathers of his armor. They were covering his body, attempting to smother his mouth and nose and eyes. Germs conspiring to bring him down again, to lay him low.

Irons was standing in front of him, his hand still on the rookie's sleeve, staring up into the tinted visor of his helmet. "Rookie?" he said quietly. "DePaul?"

DePaul stepped back, brushing Irons's hand—and a whole culture of germs—away from his sleeve. "Get away from me!" he said, reaching for his own helmet and yanking it from his face. "Keep them away from me!" His last words came out almost as a scream.

Irons was quick; a lifetime on the streets, including regular excursions into the dangerous Outlands and the Tartarus Pits, had kept his mind keen. He turned on his heel, facing the crowd that remained watching the strange scene play out, and there was authority in his voice when he spoke. "Everyone is to return to their homes—whatever that might mean—right now," he shouted over the hubbub of the marketplace. "And I mean everyone. I see anyone still standing on this street in thirty seconds and I will arrest their dead body after I've shot it full of holes—get me?"

For a moment the crowd seemed unsure, glancing at one another, looking for a cue. Then, almost as one, they turned and fled, hurrying from the scene as swiftly as their legs would carry them. Vendors left their stalls, exotic dishes sizzling and charring, juices spitting as the heat excited them.

Irons ignored it all, trusting his authority to carry the situation as he turned back to his rookie partner. DePaul was still standing as he had left him, helmet lying sideways on the ground beside a market stall. He held one arm out before him and seemed to be studying the leather of his uniform.

"DePaul? What's going on here?" Irons demanded, employing that same tone of authority that he had used on the crowd moments before.

DePaul looked up past his own arm, his haunted eyes meeting with Irons's mask. "They're everywhere," he said. "Sticking to me, trying to kill me."

"Who's everywhere?" Irons demanded. "Who's trying to kill you?"

"The dirt," DePaul spit. "The germs, the viruses, the unclean shit that's everywhere around us. Don't you see it? Can't you feel it?"

Irons took a step toward his rookie partner, holding his arms out in a nonthreatening gesture. He had seen men crack before; good men, ones who should have made good magistrates. He had seen good magistrates shoot innocents out of fear, and he had seen brilliant magistrates moved to desk positions because they just could not face another day out there on the streets. He reckoned that he had seen it all, until he saw DePaul—the most brilliant rookie to ever come through the training program—crack as they stood in the squalor of a Tartarus Pits market.

"We're going to go back now," Irons said gently. "Back to the Magistrate Hall on Cappa Level. Grab your helmet and we'll walk back to the elevator."

DePaul just stood there, staring wildly at his gloved hands, his wrists, his arms. He was looking at them as if they were alien to his body, or as if they were covered in poison.

"DePaul," Irons said, putting a little of that authority into his voice. "Grab your helmet, lad. When you leave here you'll do so looking like a mag. Is that understood?"

DePaul looked up at Irons for a moment, a flash of blue eyes in his sunken face, the dark bags still visible under his eyes from the sickness that had felled him two weeks earlier. He seemed bewildered, as if he didn't quite realize where he was.

"Helmet," Irons said again.

Obediently, DePaul bent down and snatched up his helmet, brushing the dirt from it.

"Put it on your head, boy," Irons told him.

DePaul looked askance at the older mag through narrowed eyes. "It's dirty."

"Put it on," Irons repeated. "If you don't do it, I will shoot you right here. You leave the pits like a magistrate or you don't leave at all."

DePaul held his breath as he put on the helmet, body trembling, his eyes closed in fear.

MAGISTRATE PSYCHOMETRIC REPORT *D-1011-r*, Code, De-Paul (rookie), Cobaltville. Awaiting Active Badge of Courage. Training Scores: 10, 10, 10, 10, 10.

Intelligent, loyal and unflinching. Has strong curb on emotions. Suggestibility low. Attitude scales incomplete. Concerns raised over mental health, seems traumatized by recent infection. Short-term observation prescribed. Caution recommended.

GRADUALLY, DEPAUL'S mind came back to the present, his eyes focusing once more on the bleak desert that stretched before him in all directions, rocks and cacti and dirt laid out beneath the sinking sun. He had been clinging tightly to the steering wheel as he recollected his experience in the Tartarus Pits, and the insides of his gloves were slick with sweat.

Soon now, he would bring his final judgment to the Tartarus Pits and to everyone else in Cobaltville. Soon all the lawbreakers and corrupt administrators and the filthy baron would reel from his decision, as he passed sentence on the whole ville.

And after that? Well, the world was full of lawbreakers, criminal minds scheming to destroy the fabric of moral society. With his biologically engineered plague, he would cast judgment on every man, woman and child on the planet. The final judgment would wipe every lawbreaker from the face of the Earth, finishing the job that the nukecaust had started. And then he could start things fresh, cleansed from all the germs and bacteria and human detritus that befouled this perfect blue-green mud ball of a planet.

The twin SandCats continued their passage across the empty desert, plumes of dust billowing in their wake, bringing the final judgment to Cobaltville, and to the world.

Chapter 19

At the bunker in the Sonoran Desert, Cerberus physician Reba DeFore and her two associates were studying the health of the mysterious prisoners that Kane's team had discovered in the room of cages. They had sedated those who seemed to be in real pain, partially in an effort to be humane, but also to help make recording and studying their symptoms easier.

Not wanting to move far from the source, DeFore set up a mobile analysis lab in the sleeping quarters of the underground base, placing Sela Sinclair on guard duty outside the base itself. Sinclair was a long-standing member of the Cerberus organization. A lithe, muscular woman with dark skin and short hair weaved in braids, Sela was another of the cryogenic freezies who had been discovered on the Manitius Moon Base. Sinclair had been an Air Force lieutenant in the twentieth century, and she was one the most capable combatants in the Cerberus team.

Of the twelve people they found in the compound, six of the cell inhabitants were already dead, including the one shot by Grant. Four more were close to death, by DeFore's reckoning, while the last two were in a declining spiral of health that had already taken a grave toll on their mental well-being. With Grant infected by the same virus, it was crucial to learn exactly what it was they were suffering from and how medical science might combat it.

DeFore and her two assistants set up portable monitors for the sick, injecting a simplified version of the transponder nanotech to assess the victims' health. Their patients—though DeFore struggled to apply the term to these human wretches—complained, but they had little energy to fight. She tried to be gentle, promising them this was for their own good.

"This is horrible. I've never seen anything quite like this outside of the medical journals," DeFore said, speaking with a lab tech, Gus Wilson, as they studied the results of their initial tests.

Wilson shook his head. "It looks like it's already in end stage," he said, emphasising his words with a whistle that was muffled by the protective mask he wore. "Poor devils don't have long to live." A handsome young man barely into his twenties, with unruly locks of russet-brown hair, Wilson could be a little intimidated sometimes by the array of knowledge on show at the Cerberus facility, preferring to keep to stock checking and less hands-on duties if he could. But he was a diligent worker and had taken this field assignment at Lakesh's urging.

"No," DeFore said, with a solemn shake of her head. "It seems that wherever Kane and his team go, they find things I never imagined still existed. This appears to be a virulent strain of the bubonic plague. However, it's being transmitted by the exchange of bodily fluids in preference to airborne particles."

"From Brigid's report, Grant was infected by one of these—" Wilson gestured toward the cage room

"—poor people vomiting at him. She said it took less than two minutes for the virus to take hold."

DeFore nodded, professional concern on her features. "Could be a flinch response, but as soon as it gets in the system it doesn't take long to kick in," she said. "These people are in the end stage of the cycle, as you say, but how long did it take them to get there? Weeks? Days? Hours? Without that information it will be hard to treat Grant."

The third member of the team, Karen Stapleton—a lanky woman whose strawberry-blond hair had been tied back in a high ponytail beneath her protective helmet—entered the mobile lab then, holding a sheaf of paperwork. "Ten days," she said, answering DeFore's question.

The two turned to their colleague, understandably surprised. "What did you say?" DeFore asked, not quite believing what she'd just heard.

Karen flipped through the papers she was holding in her gloved hand. They were bound computer printouts, text with graphical analysis, and as she turned the pages the others could see that a number of additional notes had been added by hand. "It's an experiment into using a weaponized virus," she explained. "The guy running the experiment made copious notes. It looks like he was trying to perfect the strain to ensure it was both virulent and highly contagious. Everything's in here, from the early tests on rats to the full-blown breakdown of his findings with each strand on his human subjects."

DeFore let out a heavy breath at this last. "Ghastly. Why?"

"Doesn't say," Stapleton replied. "It's just a diaried

report on tests and findings. It's very meticulous. The guy's utterly methodical."

"While experimenting on humans like animals," DeFore said grimly. "What drives a man to do that, I wonder?"

The question hung in the air as the pained moans of the experimental subjects echoed along the grim corridors of the underground bunker.

"YOU MEAN OUR crazy ex-magistrate plans to unleash some kind of virus like the one we discovered in Freeville?" Kane asked. He was barely able to contemplate what Brigid had just said.

"We discovered that he *monitored*," Brigid told him. "And he most probably released it, too."

"That's…"

"Crazy?" Brigid taunted. "Isn't that exactly what you just said about the magistrate psychometric report this guy received?"

"We're speculating," Kane said dismissively.

"Based on the facts we have," Brigid told him hotly.

Lakesh held his hands between the two of them, drawing their attention. "What Brigid says does make a certain degree of sense, friend Kane. If your frightening mask man is a rejected magistrate, then he would have the training and insight to work with the viruses in the compound, and he could quite probably have the motivation to use what he found in the form of a chemical weapon."

"To do what? Take revenge on the magistrate who assessed him?" Kane asked. "I don't buy it."

"No," Brigid said. "To continue being a magistrate.

Imagine if you had a weapon that could punish the guilty, execute everyone who ever committed a crime."

"Such a weapon doesn't exist," Kane stated.

She leaned close to him, speaking suggestively. "It does, my dear ex-magistrate," she said. "It just depends on who you think the guilty are."

Kane looked at her, his brow furrowed as he worked her words over in his mind. "But this...virus he's planning to unleash kills everyone without distinction. You saw Freeville, Baptiste—it killed everyone."

"Exactly. It just depends on who you think the guilty are," Brigid repeated.

"Okay, psych report failed," Kane realized. "Failed mag wants to kill everyone in case they committed a crime. No, in fact, I see it now—he knows they committed a crime."

When he saw Brigid, Lakesh and Brewster Philboyd looking at him strangely, Kane elaborated. "There was this rationale among the mags, that everyone was guilty of something. You just needed to dig deep enough to find out what that something was."

"Even magistrates?" Brigid asked.

Kane appeared to be deep in thought for a moment before nodding. "Has to be. Two of the best got drummed out of Cobaltville for poking their noses where they weren't supposed to be."

Lakesh smiled and so did Brigid. Brewster Philboyd laughed a moment later—too loud, and suddenly self-conscious, as he realized to whom Kane referred.

SHIZUKA SAT WITH Domi in the Cerberus canteen, nursing a cup of green tea that was slowly going cold. The room was a large area, dominated by long, wipe-clean tables that could seat sixteen people each, as well as a number of smaller, more intimate tables. Narrow windows ran along the top of the room in horizontal slits, bringing in a little sunlight in the daytime that was amplified by artificial lighting. The room was well-populated at this hour of the evening, as it was dinnertime for many. But somehow Shizuka felt alone at the large table that she and Domi had taken over a corner of.

"Tea's getting cold," Domi said, sipping her own.

Shizuka looked at her cup, disinterested. "Is it? I hadn't noticed."

Domi reached across the table and touched the samurai woman on the arm, making her look up. "Hey, Grant will be all right," she said.

"We don't know what it is that he has contracted," Shizuka replied. "We don't know the incubation period, the full range of symptoms, the…the inevitable effects."

"There are no inevitable effects where Grant and Kane are involved," Domi assured her. "Have known those two long enough to know that. They've made a career of bucking the odds."

Shizuka breathed heavily through her nostrils, as if expelling the weight of worry that sat on her. "But you can only beat the odds so many times," she said. "Eventually—"

"You need more tea," Domi blurted, refusing to let the woman finish. It was as if saying the words out loud would somehow be it, the curse cast, Grant's destiny assured.

"No, I don't," Shizuka said, and she pushed herself up from her seat. "I need to be with Grant. And he needs me."

With that, she made her way swiftly from the can-

teen, weaving lithely between the tables and the personnel who were engaged in lighter conversations over their
hot meals. Domi watched her go, a sense of admiration
welling within her. Whatever else she may have felt
about Grant over the years, it was clear he had made the
right choice in Shizuka. She was strength personified.

"So THIS MOOK gets drummed out of Cobaltville," Kane
mused, "and then he gets hold of a weapon that could
potentially destroy a whole ville."

"A weaponized virus," Brigid said, nodding in agreement.

"Where does he go?"

She smiled. "Back home."

"Exactly," Kane said. "The SandCat bolted to the
east, putting it in line with Cobalt. The guy's still using
all the paraphernalia of his old occupation—the colors,
the vehicles—it's all Cobaltville Magistrate. So he's
nursing a grudge."

"Or crazy as hell," Brigid said.

"Probably both," Kane concluded, "given the way
he spoke to us. This guy thinks he's still a mag, but the
way he talked about final judgment makes me think he's
planning something big. And this weaponized disease
is just that, isn't it?"

"You think he plans to use it to infect Cobaltville?"
Lakesh said, in evident surprise.

"I think it's a possibility," Kane stated, and Brigid
nodded again.

"He was treating human subjects like…lab rats," she
said. "Our mystery man has no compunction about hurt-
ing people."

"But if this virus is as virulent as you've witnessed—" Philboyd began.

"No, we don't know that for certain," Brigid said. "We've seen the results—"

"And seen Grant get struck down by a concentrated burst of it," Kane added.

"But we don't know how long the incubation period is," Brigid finished.

Lakesh looked pensive. "Whatever the case, I believe it's time we trotted out that old saw—that sooner is better in this case."

"Agreed," Kane said. "Plus, if we can track this guy down, we may be able to get some insight into what to do about Grant."

Brigid swallowed hard at those words, looking to Kane for reassurance.

"Let's find the guy first," Kane told her, recognizing her need for comfort.

Lakesh began consulting a map, checking the location of Cobaltville and the relative parallax points—a network of destinations connected via the quantum web that could grant instantaneous access to a place—as the others discussed the situation.

"You're still wanted fugitives within the barony of Cobaltville," Philboyd reminded Kane and Brigid.

"As if we could forget," Kane growled. "But that ville's sealed up tighter'n a mag's armory. No one's going in there without proper authorization."

"So you'll need a cover story to get inside the ville," Philboyd said. "I'll contact an old friend on the inside, Colin Phillips."

"Sure," Kane agreed, nodding. "The guy owes us big time."

Lakesh tapped a few keys on the nearest computer and brought up a representation of the map he had been consulting. "We can't put you inside the ville—that would be far too dangerous, because we cannot look ahead to see what you'd be jumping into. I propose a destination of seventeen miles out."

"Can't you get us closer?" Kane asked.

"Parallax points around that area are patchy," Lakesh said regretfully. "But I understand our R & D department may have something to make the journey a little easier. Something they've been itching to try."

Kane looked at the dusky-skinned leader of Cerberus, his expression unreadable. "Whatever it is, it better not blow up or catch fire."

Lakesh's brows knitted in confusion. "What are you trying to say about our research people, friend Kane?"

"Nothing they don't already know," he said. Then he turned to Brigid. "Come on, Baptiste—let's go get ourselves prepped and armed while these two figure out our way in."

As they left the room, heading for the armory, Lakesh could hear Kane explaining the situation to Brigid: "Once we enter Cobaltville we'll need to act stealthily, catch this maniac and slip out without getting dragged into the local politics. Like Brewster said, we're still wanted fugitives in Cobaltville—you and me."

"And Grant," Brigid reminded him, a hint of regret in her voice.

WHEN SHIZUKA RETURNED to the medical wing of the Cerberus redoubt, her face was fixed in a grim expression of determination.

Grant had been sedated and moved to a white-walled room occupied by a single bed, where his sleeping form was being tended by Dr. Kazuko and his assistants. All three were wearing surgical masks that covered the bottom half of their faces. A large observation window looked into the room from the administration area of the medical wing, and Shizuka stood watching Grant through it for a few moments until Dr. Kazuko noticed her. He held a hand up to advise her to wait, and joined her a couple minutes later, after he had finished ministering to Grant.

"How is he, Doctor?" Shizuka asked.

"Stable," Kazuko said grimly, drawing down his surgical mask so that it hung below his chin on its ties. "We're feeding him nutrients and keeping him sedated for now, while we run a few tests, but all I can really tell you is that his condition is not deteriorating."

"That's good," Shizuka said, though she sounded uncertain.

"His health appears to have dipped very rapidly at the point of contraction," Kazuko explained. "Running through the transponder records, we can see his normally strong readings dropped sharply once he was infected by this unknown malady."

"How sharply?"

"I would estimate his health is at 40 percent of what it was when he went into that bunker," Kazuko said grimly. "We've flushed his stomach, but without the drugs we have administered, he would be in tremendous pain."

Shizuka bowed her head once, nodding acceptance of this grim fact. "I will see him now."

Dr. Kazuko shook his head. "That is inadvisable," he

stated. "The less people who have contact with Grant, the better—for everyone."

Shizuka's hand snapped out, plucking the surgical mask from Kazuko's chin. The doctor was drawn forward as the mask was wrenched from his face, until at last the ties snapped.

"You will bring me a mask," she said, firmly, "and I will sit at Grant's side, as is expected of me. The risks to me are unimportant, Doctor."

"But if you contract this virus—" Kazuko began.

"Then you will be blessed with two patients on whom to practice your not inconsiderable skills," Shizuka told him.

Dr. Kazuko bowed a formal assent, and strode away to obtain a mask for Shizuka. He had worked closely with the leader of the Tigers of Heaven for many years and had never seen her lose her tight rein on her emotions like that.

OUT IN THE hidden bunker in the Sonoran Desert, Reba DeFore was busy running through the results of the analysis of the patients in the room of cages. There were ten people in there, and some had fought bitterly against any type of testing, but it was necessary if she was to get to the bottom of this infection.

"Bad news, Reba," Stapleton said, marching in from there. "Two more dead."

She says it as though she's reciting a weather report, DeFore thought. Have we really become so desensitized to horrors such as this?

"Reba?" Stapleton prompted.

"It's bioengineered," DeFore said, looking up from the portable computer screen. "Virulent and easy to transmit from person to person, primarily transferring in contaminated spittle."

Gus Wilson adjusted his helmet absently, his pale eyes flicking nervously to the open door and the corridor that lay beyond. "Is there anything we can do for those people in there?" he asked.

"Two dead," DeFore said. "Two others dead before we got here, and probably more that have already been disposed of. I don't think there's time."

"Then we can't save them, is that what you're saying?" Wilson asked.

"The results of their tests show that they are too far gone," DeFore told him sadly. "All we can do now is make them comfortable while they live out their final hours or days, whatever they have left."

"I would hate to die in a bunker, like this," Karen Stapleton said coldly. "I always feared dying in the Cerberus redoubt. When Ullikummis attacked us, I thought that fear was going to come true."

DeFore nodded, containing the shakes she exhibited whenever that devil's name was mentioned. She had suffered at the hand of Ullikummis, had been close to a breakdown after his attack on Cerberus. It still haunted her sometimes; at night, when she was alone.

"They should see the sun again," Stapleton suggested. "We could walk them—"

"No," DeFore insisted, cutting the other woman off. "The virus is too dangerous. The risk of infection, even out here in the desert, is too great. I'm sorry, but no."

"Then they'll die here," Stapleton said, "caged like animals."

DeFore reached into her medical case and drew out

a vial of liquid. "We'll sedate them." She didn't mean to help them sleep, but rather to put them to sleep. It was a tough choice, and one that would stay with her a long time after they left the bunker.

Chapter 20

Cobaltville Observation Post 17 was located on the west wall and was manned by two magistrates who controlled the gate there. It was a dull post and being assigned to man it was considered an unspoken demotion.

The tower was surrounded on all four sides by armaglass windows, and within, there were several monitor screens granting pinpoint-specific camera views of the area. The sun was approaching the horizon, a bright golden ball creating a dazzling scene through the west-facing windows. Magistrate Meers sat in one of the two chairs in the observation tower, bemoaning what he had done to get on the wrong side of his superior.

"I tell you, Stovepipe, I didn't even know the skirt was there," Meers told his partner as he oiled his field-stripped sin eater on the desk before the monitor bank. "She just come up behind me and—whack—swung her sugar daddy's false leg at me, right across the noggin. What am I s'posed to do then, right?"

Magistrate "Stovepipe" Stover had his back to Meers and was peering through the windows at the rear of the observation post, where they looked down on the coil of streets that made up the Tartarus Pits. He was watching a gaudy slut working her patch of the street. He figured she was maybe seventeen, with a body trim through hunger, but wearing it well. She was dressed in a spar-

kly bandeau top, miniskirt and diamante-trimmed cow-
boy boots, and she took the arm of any male passerby,
offering a dazzling smile as she plied her trade. Stovepipe was wondering how many men she slept with in a
day, and his mind was busy conjuring images of what
she did with those clients and just how depraved things
could get. He had heard Meers's lamentations before,
could probably recite the words and sing the chorus if
he'd been asked to. As it was, he just made a "hmm"
noise that seemed to satisfy Meers as a cue to continue.

"That's right," he stated. "I turned and shot her,
straight through the gut. I mean, my helmet cracked
and there's blood on the visor, plus I'm seeing stars
from where she'd hit me. How was I to know it was an
underage kid? Still a perp, right?"

Stover nodded. "Still a perp, underage or not," he
agreed. The gaudy in the street below had linked arms
with a guy in a long, tailored jacket that flared below
the waist, almost like a peacock's tail. She led him to
her hovel just off the street, disappearing from view.
Man, what Stover wouldn't give to be that guy right
now, instead of stuck here in a dead post.

"'S'right," Meers said. "Anyway, the family kick up
a big stink, and Supervisor Hill chucks me out here till
the heat blows over."

"And that was two years ago," Stovepipe recited,
turning back from the windows to face his partner.

Meers was putting the sin eater back together piece
by piece, his helmet resting on the desk beside him.
He looked up. "Two years, one month and nine days,"
he said. "Idiot's forgotten all about me, that's what it
is. You'd think they'd be crying out for a good magistrate in the ville, someone to go pass sentence on some

of that human detritus in the pits. A man could really clean up there."

"He sure could," Stovepipe agreed. He was still thinking about the gaudy slut with the trim body.

"What about you?" Meers asked, although he continued, answering his own question before Stover said a word. "Two months now, is it, since you got demoted from east sector patrol? Man, that bites. East sector is a good gig, lot of—"

Stover stopped him with a gesture, pointing to the monitor desk, where a green light had just winked on. "What's that?" He stepped to the desk and sat down in the empty chair, tapping out a command and bringing up a live camera view of the section in question. There was a SandCat heading toward the ville, leaving a trail of dust in its wake.

Meers leaned over and eyed the image on the screen. "One of ours?" he asked.

"Were we expecting anyone today? Outland patrol, maybe?" As he spoke, Stover was trying to remember the week's schedule and whether there had been any reference to a patrol returning. He vaguely remembered something was happening on Thursday, then realized he didn't actually know what day it was today, as they all kind of melded together after a few weeks on observation post duty. "You know what day this is, Meers?" he asked.

"What? Baron's birthday?" Meers asked, mystified by the question.

"No, day-of-the-week day?" Stover elaborated. As he said it, he realized he couldn't recall anything about a returning patrol. "Doesn't matter. Let's go check it out."

Stover grabbed his helmet and sidearm from the

locker—which was open, naturally—and made his way down the stairs that ran inside the observation tower, with Meers trotting along a few steps behind.

IN THE CAB, DePaul eased his foot off the accelerator and let the SandCat slow as it approached the observation post at the west side of the Cobaltville wall. There were tall towers located at each of the four corners of the ville, but these could not cover the whole area in its entirety. Instead, smaller observation posts were placed at intervals along each wall, guarding for the lesser items of traffic that passed into and out of the ville, checking the credentials of outlanders with work visas who regularly topped up the Tartarus Pits, keeping population numbers stable.

DePaul approached alone. He had sent the drone car away, commanding it to hide nearby until called.

DePaul had chosen this observation post specifically. Located where it was, well out of the way of the main traffic routes, it was a sleepy post that was used only for the transport of waste product from the ville. Furthermore, its location was such that it was drenched in the rays of the afternoon sun, ensuring that its operating magistrates would be staring straight into that golden ball when he approached. It was classic military strategy, keeping the sun behind him to blind the enemy.

As he drove closer to the ville walls, he saw two figures emerge from the base of the observation tower—the full complement of its personnel. The mag to the left wore his helmet, hiding everything but his mouth and chin beneath its sleek lines, while his partner was more casual, carrying his under his left arm, revealing a mop of tight blond ringlets atop his head.

Seeing the mags, DePaul crossed his hands over the steering column and stroked his thumb along his right sleeve, checking that the sin eater was still there. The weapon had been in the SandCat when the intruders had arrived in his laboratory, and he had been forced to improvise, using the Streams of Judgment against them, as he planned to do to all of Cobaltville. But first, he needed to gain access to the ville itself.

One of the magistrates, the one in the helmet, stood directly in the path of the SandCat, framed in its windshield with palm held up as DePaul approached. DePaul touched the brake, bringing the SandCat to a halt.

MEERS WAITED BY the door to the observation post while Stover flagged the SandCat down. The vehicle was covered in dust churned up from the desert, and it looked real beat-up, with a hunk of the grill missing and bullet scoring running along the right wing, plus scrapes across the magistrate shield that was displayed on the side.

Stover walked around to the driver's door and tapped on the window. "ID and state your business," he said, before stepping back.

As he did so, the gull-wing door popped open, swinging up on its soft release. Inside sat a magistrate like none the other two mags had ever seen before. He was dressed in regulation black, including what appeared to be a uniform raincoat that was worn when the Cobaltville weather was bad. But in place of the standard helmet, he wore one that covered his full face, encasing his head in its weird structure, a beaklike protrusion emanating from the nose.

"Long journey, huh? Going to need to see your

ID, brother," Stover stated, watching the mystery mag warily.

Crossing his right hand over his chest, DePaul commanded the sin eater into his palm with a practiced flinch of his wrist tendons, and fired the trigger, sending a triple burst of 9 mm bullets into the magistrate's chest. The man went down in the hail of bullets, slumping backward before sinking to the ground.

The other mag looked surprised, but he moved quickly, his instincts kicking in. He was raising his right hand, his own sin eater rocketing into his grip in the blink of an eye. DePaul leaned out of the cab and blasted, his arm moving in a smooth arc, squeezing the trigger at its optimum point and sending the bullet straight into Magistrate Meers's forehead. The back of Meers's head exploded, sending a burst of skull and brain matter out across the wall of the observation post in a grim smear.

DePaul was out of his seat by then, stepping onto the soil and drawing his weapon around to target the first mag again.

The man was lying on the ground grimacing, his chest armor singed where the first bullets had struck. Stover was scared, and he was trying to bring his own weapon into play, raising it to target the intruder in the fright mask. As he raised his blaster, DePaul stepped forward and sent a bullet into his right wrist, severing the tendons there and shattering the bone through the leather of the glove. Stover's sin eater cracked apart with a flash of exploding propellant, and he shrieked in pain.

DePaul leaned down, raising his left hand close to Stover's face. Then he triggered the catch there and a burst of dark, viscous liquid jetted out into the man's wailing face.

Stover choked as the liquid rushed into his open mouth and down his throat.

DePaul had no compunction about killing mags. They were as guilty as anyone else in Cobaltville. No man was guilt-free—Irons had taught him that. If you looked deep enough you would find some blemish on the record of even the most seemingly innocent man. Avarice, greed, lust—not even magistrates were immune to these vices. And even if they didn't act on them, they were still guilty in thought, and thought was only precursor to deed, after all. If they deserved it now or if they deserved it ten years from now, it didn't matter. Preemptive law enforcement was the most effective of all, wasn't it?

DePaul watched for a moment, emotionless, before releasing the trigger of the plague agent. The aperture sealed and the rush of dark liquid stopped. DePaul marched past the other mag, the one with his brains now decorating the side of the observation post, and strode inside. His boots clattered as he hurried up metal steps, reaching the monitoring room in just a few seconds. Then DePaul triggered the gate release, using an old magistrate code, but one that had not changed in ten years, since he had last been on the force.

Down below, a grilled security gate, perfectly camouflaged to blend with the wall behind it, slid back on oiled runners, revealing access to the roads that the waste trucks used once a month.

DePaul was back down the stairs and outside the observation tower in no time. Stover was lying on his side, gagging from the gunk that had adhered to the inside of his windpipe. DePaul stepped past him and started up the SandCat's engine once more, settling into the driver's seat and tapping the recall button for the drone SandCat to follow. He slipped the rig into reverse, bumping the caterpillar tracks over Stover's sprawled body, where the magistrate lay, trying to catch his breath. Then the SandCat lurched forward with an animal roar of engine, disappearing through the gate and into Cobaltville, closely followed by the drone. As DePaul passed, the security gate shuddered back into place, sealing behind the SandCat.

He was in.

DePaul used the service roads to travel deeper into the heart of the ville, following the winding paths that the garbage took so that it would never be seen by the residents of Alpha, Beta and Cappa Levels; as if waste was somehow too offensive and might sour those people from their valuable work contributing to the ville. The drone SandCat followed obediently.

He reached Delta Level without incident. His Sand-Cat was beaten up, but it was still a magistrate vehicle, stolen when he had jumped two mags on patrol outside the ville walls six years before. He had killed them, though one had taken a while to die and had pleaded long after DePaul had stopped listening.

He found an empty bay in Cappa Level, where the magistrates were based, making the area much more dangerous to be caught wandering around in. After parking the SandCat, he worked his way deeper into the ville on foot. The drone SandCat located its own space and shut down.

Anyone who saw DePaul they would shy away from his appearance, he figured, or he would merge with the shadows if he spotted a magistrate. Mags were easy enough to spot even from a distance; they had a certain walk, a confidence that normal citizens did not have. DePaul ducked aside a few times to let them pass by.

The drone SandCat had a remote in it, which he could activate when he was ready. For now, he needed rest. Tomorrow would be big and he needed somewhere to bed down, far from any magistrate's prying eyes. As if he could sleep.

The two mags at the gate would be discovered soon enough. Once their shift ended, their bodies would be found by their replacements, or it would be noted that they had not returned and a search squad would be assembled. DePaul had little fear of capture on that score. The gate had sealed behind him and no outlander knew the codes to the trash gates. They would look outside the walls in any case, not within.

He made his way to an exclusive elevator, tapped in the mag override code and stepped inside. It was good to be home.

Now to find a place to lie low. Somewhere they wouldn't look; somewhere out of the way. DePaul pressed the button for his destination and started to ascend.

MARINA GLASS WAS thirty-nine and beautiful. She had long dark hair that cascaded in curls halfway down her back. Her dark eyes matched her hair. They were inquisitive, intelligent eyes that, when they looked at you, would melt your heart. At least that's how Sam Jeffries felt whenever she looked at him.

Sam was a year younger than Marina, but his hair was already receding at the temples and he had noticed speckles of gray appearing in its once black sheen. It made him feel old.

Marina felt old, too, in a way she could put her finger on without hesitation. She was thirty-nine and had not had children. She wanted kids, had wanted them from the moment she'd left education and home and her three sisters, with whom she'd grown up. Her sisters all had children—one each, two girls and a boy. Even her younger sister, Franny, had a little boy now, an adorable ten-month-old blob of giggles and gurgles who melted her heart just the way that she melted Sam's every time she looked at him.

Marina wanted kids. But she was an archivist in the Cobaltville Historical Division and the job came first; that's what her supervisor said, and he assured her that it had come straight from the baron's mouth.

No one had seen the baron in a while now, not for years, in fact, but Marina didn't know that. She was too low down on the food chain to warrant the baron's attention when he had been here, so whether he was around now or not made no difference to the way she viewed him.

Like all the walled villes, Cobaltville had a specific population quota, which it rigidly maintained. That meant that any procreation was strictly regulated, and having children was a communal decision based on the needs of the ville as a whole.

Marina had applied for a child license eighteen times since she had turned twenty-one, and eighteen times she had been refused. Her nineteenth application was in, but she didn't have much hope now. She was good at her job and her job was essential, diverting information and rewriting predark history to make it more palatable to the public.

And she was thirty-nine.

Which meant that, biologically, her window to have kids was closing. Soon there would be so much longing inside her that there would be no room for a baby to grow.

So she'd met Sam, who did something crucial with IT, and she'd wooed him. Wooing men was easy, she discovered. A stolen glance, a brush of fingertips, a smile at just the right moment. That and a too-tight blouse on the day when her computer sighed its last was really all it had taken.

They had met outside of work, tentatively at first, and never telling their supervisor or anyone else in their division. Marina had insisted on that. "Workplace affairs are so gauche," she'd told Sam when he asked why. But the real reason was she passionately wanted a child and didn't have a license to get one, so the only way to do it was to have sex.

Marina made it pretty clear on the first date that she was keen to sleep with Sam. They had made love that first night, with the lights off and the sheets over them, pressed together in desperation—hers for a child, his for her body.

After that they had met a lot, but always in secret. There was little need for them to go out and be seen, and with the right words and the right underwear, Marina discovered that Sam hardly needed convincing to stay inside and fumble under the covers.

So they made love night after night, meeting after work four nights in every five, liaising whenever they could.

That afternoon, they had both left work early, skipped dinner and met at Marina's residential block as the sun set. Her place was a small, single occupier apartment, with a small bedroom that opened onto the compact kitchenette. Sam knocked once on the door— unnecessary, because all apartments in Cobaltville were unlocked, as they had always been since the instigation of the Program of Unification; but he liked to knock anyway, another gesture to days long passed.

"Be still, dear heart," Marina called from where she sat in the lounge, watching the door. She had been re- writing ancient poetry to pass the censor all week at work, and was trying to get the sense of it into their lovemaking.

Sam pushed the door open just far enough to enter, stepped inside and quietly closed it behind him. He let out a breath of admiration when he saw Marina. She was sitting surrounded by scented candles, shades drawn, her body luminescent in the firelight. She wore a cerise-pink dress that cinched tightly across her breasts and barely covered her hips, and she had teased her hair so that curling strands tumbled down past her ears and cheeks, a single curl just beside her right eye.

She was pleased to see him, too, the way he dressed just for her—or at least she imagined he had. He wore a white, buttoned-down shirt with a high collar, and a vest over it, in a deep maroon like wine. His pants were dark, with a matching stripe of maroon woven into the fabric, one stripe running down each seam. His hair was brushed and parted, and he had shaved, leaving that telltale plumped look to the skin on his cheeks and chin. He smiled; straight teeth, full lips.

Sam could not take his eyes off Marina. She looked

more beautiful every time they met. More beautiful and more appetizing. You look delicious, he wanted to say. But what he said was "Something smells delicious," and he made a show of inhaling through his nose.

"Dinner," Marina whispered in her treacle voice, "will be chicken in a pseudo-alcoholic sauce. But it's too early to eat yet, isn't it, sweet Sam?"

He nodded eagerly, pacing across the room to her. He felt hot, and not just from the candles—he was hot in all the right places. "Far too early," he said, admiring the glistening, smooth legs that were stretched along the sofa. "But how will we spend so much time until it's ready?"

Marina's answer was to reach up for Sam, place her arm behind his neck and pull him toward her. He could smell the candles as he came close, and the musk of her scent—illegal but still available if you ventured into the Tartarus Pits or had a contact who would.

Marina pulled his pants off first, and Sam took his shirt off over his head. They made love on the couch, Marina still wearing the dress she had sourced from Historical—a copy of something some starlet had worn on the red carpet of some show's premiere two hundred years before, hitched up so that Sam could gain access to the place between her hips where all her longing had taken root after eighteen barren years.

The room had a smell to it afterward; a smell of sweat and bodies and chicken cooked too long in pseudo-alcohol until the sauce had begun to burn. They ate it anyway, sitting in one another's arms, bodies coiled together like the coiling flames in the room's slight breeze.

Marina wiped sauce from Sam's chin and then

licked it from her finger, her eyes still on him. "I love you," Sam said. "I never want to leave this spot, leave your arms."

Marina looked at him, feeling the warmth inside her where he had spilled his seed once again, wondered if she would feel the difference when it worked—if it worked. "Then don't leave," she said. "But we'll get hungry one day."

"And maybe they'll find us dead, like this," Sam said, "all for the sake of a chicken dinner we couldn't be bothered to reheat."

Marina laughed at that. "Angling for seconds?" she teased. She hoped that he was; she wanted him strong and healthy, good father material.

Before Sam answered, the front door to the apartment crashed open and a figure came striding in, dressed in black, a helmet over its face.

"Oh no! Magistrates!" Marina yelped, staring up at the ominous stranger.

But it wasn't a mag, or at least it was one unlike any that Marina or Sam had ever seen before. The figure wore what looked like a magistrate raincoat, black with the familiar red insignia at the breast, coupled with a helmet that covered its entire face and looked like something out of a nightmare.

Before either of them could say another word, the mag raised his right hand, the sin eater materializing there even as he did, and fired, two shots, pumped straight to the head of his victims.

DEPAUL TURNED BACK from the scene of carnage, reaching for the front door and sweeping it closed. He didn't want anyone to see what he had done to the two lovers, that he had executed them. Their names and details flashed across his Heads Up, but he didn't care.

Doors were always open in Cobaltville—that was the law, ever since the introduction of the Program of Unification and its wondrous rules for a harmonious existence. Nothing had barred his way. He could have chosen any of a hundred different apartments, a hundred different doors, and walked in and shot whoever he found inside. What would it matter who he chose? They were all guilty, weren't they?

The woman lay with her head tilted back, blood in her dark hair, vacant eyes staring up at the ceiling. The man must have turned as the bullet struck, and he had lost the side of his head, just beside his left eye, leaving a gaping red wound where his temple should have been. Both were dead.

"Illegal sexual liaison," DePaul muttered, recognizing the signs. "Seen it before. Consider your relationship terminated."

The candles flickered as he passed through, checking the other rooms of the apartment to confirm that they were unoccupied. They were. The place would do. He could set up his base here, rest until the next day, until he was ready to strike.

Chapter 21

It was an ordinary patch of the Sonoran Desert, barren and unearthly still beneath the sliver of moon that lit the sky. The terrain, undulating like the creases on a bedcover, stretched as far as the eye could see. The only sound was the haunting moan of the desert winds as they coiled across the sands, whipping up particles and dropping them a few yards away, like some elaborate game of pick-up sticks.

Suddenly, a swirl of impossible light came into being, cutting a hole in reality as it formed a single, spiraling whirlpool of colors, a rainbow window into infinity. Colors swirled and merged within that whirlpool, and witch fire played across its vast depths. The swirl had proportions impossible for the human eye to comprehend. It seemed to sprout from the ground in a cone, but that swirling cone was mirrored beneath it, sinking deep into the soil to create an hourglass shape.

Two figures emerged, stepping out of nowhere and onto solid ground even as the hourglass swirl collapsed in on itself and disappeared. The two were Kane and Brigid, and between them stood a one-foot pyramid cast in metal, with a chromium sheen. The pyramid, a travel device called an interphaser, had cut a hole in quantum space, instantly propelling the two Cerberus agents from the Bitterroot Mountains of Montana to the edge of Cobaltville.

The teleportation device was based on ancient plans devised by an alien race, and the scientists of the Cerberus organization had spent many man-hours figuring out how the system worked before it had been put into field operation. The units tapped parallax points in a network that stretched all the way across the globe and even to other planets, parallax points that acted as doors to locations the world over. Dependent on naturally occurring sources of energy, these points were one of the few limitations on the interphaser's use; only a set point was available for travel to a given location. They had existed for millions of years, and many of them had been treated as sacred places by the ancients, who had sensed the power that coursed through them.

"Cold night," Kane remarked as he stepped from the interphase window and onto the desert sand. His eyes were already keenly searching the area, spying the distant lights of Cobaltville, standing proudly on the horizon like an ornate chandelier.

"Desert's always cold at night," Brigid stated as she bent down to pack the interphaser. The compact unit could be carried in a specially designed case, light enough for one man—or one woman—to travel with. While Brigid had brought the case, which featured a padded and molded interior within which the interphaser sat, she did not intend to carry the unit to Cobaltville. Instead, she would hide it somewhere out here in the desert, buried close to a landmark that she would automatically commit to her eidetic memory. This was standard practice when they were out in the field like this; it saved not only on carrying the bulky attaché case, but also on having to answer any awkward questions about the revolutionary device if they were discovered in hostile territory. And, with their fugitive status within the barony, Cobaltville could certainly be defined as that.

While Brigid packed away the unit, Kane first activated his night-vision goggles, then got out a compact device he had brought with him for the occasion. Flat-packed for ease of transport, the unit required reconstructing at the destination point after the quantum jump.

Initially, it looked something like a narrow strip of metal, four feet in length, a foot across and about six inches deep. Kane flipped up a hinged section at one end of the metal strip—the front—and pulled up an extending bar until it stood approximately four feet in height. The bar ended in a control stick with a handle grip within which the user would place his or her hand, so that the grip sat around it almost like a clamp. Once the grip was locked in place, Kane set the main strip on the ground, stood on one end and kicked at the back. A hinged flap opened, revealing a small propulsion system.

Kane tested it once, standing on the back plate and sending power through the system. He felt the unit shudder beneath him and start to rise, until it hovered a few inches above the ground. The device, something the technicians at Cerberus had whipped up recently, was a prototype, still in the experimental stage. Roughly the size of a scooter, it worked by repelling the earth's natural magnetic field to hover above the ground. Powered by a small air propulsion system, the device worked a little like a Florida airboat, sucking in air at the front, then spewing it through a fan at the rear to create momentum. The techies had not come up with a name for it yet, but Kane was already calling it a jump-board. He was excited to finally get a chance to field-test it, though he tried his best not to show it—not in the least because both he and Brigid were worrying about their partner, Grant.

"So, whaddaya say?" Kane drawled. "Wanna go for a ride, Baptiste?"

She looked up from where she had been hiding the interphaser among a tiny grove of cacti that had budded around a few small rocks. "Beats walking," she said.

Kane commanded power to the rear fan. "Don't get too excited," he deadpanned as Brigid stepped on the board behind him. "Now, hold on tight."

She wrapped her arms around his chest and a moment later the pair were gliding across the desert sands toward the distant lights of Cobaltville, traveling along at a respectable fifteen miles per hour just two inches above the ground.

"At this speed, it'll be over an hour before we reach Cobaltville," Brigid said in Kane's ear. There was no need to shout; the engine was silent and the fan powering it made nothing more than a slight shushing sound as it churned up the particles of sand in its passing.

"Couldn't get any closer," Kane reminded her as he sent full power to the engine, picking the speed up to about 20 mph. "And it still beats walking."

"You're right," Brigid agreed. "For top field agents, we do seem to spend an inordinate amount of time trekking across deserts."

The jump-board continued, whirring across the sand toward the distant towers of the city.

KANE AND BRIGID had been traveling twenty minutes when the jump-board caught on something and threw them both without warning. They caromed through the air before crashing to the dirt in a patch of unremarkable desert.

Cursing, Kane rubbed his jaw and rolled onto his back. "Baptiste? You okay?"

She groaned something that sounded like an affirmative, and Kane went about the slow process of gathering his wits and forcing himself to sit up.

They must have hit something. Something low, something he hadn't seen. Moving his head slowly, Kane looked around. Brigid was sprawled a few feet from him, facedown in the dirt, but stirring slowly. He saw the jump-board, too, idling where it had stopped. The accelerator acted as a dead man's switch, shutting off the moment that his foot had left the pedal. He noticed something else there, as well—a narrow line of wire pegged three inches above the ground, barely visible in the faint starlight. A tripwire—someone had planned this as a trap, probably for animals.

Even as Kane spotted the wire, a new voice called from behind him, a sneering voice full of bravado:

"Well, well, what have we here?"

Kane turned, silently cursing the giddiness he felt as he moved his head. He had taken quite a fall, he realized absently, as he eyed the strangers standing there.

There were seven of them, garbed in ragged, sandy clothing that perfectly blended with their background, camouflaging them from casual view. Kane knew the type at a glance—bandits, predators, the kind of scum who inhabited the Outlands and preyed on the weak where no one would reach them, ambushing caravans and traders on their way to the ville. Back when he had been a mag, he had covered a few patrols out beyond the walls, dealing with groups like this who had become too bold and were threatening trade routes. Still, he was surprised to see them operating so close to the ville.

One of the other bandits, dressed in a wool jacket with a woollen hat pulled low over his brow, swore in disappointment. "Only two of 'em, Lance? Slim pickings."

"Slim's better'n none, Argo," the man who had spoken first—and whom Kane assumed to be the leader—replied. Then he turned back to Kane with a swagger, pulling down his scarf to reveal as much of his face as his goggles didn't cover. "Nice piece of machinery you had there." His cargo pants and the tails of his beige frock coat were crumpled, his hair was a curly mop, and when he removed the scarf, Kane could see he hadn't shaved for days. One of his top incisors was a silver false tooth that glinted in the starlight as he spoke.

"Thanks for your concern," Kane said, "but I think it'll be okay. It's pretty hardy." As he spoke, he assessed the group, looking for bulges where weapons were stashed. He judged that they were all armed; most of them had at least one blaster on show.

One of the bandits strode past Kane toward the jumpboard. "Damn flimsy, if you ask me," he spit. "Hardly anything to it. What's it do?"

The leader stood over Kane, bending his knee to lean forward. "Well? You heard Frith. What's it do? Quick now, chop chop."

"It's a transport," Kane said, his eyes roving across the others, keeping track as they spread out.

"What's it powered by? Got fuel?" he asked.

Kane watched as two of the group reached for Brigid, pulling her groaning body up off the ground. "Hey," he called, pushing to get up.

"Hey, eyes here, tough guy," the bandit leader said, shoving his outstretched palm against Kane's forehead and pushing him back to the ground. "I said, do you got fuel? Well?"

"Don't know," he answered, faking more wooziness than he felt, stalling for time. Bandits stripped down vehicles they trapped for parts, he knew, and they would either use or sell any fuel they found. "Power cell runs it, rechargeable."

The leader glared at him before turning away, shaking his head. "Power cells," he grunted. "What's wrong with old-fashioned burning oil?"

As he muttered to himself, one of his crew spoke up. "Got a live one. Looks healthy," he said, jabbing his thumb at Brigid. "Good meat there, should fetch a good price."

Some groups were not above slave trading, and there were some particularly disturbing stories of what happened to those slaves once they were out of reach of the ville mags.

"What about that one?" the speaker asked.

The leader leaned close once again, eyeing Kane the way a man might eye a horse he intended to purchase. "Looks strong, but still got a bit of fire in him, I reckon," he said. "We'll get that beat out of you in no time, my friend," he added, smiling solicitously at Kane.

"You reckon?" Kane asked, pitching his voice low enough that the bandit had to strain to hear it.

The leader laughed. "Woo, doggie," he cheered, "that's just the kind of fire I mean. Come on, meathead, get up. We got places to go and your little scooter won't carry all of us, now will it?"

Kane teetered for a moment, pushing himself from the ground. As he did so, his right arm swung forward and a sudden burst of 9 mm bullets seemed to launch from his hand in the darkness as he commanded the sin eater into it. The shots sounded loud in the bleak desert, their report echoing across the plains in a staccato rhythm.

The lead bandit fell at Kane's initial burst, clutching his chest as he slumped to the ground.

Kane was moving immediately, tumbling in a crouch-walk as he found his next target and squeezed the trigger. He saw the bandit stumble and drop, even as he spun to locate his next target.

Around Kane, the raised voices of the other bandits were only now exclaiming in surprise. "This one's got a blaster," one said.

"Chill him!" another cried, emphasizing his statement with a blast from his own pistol, a Detonics MTX double stack design.

Shots rang out.

Chapter 22

The bandit's bullet went wild, missing Kane by several feet.

Kane was moving again, using the cover of darkness to generate some distance between himself and his attackers. Gunshots sounded out across the plain, bright flashes of propellant in the darkness.

He moved on silent feet, scampering away from the scene, putting as much distance as he could between himself and these lawless outlanders.

Kane was thirty feet away from the jump-board crash site, thirty feet from Brigid, and all too conscious that he had left her with those rogues. Two were down, but that left five stalking in the darkness.

He knew these people, knew how they thought. First they would hold their position, thinking that they could repel the attack of one man hindered by the darkness. Then, when he didn't reappear, they would fan out and try to locate him, while the smartest of the group would run for cover with the booty.

It was a fair strategy on their part, except they hadn't factored in one thing—he wasn't lost in the darkness. Kane pulled the polymer lenses from his jacket pocket and slipped them over his eyes, waiting the fraction of a second it took for his eyes to adjust. There were the bandits—five of them—sure enough, still congregated at the jump-board crash site, with Brigid still reeling from being thrown to the ground. They were discussing their next move, pacing around in a small area. Two of them had night lenses on, bigger rigs than his, one of them handheld. Kane ducked down, flattening his belly against the sand. Through their lenses he should be mistaken for just another hillock of sand—at least long enough for him to make his move.

As Kane waited, watching the group of outlaws, he activated his commtact. "Baptiste? You awake?"

The response came back almost instantly—a double tap as she clicked her tongue. Which meant she was all right.

BRIGID WAS KNEELING on the sand, forced to lean precariously forward as one of the bandits held a knife blade to her throat. When she heard Kane's words tickling her cochlea through the medium of the commtact, she replied by clicking her tongue twice, hoping he would get the message. More than that, even subvocalizing, was too risky.

Come on, Kane, she thought, where's all that magistrate bravado when I need you?

Around her, the remaining bandits were having a heated discussion about what to do next.

"Lance is dead," one of them confirmed as he crouched over their leader's body; his voice cracked, making Brigid suspect he was just an adolescent playing with the big boys. "That flaming roamer shot him."

"Take his goggles, Joey," one of the others instructed. "Pass 'em to Dill."

The adolescent did what he was told, removing the eyewear from atop their dead leader's head and handing them to another of the group, who had no night goggles of his own.

"So, what?" asked the man who had taken them. "We just going to take this?"

"We've got his girl," said the man standing behind Brigid. "He'll come back for her, count on it. When he does, we'll skin the bugger alive."

Brigid subtly shifted her weight, pulling the man behind her an inch forward, and closed her eyes. She wanted to be ready for Kane, ready to drop this guy with the blade before he could slit her throat.

KANE SENT THE sin eater back to its hidden holster and waited, belly flat to the dirt. It took less than a minute before the bandits began spreading out, searching the area, just as he had predicted. He watched through the night lenses, keeping his eyes on each of them, assessing their movements. Four of them had split from the site of the initial conflict, spreading out and walking roughly in the direction Kane had taken, coming toward him. The other one was still waiting with a knife to Brigid's throat, holding her as leverage should Kane return. He smiled at that—the guy didn't know what his captive was capable of.

There was an art to this, Kane knew.

He coughed, keeping the sound low.

Three heads turned at the noise, not quite sure if they had heard or imagined it.

That's it, Kane thought, just a little closer. He reached into one of the utility pouches affixed to his belt, pulling something loose. It was a small spherical object with a metallic casing, similar to a ball bearing, roughly an inch-and-a-half in diameter.

"I thought I heard something," one of the bandits was saying as they moved their search closer to Kane.

"Yeah, me, too," replied his colleague. "This way."

Three of them were walking nearer, hunkered down a little as if that would save them from attack. Kane rolled the sphere across his hand, back and forth, waiting for his moment. With his other hand, he was placing earplugs into his ears, dulling the noise around him. Any moment now...

They were fifteen feet away, close enough that the two with night lenses should be able to spot him at any moment.

"Hey!" one of them shouted, raising his blaster as he spotted Kane. "He's—"

At the same moment, Kane broke the seal on the sphere and tossed it ahead of him, just a few feet. As he threw it, he turned his head, squeezing his eyes shut tight.

"What is th—?" another bandit began.

Then the thing went off, exploding in a bright burst of dazzling light. The sphere was called a flash-bang, a standard piece of kit for Cerberus field teams. Small and light, making it easy to carry, the device contained a miniature charge that, when triggered, sent out a lightning-bright burst of light coupled with a sound like thunder. The compact objects were nonlethal and could do little actual damage, but were ideal to startle and confuse opponents by temporarily blinding and deafening them.

Startled screams accompanied the explosion, as the bandits were caught totally unaware. Kane heard them even through the earplugs he wore.

He leaped up as the fearsome light began to fade. In

its wake, he saw that it had been bright enough to temporarily blind all three bandits close to it, leaving them staggering in confusion.

One began to fire his pistol, shooting blindly, his targeting based on what little muffled sound he could pick up in the wake of the deafening explosion. His companion went down in a volley of friendly fire, while the other one screamed a second time as a stray bullet clipped his leg, sending a spray of blood across the sand.

The sin eater was back in Kane's hand now. He shot the bandit with the blaster while still on the hoof, kept moving as the man crashed to the sand, a chunk of his skull erupting in a mess of blood, brains and bone.

BRIGID HEARD THE pop of the flash-bang, saw the brightness of its explosion even through the closed lids of her eyes. She had guessed Kane's play, suspected he would use a flash-bang in the situation. Maybe she had known him too long, she lamented, even as she let herself sag backward, using her weight to overbalance her opponent.

The two of them sank to the ground, his knife slipping away from her exposed throat as she shifted her head.

He recovered quickly, twisting the knife and trying to regain the upper hand. But Brigid was slippery as an eel now; she wriggled out of the man's grip, shoving against the arm that held the knife and forcing it away from her like the safety bar on some hideous carnival ride.

The bandit grunted, then came at her again with the knife, scampering across the sand on his knees from where he had fallen.

Brigid was on the ground, too, but she moved quicker, seeing the metal blade glint as it caught a fraction of moonlight before driving toward her gut. She sank back, pressing herself down against the sand, and kicked up and out. Her toe struck the bandit's arm with a satisfying thunk, and she heard the man curse her for a gaudy slut.

"Such language," Brigid taunted. "No wonder you became a loser—what else was there to aspire to?"

"I'll skin you alive," the bandit sneered, scrambling up from the ground to a standing position, then barreling across the dirt toward her.

Brigid was up on one knee now, and she turned her body as the man reached her, snapping her hand out to grab his knife arm before shifting her weight and throwing him over her shoulder. He slammed against the ground on his back, expelling a grunt of breath as he landed.

Brigid leaped up like a pouncing jungle cat, scrambling on the shifting sands as she ran at her opponent. He was heavier than her and stronger, but she had been trained by both Kane and Grant.

The bandit was still on the ground, struggling to right himself. He saw her running at him and he lifted his arm, jabbing at her with the knife. She sidestepped, then snagged his forearm, flipping behind him in an instant.

The bandit yowled in pain as she put pressure on his knife arm, and then came an awful snapping sound as she broke his ulna and radial bones, disabling his attack.

"You freakin' bitch," he sobbed, pawing at his limp forearm. "What did you do to me?"

"Taught you a lesson in manners," Brigid said, standing upright once more and taking a few steps away. "It's rude to point—especially with knives."

The man's head sagged. "Stupid mutant bitch," he muttered.

Brigid only just saw it—the momentary glint of metal in the starlight as he snatched something hidden at the small of his back with his left hand. She had only a fraction of a second to react as a bullet cut the air from the hidden pull-out blaster.

KANE WAS SPRINTING for the next man, the last of those who had spread out to find him. The bandit was bent over, rubbing at his eyes where he had caught a glimpse of the dazzling flash-bang, but he still had the wherewithal to get a shot off at Kane.

Kane heard the whizz of the bullet as it cut the air, missing him by several feet. He kept running, sin eater raised.

The bandit fired again and Kane rolled, weaving to make himself a more difficult target. As he righted himself, he stroked his trigger, sending a 9 mm bullet toward his foe. The bullet clipped the bandit's right shoulder, sending his aim wild as he tried to blast Kane again.

The man howled in pain but kept moving, whipping up his left hand to steady his wounded right arm, firing again.

The bullet sailed close to Kane's ear as the ex-mag ducked his head, charging toward his attacker. Then he was on the man, bowling him over.

The bandit grunted, flying off his feet before crashing down in the dirt. Kane whipped his weapon up and blasted the guy in the chest.

INSTINCTIVELY, BRIGID dropped to the ground even as the bullet left the chamber of the Derringer 22. The bullet zipped past overhead, the noise of the shot cutting through the air like a thunderclap.

The Derringer was a small, stealthy weapon, designed to be hidden. It was intended to surprise opponents, ideally, to fell them with a single shot before they realized what had happened. Because of its size, it was often seen as the kind of blaster a woman might carry in her purse. The silver barrel was tiny, shorter than the bandit's index finger at full extension. The pistol had a lot of kick, and Brigid moved as the bandit recovered for a second shot. The Derringer had a manually operated hammer, which had to be cocked before the weapon could be fired again. That would take a second or two; Brigid had that long to reach and disarm her opponent.

She sprang from the ground, running at a slant, head low. Across from her, the bandit was drawing back the hammer, fixing it into place with an audible click. He had the blaster raised, teeth clenched in a grimace as he targeted his charging opponent.

And then—bang!—the Derringer went off at the same instant that she slammed into him, knocking him back. He landed on his broken arm with a high-pitched shriek of absolute agony, while Brigid rolled and rolled, turning over in the dirt with the force of her momentum.

A second later, she pushed herself up from the ground, brushing sand from her legs. The bullet had missed by inches, spiraling off into the dark night.

The bandit fearfully tried to recock the Derringer again, but was in too much pain to work the mechanism now, his right hand quivering with adrenaline and agony. He looked up when two shadows crossed his line of sight. It was Brigid and Kane, his would-be victims, she with her TP-9 semiautomatic in her hands, he holding a sin eater, the magistrate weapon of office.

"I'd suggest you drop the blaster," Kane said, his voice little more than a growl.

"Or we can drop you," Brigid explained, "so you can never hold it again."

The bandit seemed to think this through for a moment before he nodded painfully, wincing as another spear of agony spiked through his broken arm, then dropped the Derringer to the ground. "I didn't…" he started, shaking his head. Whatever it was he didn't do or mean to do was lost in a mutter.

Kane picked up the Derringer and pocketed it before he and Brigid made their way back to the crash site and the waiting jump-board. They had lost eight minutes to this altercation, eight minutes when they could have been closer to Cobaltville and the likely location of the plague outbreak.

Chapter 23

Kane and Brigid continued on toward Cobaltville, leaving the scene of carnage behind them. Two of the bandits were still alive, but both were wounded and they had been disarmed. If anything, they would fall victim to their own kind now, in a kind of poetic justice. As Kane had put it earlier, it was a dog-eat-dog world outside the ville walls.

Thankfully, the jump-board had suffered no damage in the crash. Its air propulsion whirred smoothly, taking the two Cerberus warriors to their destination. They were dusty with sand by the time they arrived.

Before long, the brightly lit towers of Cobaltville loomed before them. It wasn't easy to obtain access into the isolated city surrounded by high walls. Papers needed to be checked, and anyone who didn't belong was immediately turned away by the sharp-eyed magistrates.

Two hundred yards from the walls, with watchful eyes no doubt already on them, Kane powered down the jump-board and folded it, cinching it to his back on its carry strap. Then he and Brigid strode toward the south gate, where their contact should be waiting.

Two magistrates operated the sentry post at the gate, with two more on duty in the high tower. All of them were armed, and there were larger swivel guns in the tower that could pick off a transport at a hundred yards.

As he approached the sentry post, Kane raised his arms in surrender, and Brigid followed his lead.

"Hey, fellas," Kane began. "Maybe you can open the gates. We've got a little business inside and we're on a tight schedule."

The magistrate on guard duty appeared emotionless behind the intimidating visor and helmet he wore. "A little late to be entering Cobaltville, citizen. Purpose of visit?"

"Medical," Kane said. "I'm Dr. Gander, this is my assistant, Lexa. We were called in for research analysis, but our transport gave out just a couple of miles out. You know how it is."

The magistrate studied him with grim indifference. "Do you have papers?" he asked.

Kane made a show of reaching into one pocket before patting down the others in his jacket and pants. Coming up empty, he turned to Brigid. "Nurse?"

"Not me," she said confidently.

Kane turned back to the guard. "Ah, must have left them on our transport."

The mag remained unmoving, standing proudly before the sealed gate into the ville. "Enjoy your walk, citizen. We'll see you again in two to three hours."

Kane made a face. "Aw, c'mon! You seriously don't expect us to trek all the way back to—"

"That is exactly what you will do, citizen," the magistrate stated.

Kane turned on his heel, somewhat reluctantly, as if set to leave. "Come on, nurse," he said to Brigid.

He took two steps and stopped before turning back to

the magistrates at the sentry post. "My man inside will have a copy of the paperwork," he said, as if struck by sudden inspiration. "Maybe you could page him. He's expecting us—matter of life and death, you know?"

The mag stared at Kane through the tinted visor of his helmet, weighing the implications of the statement. "Life and death?" he muttered to himself thoughtfully. Then he nodded, reaching a decision. "Who is your contact?"

"Colin Phillips," Kane stated. Phillips was a Cobaltville physician who provided health care not only to the privileged, but also went down into the Tartarus Pits to assist the less fortunate. He had had dealings with Kane and his team before, during a mission of mercy to bring much-needed medical supplies to the desperate who lived in the pits. Phillips was the leader of a ragtag group of physicians and remained a staunch ally to Cerberus.

Kane and Brigid were taken to a holding area located just inside the gate. The room featured thick armaglass windows and metal plate walls, and was by and large impregnable. No one would be released from here without official consent.

"Well, here we are," Kane muttered to Brigid. "Belly of the beast."

The mag called Phillips arrived in person at the south gate a few minutes later. Cerberus had already contacted the physician and briefed him on what was required. He was a stocky, middle-aged man whose sunken face showed the weight of years and responsibility. His dark hair had thinned to a few wisps over his pate, but his hands were the steady hands of a surgeon.

"Ah, my colleagues," Phillips began without a hint

of hesitation. "Dr. Gander, so good that you could come so soon."

"Doctor," Kane said, shaking his hand.

"I understand there was some kind of mix-up with your official papers?" Phillips said, and he turned to the magistrates on duty. "I have my copies here for your examination." He handed over two sets of official-looking papers and waited. Phillips's work in the Tartarus Pits meant that he operated at the edge of ville law, and he had contacts enough to procure fake papers for Kane, Brigid and anyone else they cared to smuggle in—for a price.

While one magistrate guarded the group, the other ran the papers through his computer and confirmed that they were correct, and that the relevant documentation had been filed in the system—once again, the work of the Tartarus underground. An illegal hacker had sown the back-dated files into the magistrates' system so they would be there when checked.

Once the papers had been approved, Kane and Brigid were free to enter. They left the holding pen with Phillips, who led them to his transport—a small four-wheeled vehicle that consisted of an engine, two seats and a small luggage area. Being the smallest, Brigid wedged herself into the luggage space behind the seats.

"Sorry I couldn't bring anything larger," Phillips told her as he glided through the streets of Cobaltville. "Short notice, you see?"

"We appreciate that," Kane said, speaking for both of them. "It's good of you to stick your neck out for us like this, Colin."

"It's the least I could do for the people who saved my

life," Phillips responded, switching lanes and taking an off ramp into the heart of the mega city.

When Kane, Brigid and Grant had last been in Cobaltville, bringing medical supplies to Phillips, they had run into a group of ne'er-do-wells led by a rogue named Lombard. An ex-magistrate, and a bloodthirsty one at that, Lombard had very nearly killed Phillips and his people before being stopped by the Cerberus team.

Within the walls, Cobaltville was made up of wide-based towers that housed the various people and divisions that operated in the ville. The buildings were linked by pedestrian walkways, and much of life within the city was conducted without ever really leaving those structures. What roads existed were sunk beneath the towers, and used primarily by service vehicles transporting goods and disposing of waste as required. The magistrates had vehicles, of course, but most normal citizens did not, and would never have need of one.

"So, Lakesh tells me you've run into some kind of viral disease you think is loose in my ville," Phillips said.

"It's still speculation," Brigid explained, "but there's a significant risk that someone is about to release a weaponized version of the plague here."

Phillips was shocked. "Why?" he asked. "Why would someone do that?"

"Now, that's where it gets tricky," Kane answered, and he and Brigid began to outline everything that had happened to lead them to this point.

The doctor's vehicle hurried on through the empty streets, making its way to the Tartarus refuge that Phillips volunteered for.

Chapter 24

Reba DeFore joined Dr. Kazuko in the Cerberus medical bay as soon as her team returned to the redoubt. "How is he?" she asked breathlessly.

"I sedated him two hours ago," Kazuko explained as DeFore peered through the observation window into the room where Grant was recuperating. He lay asleep in the lone bed in the room, with Shizuka sitting by his side, a surgical mask cinched over her mouth and nose. "Life signs are holding steady, breathing's good, some rattling in his chest from mucus, but otherwise he's holding in there."

DeFore looked relieved. "Thank you," she said. "I assume Shizuka's been here the whole time?"

Kazuko nodded. "She was quite insistent."

SEDATED, GRANT slept a restless sleep, sweat beading on his brow.

Shizuka sat with him in the private room, watching him with concern. She was like a mother lioness with cubs, protecting them, ready to pounce on anything that came too close. But this was an enemy that had already come too close—an enemy that could not be driven back with swords or fists or bullets.

DEFORE POPPED INTO a private changing room, washed and pulled on a clean set of scrubs. Then she made her way to Grant's room, pushing the door gently so as not to wake the patient. Shizuka glanced up as it moved, and her face looked fearsome, eyes narrowing above the surgical mask on her face. Always the warrior, DeFore reminded herself.

"Reba," Shizuka said, bowing her head. "When did you return?"

"Our Deathbird landed not fifteen minutes ago," the Cerberus medic explained, keeping her voice low. "I came as soon as I could."

"Thank you."

"How is Grant?"

"Restless," Shizuka said, "but that's Grant for you. He's fighting whatever it is that hit him, I am sure, but Dr. Kazuko feels this is a battle he cannot win alone."

DeFore nodded solemnly. "I've just got back from the site of the infection," she said. "I had a chance to analyze what went into Grant's system, and I think he has a strong chance if we can move quickly."

As she spoke, Kazuko joined the pair of them, a surgical mask covering the lower half of his face.

"What is it, this thing that affects Grant?" Shizuka asked.

"It's a type of artificial virus designated only by a number," DeFore explained. "It transmits through the sharing of bodily fluids, most especially spittle, and is very fast acting. It was created in the twentieth century as a by-product of an immunity research project, but it's been mutated and refined since then to make it more virulent.

"The virus works like a very quick acting cancer, filling the lungs with a poisonous compound so the sufferer cannot process oxygen properly. That's why the victims have dark saliva—it's the effect of the poison."

"But you said it could be stopped…?" Shizuka asked.

"If we catch it soon enough, then yes," DeFore confirmed.

"He is already on a drip feed to replenish lost protein," Kazuko stated, "and I pumped his stomach to clear as much of the disease as I could before it took further hold."

"Good," DeFore said. "We'll need to up that dosage immediately, and get to work tackling the infection with radiation therapy, force it into remission."

Shizuka looked back at Grant's sedated form, her brow furrowed. "Grant-san is already in its grip," she pointed out. "Are you certain—?"

DeFore nodded firmly, almost as if she was trying to assure herself. "Grant has been dosed his whole live with the strongest immunization shots around," she said. "As a mag, it was common practice for him to be immunized against any possible disease floating around in the Outlands beyond the ville walls. Plus, he's strong—physically, he's in prime condition, and he's exceptionally healthy. If anyone has a chance, it's Grant."

Shizuka nodded solemnly, her eyes downcast. "I have fought with Grant through many obstacles," she said, "but now he fights an enemy whom I must defer to your greater wisdom to defeat. However, if you will allow me the honor, I would choose to remain at Grant's side, where I can be with him while he fights, providing spiritual, if not physical, support."

DeFore looked at the brave samurai woman and nodded. "We would appreciate that," she said, "and I'm sure he would, too."

AN UNCANNY SILENCE seemed to have overtaken the Cerberus redoubt. Word of Grant's condition and the radiation treatment he had been rushed into had got out, and the news of the mission that his partners were now on weighed heavily on the minds of all personnel. Cerberus was a family—a large and sometimes dysfunctional one, but a family all the same.

To DeFore, the silence conveyed the sense that she was being watched, that everyone was waiting for the news she would bring about Grant's condition. She checked him out, a surgical mask over her face, while Dr. Kazuko waited quietly to one side and Shizuka looked on from the edge of the room.

"Grant is a healthy specimen," DeFore said, "and has built up a natural immunity to a plethora of diseases. He reacted badly to the initial attack—little wonder, as Brigid says he was drenched in infectious detritus when he was struck by the infected subject. That's roughly equivalent to being poisoned, so it's little wonder his system almost shut down.

"But from what I see here, I think he's fighting back now, his natural immunities going some way to stave off the infection, the radiation having destroyed what we could find."

"Thank you." Shizuka mouthed the words to the air.

"We'll flush Grant's system with a cocktail of antibiotics," DeFore continued, "while keeping him strong to fight the infection internally. He's been doing what he can with that, but we can help him."

Dr. Kazuko wrote down several notes on a computerized clipboard, running through antibiotics and dosage levels.

"Furthermore, we'll need to monitor him at hourly intervals for the next half day."

"Understood," the doctor acknowledged.

As he hurried away to begin gathering the drugs that would fight Grant's infection, DeFore turned to Shizuka, her expression wrought with concern. "He's not out of the woods yet," she admitted. "That will take time."

"Grant-san is strong," Shizuka reminded her, "and his heart is pure. In the end, that must be enough."

The Cerberus physician nodded, accepting the warrior woman's point. "For now, all we can do is monitor his progress," she said, "and hope."

Chapter 25

There were two dead bodies in the living room, but DePaul ignored them. He had trained as a magistrate; death held no revulsion for him.

He stood in the tiny apartment, staring out through the bedroom window at the towers of Cobaltville, seen through his own dark reflection on the glass. His face was reflected there, the face he had worn for longer than he could remember, so long that it had become a part of him, its sharp black lines like an insect's face or a bird's. He could no longer remember a time he had not worn that face, with its black covering, round eyes and beaklike nose. It was a part of him, as much as his own limbs, protecting him from the sickness that loomed in every breath of air, every touch of breeze on skin. His skin had not touched the air in eight years. Even when he bathed, he did so in a hermetically sealed chamber with its own regulated environment made up from distilled chemicals, oxygen split from sterilized water, boiled over and over to ensure it was clean.

The lights of the ville cast great arcs of gold across the towers, like golden fingers reaching up for the sky. DePaul smiled as he observed them, old sights renewed, not changed one iota from when he had lived here, before his exile.

He thought back, recalling the day the decision had been made for him to leave Cobaltville.

Ten years ago

SALVO SAT BEHIND his desk, thumbing through the psych-division report.

Dressed in his rookie uniform, DePaul stood at attention, hands behind his back, waiting for him to finish. If Salvo took two minutes or two hours it would not matter—DePaul would wait; that's what he had been trained to do.

He had augmented his uniform with a standard surgeon's mask, its ties hidden beneath his helmet, the white mask itself cinched tightly over his exposed mouth and nose.

There was a window behind Salvo, looking out on the high walkways of Cobaltville and up to Alpha Level, where only the baron and his most devoted and trusted administrators were allowed to tread. Eyeing the highest levels, DePaul wondered if they were clean. Whether anyone had ever caught a disease up there, or if it was protected from everything in the ville and what lay beyond.

"DeSouza in Psych reports you were a good prospect," Salvo said, bringing DePaul's thoughts back to the present. "But that thing you picked up out in mutieville—" he used the term flippantly; there was no mutieville, just ranches and pest holes where the muties struggled with the rest of the Outlands scum "—knocked you for a loop for quite some time."

"Nine days, sir," DePaul said, hating the feel of his hot breath against the surgical mask. "I was out of the field for nine days in total, and I would have returned sooner had the doctors allowed me to."

Salvo inclined his head, accepting the point. "Your dedication to the Magistrate Division is not on trial here, rookie. Your emotional capacity to function under pressure, however..."

"Sir?"

Salvo held open the report and tapped a page. "It's compromised. Very compromised. The incident in the Tartarus Pits on Tuesday. According to Irons you had to be evacuated from the location with an armed escort. Irons said that you had put both yourself and him in jeopardy with your aberrant behavior."

"My behavior was not aberrant, sir," DePaul insisted. "I was surrounded by filth. It was a natural and entirely rational response."

Salvo shook his head slowly, wearily, as if it weighed more than his neck could support. "Listen to me, DePaul," he said finally. "We immunize all citizens, including magistrates, against a whole host of diseases because there is so much crap floating around out there. But we never catch all of it—and even what we do, it sometimes takes a person's body a few days to shrug off, especially what they pick up outside ville walls. I've seen that before—it's normal, it happens. It happened to me, nastiest darn rash you ever saw, went right across my chest and burned like an acid-spitting mutie. But it passed, and yours did, too."

"I know that, sir," DePaul said, struggling to keep the edge of irritation from his voice. "I am fine."

Salvo looked sorrowfully at the rookie, and despaired when he saw the surgical mask. "Your scores are impeccable, your initiative is above question, but I cannot place a magistrate on the streets who may put himself and others in jeopardy."

DePaul was taken aback. There was so much crime out there; everyone hid something. Without good magistrates the system broke down, and then it would be anarchy, just like it was outside the ville walls. "With respect, sir," he began, "I believe in the Baron's Law and I truly intend to make a difference."

"And you'll make that difference from a desk, DePaul," Salvo told him. "It is with regret that I say that I cannot put you out on the street. For now, you're on desk duty in a probationary capacity. We'll evaluate in three months, and again in six. If Psych sees no improvement, then we may have to reconsider your position here entirely. That is all."

DePaul stood for a moment, his superior's words jabbing at him like knives.

"That is all," Salvo repeated, looking up from the paperwork he still held.

"Yes, sir," DePaul said, saluting. He turned and left the office, feeling empty as he strode down the corridors of Cappa Level, where the magistrates were headquartered.

A DESK JOB. No, not just a desk job. A probationary desk job that might be rescinded at any time. It was ridiculous, DePaul thought as he sat in his quarters. What good could he do behind a desk? That was where old men sat, brave mags who had got wounded in the line of duty. It was no place for a rookie who had graduated top of his class in every field.

He had been trained for this job since birth, had one name—DePaul—like his father before him; would assume his father's role the moment the old man retired. That retirement was in just a few weeks, DePaul knew—not that there was a sentimental attachment there, merely that the date was lodged in his mind from when he had been told he would be taking over. Only now he wasn't taking over, after all, not really.

Crime was rife, the dirt and the wickedness creeping out of the shadows, determined to strike good people down. As it had struck him down at the mutie ranch, where he had picked up that infection and lost days on the beat.

He had not gone soft. He was still able to do the job, enforce the law, execute its abusers. He would kill a mag if he knew the man was doing wrong, his belief in the law was so strong.

A desk job, he sneered, reaching for the lock-up drawer where he kept his sin eater and ammo. That was not the glorious future he had in mind.

THE COMPOUND, a storage facility for SandCats and the other ground vehicles magistrates used, was located low down in Cappa Level, with ramped roads running through Cobaltville. Air vehicles were located in another tower, much higher up, where they could be launched with ease.

Thirty SandCats were parked in bays in the low-ceilinged room, and the air was suffused with the smell of fuel and grease and oil.

Only magistrates ever came in here, since no one else could get this deep into Cappa Level without being challenged. Even so, the facility was guarded, with two mags on the walk-in doors, another posted by the exit gate and armed with a UT Blaster—UT being short for

Undertaker. The weapon was like a portable Gatling gun on a sling, and it took some strength just to wield the thing. There were other magistrates in the garage compound, too, plus five mechanics fine-tuning engines and checking over tires for damage, two more support staff wiring the electrical system in a damaged rig that had taken too much punishment out near the east wall.

DePaul watched them from the door, his eyes masked by the tinted visor of his helmet. He was in full uniform, which would get him so far, though he knew it would not help him entirely. He would need to be efficient and ruthless if his plan was to be successful. See them as lawbreakers. Every man was a criminal if you dug deep enough.

DePaul marched into the garage, drawing the door closed behind him, and headed over to the admissions desk, glancing at the open doorway behind it. That led to an office where another mag was waiting, going through paperwork relating to the upkeep and servicing of the vehicles under his command. The man could be seen clearly through the open door, in full uniform, but with his helmet removed, feet propped up on his untidy desk.

The magistrate at the front desk looked up, putting down the technical booklet he had been reading, which outlined the latest developments in magistrate firearms. Its cover showed a blueprint of the UT Blaster, the weapon being trialed across Cobaltville this quarter. "Name and rank?" he asked. If he wondered about the surgeon's mask that DePaul wore, he did not comment on it.

"Irons, full shield, twenty-six years served," DePaul recited. "Require a SandCat for an exploratory mission."

"SandCat, sure," the mag at the desk said, typing the request into his terminal, the screen inset in a well so that its top barely poked above the desk's surface. "'Cats in bays 12, 14, 15 and 19 have just been checked over and refueled, and are free. You can take your pick."

"Thank you," DePaul said, his eyes switching to the parking bays. This was proving easier than he'd expected, he thought as he began to pace toward the nearest of the available SandCats, waiting in bay 15. He was three steps toward it when the mag at the desk called him back.

He was checking through his itinerary on the screen and slowly shaking his head. "Not showing anything here, Irons," he explained. "Are you sure you have the right day?"

DePaul flinched his wrist tendons and his sin eater popped into his hand, firing its first shot even as the guardless trigger met his finger. The mag at the desk went down in a burst of bullets, slumping over his desk as the titanium-shelled slugs cut through his helmet and body armor.

The alert went up at the noise, the second magistrate on duty hurrying from his office with his sin eater extended, garage mechanics scampering to retrieve their weapons, running for cover.

DePaul shifted aim, blasting another shot through the door to the back office, executing the helmetless magistrate with a head shot even as he came to investigate the disturbance in his garage. The man went back and down, his feet still running even as his skull exploded in a familiar blossom of red.

DePaul continued moving, striding purposefully across the garage and picking off two mechanics as they peered out warily from their hiding positions. He had graduated top of his class, and this was just like training. The secret was keeping mental track of all the targets as they moved about the field.

Bullets whizzed across the room toward him, pinging against the armored ceramic shells of the SandCats as he ducked his head. DePaul selected his targets emotionlessly—they were all guilty of something, he knew, just the way Irons had told him. He blasted a service operative in the shoulder and watched the man drop back in a spray of blood.

More bullets crashed against the nearest SandCat and DePaul ducked down behind it, using its armaglass shielding for protection. He reloaded, listening to the drumbeat of bullets slapping against the far side of the vehicle.

Almost done, he thought. Just four more left, plus the gate man.

Hunkering down on his belly, DePaul slipped under the stationary SandCat and crawled its length, emerging on the far side, eight feet from where the mags were concentrating their fire.

When he popped up, he surprised a mechanic who had clearly been hoping to surprise him. The man was carrying a sin eater and had a patch over his missing left eye. He brought the weapon around with an exclamation of surprise as DePaul drove his own blaster into the man's belly. Overalls mangled with flesh as he pulled the trigger, holding it down for a moment, blasting a triple burst into the poor unfortunate's guts.

The mechanic sank to the floor, blood washing over his teeth.

The next one was behind a SandCat being stripped

down for parts, hunkering against a wall with fear in his wide eyes. DePaul shot him as he passed, moving like a wraith along the aisle.

As he executed another service man, DePaul heard the loud boom of heavy artillery. The mag at the gate had fired up the UT, was blasting at DePaul's shadow as he made his way through the garage.

DePaul moved quickly then, clambering into the open door of a SandCat and scrambling into the back, up into the well that led to the turret. A moment later, he had the USMG-73 machine guns powered up, and he swung the turret around as he searched for his last two targets.

The twin USMGs sounded apocalyptically loud in the confines of the low-ceilinged garage, spitting cruel bullets out at a rapid rate.

The remaining mechanic made a break for it and got caught up in the fire, his body all but cut in two as the 73-caliber bullets drilled through him.

That left just the man who had been on the gate, a fully trained magistrate armed with that vicious Undertaker Blaster. DePaul eased his finger off the twin triggers, let the USMGs cycle down with their accompanying low whir. He watched through the armaglass of the turret, searching for the mag.

Need to move quickly, DePaul mentally urged himself. An alert's gone out. Won't be long until reinforcements arrive.

Yes, and he sure as hell didn't want to be facing another few dozen angry magistrates, trained killers carrying everything the armory had to offer.

The mag at the gates reappeared, stalking between two parked SandCats, that heavy Undertaker blaster slowing him down as he tried to get behind the rogue magistrate.

DePaul scanned the area, then took careful aim, not at the mag, who was little more than a fast-moving shadow, but at a fuel store located a little way behind and to the left of him. Then he depressed the triggers and watched as his bullets rocketed away, drilling a steady stream of holes into the metal-sided bin.

The fuel exploded in a mighty blast, flipping two SandCats parked beside it and rocking the others on their suspension. DePaul's rocked, too, but he was already scrambling back through the vehicle, slipping into the driver's seat. Too close to the blast, the mag who had been posted on the gates was obliterated in an instant, body stripped down to a charred mess of meat and bone.

DePaul pulled the gull-wing door closed and pumped power to the accelerator, bringing the SandCat to life as fire ravaged the garage all around him. In a moment, he was hurtling from the parking bay, lunging toward the sealed gates at the end of the garage. DePaul stepped on the gas and smashed through the gates, ripping them from their frames as he crashed out onto the service road and to freedom. Behind him, the garage burned, alarms wailing.

He would bring judgment to the Outlands first, but he was not done with Cobaltville. Not by a long shot.

THE MISSION HAD not changed, but that day everything else had. DePaul had realized that he was the force of justice, a walking, breathing, living representation of the law, just as he had been trained. And that Salvo and all the other mags merely paid lip service to the law, could never understand the true nature of crime in its myriad forms. He had seen crime, had seen its filthy grip as it tried to strangle the life out of mankind, preying on the weak, the helpless, even the healthy. His job as a magistrate was to bring harmony, to end the fear that people were forced to live with, to pull crime out at the roots.

And now he was back in Cobaltville, back to bringing final judgment down on everyone, every damn dirty lawbreaker, everyone who had ever tried to lay him low.

The lights of Cobaltville winked like artificial stars in the darkness, framed in the reflection of the inhuman mask that had served as his face for so long. Down below, the Tartarus Pits seethed, and above them, the crimes of the sexual deviants, the selfish, the immoral and inconsiderate, the greedy who clung on to power. It was a great tapestry of criminality, spiraling all the way up from the pits to Alpha Level, a cesspool of crime that could never be fixed. Could only be disposed of forever, sterile perfection left in its place.

Thanks to DePaul, it would soon be clean, all its crime eliminated forever. Man would be grateful, if he was allowed to survive.… But that was impossible; letting anyone live risked a new outbreak of crime, a new blight to purge. Soon he would eradicate the deviance of mankind, wiping the whole world clean of crime until only he remained—the one honest man on a planet of corruption and immorality.

Behind his inhuman mask, DePaul smiled. It was a cold smile, somehow more inhuman than the mask he wore.

Until tomorrow, he thought. Until tomorrow.

Chapter 26

Phillips sat with Kane and Brigid as they worked over a map of Cobaltville, level by level. They were in a back room of the refuge, hidden deep within the heart of the Tartarus Pits.

The refuge had been cleaned, but it didn't feel clean. It felt as if years of sickness and sweat and depression had oozed into the walls and taken root there, sapping the will to live from every person who entered its miserable surrounds.

The walls were painted a soft, light brown—a color that had probably been called treacle or muffin or something like that, but now just looked as if someone had failed to fully remove feces from a white wall. The cupboards and fittings were cracked, with worked-in dirt that could never be removed, their plastic coverings yellowed from age. Sunlight didn't get down to the Tartarus Pits much, and if it had, then the place would doubtless be faded from that, too, Kane mused sourly.

Although it was still night, there were people here already: two volunteers of Phillips's acquaintance, plus three sick locals, including a kid not yet four years old, who were sleeping in the back room while their child fought a fever that had turned her skin an angry red.

"Something going around," Phillips had said when Kane asked. "We're immunized against these things, living in the levels the way we do, but the people down here are still susceptible. The kids especially."

Kane nodded. Ville dwellers were given a cocktail of immunization drugs in light of the mess that man had made of the environment with the nukecaust, and magistrates were especially immunized because they spent more time outside the walls than any other locals.

"We figure this guy's bringing in a weaponized infection to the ville," Kane explained.

Phillips shook his head in lament. "Why here?" he asked.

"We think he's got a grudge against Cobaltville," Kane said. "When we found him he was piloting a Cobaltville Magistrate's SandCat."

"They're not easy to get hold of," Phillips said, "and that's an understatement."

Brigid pushed a stray lock of hair from her face as she spoke. "We think he may be a magistrate," she explained.

"Or an ex-mag," Kane added.

"There's some evidence for this, but we're still piecing things together," she continued. "He's meticulous, wears mag armor—albeit heavily adapted—and Kane and Grant said he fights like a mag."

"Magistrate moves," Kane elaborated, "hence magistrate training."

Phillips looked from one to the other, his brow furrowed. "Where is Grant, anyway? Don't you guys usually work together?"

"Grant got hit with a faceful of virus," Kane said grimly.

"Damn," Phillips spit. "Where is he now? Does he need help?"

Kane held up a pacifying hand. "We've got it covered. Let's just concentrate on finding this nutball before all hell breaks loose."

Phillips nodded in understanding. "So where do you plan to start? Cobaltville's a large place."

"It is," Kane agreed, "but you have a network of medical people you could speak to, right?"

Phillips looked wary. "What are you thinking?" he asked.

"If we can track down the early symptoms, we may find this mook before he causes too much damage," Kane explained.

"I'll put the alert out," Phillips told the Cerberus warriors, "but if this virus is as infectious as you've suggested, I don't see it doing much good. Once it's out there, the best we could hope to do is contain it."

Brigid sighed and turned to Kane. "Colin has a point," she said. "If we don't find this guy swiftly, then we may be too late to stop whatever it is he's planning to unleash."

Kane bit his bottom lip thoughtfully. "We're wanted fugitives here, Baptiste," he said. "We may have blindsided those mags on the gate, but that luck won't hold. If we go walking boldly around the ville, someone will recognize us, and before we know it we'll have more trouble than we can handle."

Brigid pushed herself up from her chair and strode across the room. "Then we'd better move quickly," she said, "and not get spotted."

Kane was shaking his head in a definite negative. "No, we'd just be asking for trouble," he stated.

Brigid glared at him. "Aren't you usually the impetuous one, throwing caution to the winds and going in with guns blazing?"

"I want to do this right," he replied. "What we do here could be Grant's best chance."

It was the first time Kane had shown he thought that Grant was in trouble, and Brigid was taken aback by it, even though she had been thinking it herself.

"Then we'll stay stealthy," she announced, "but we need to get moving on this, Kane. Sitting here and waiting for our guy to show is the same as not doing anything, and I don't think that's an option."

Reluctantly, he nodded. "Then what do you suggest?"

Brigid looked around the room, searching for inspiration. There were warning posters about cleanliness and the spread of disease, wall-mounted visual guides that displayed the symptoms of a variety of common infections, advice on birth control. Finally, her gaze settled on Phillips. "Colin, you have access to all levels in your capacity as physician, don't you?"

"Not Alpha," he replied, "but my pass lets me go everywhere else if I'm needed."

"Then we're going to need to borrow your pass," Brigid told him.

Phillips reached into the pocket of his jacket, which hung over the back of his chair, and pulled out his coded pass. "It's yours," he said, handing it across to her. The card had an intelligent computer chip in it that allowed Phillips to enter any level, even restricted areas via the network of elevators that ran through Cobaltville.

Brigid took the pass and fixed Phillips with a serious look. "You are to report this stolen in thirty-six hours," she said.

"Is that long enough?" he asked.

"It will have to be," she told him.

KANE AND BRIGID hurried through the overcrowded Tartarus Pits, heading for the exit elevator, armed with the pass. They had ruled out the Tartarus Pits as the site of the first outbreak, not through any snobbery, but simply because a man seeking revenge was unlikely to take it out on the lowest level of humanity. Colin Phillips would remain down here to check for any signs of infection—and Kane and Brigid hoped that would be enough.

While they would have to remain out of sight of mag patrols, Phillips's pass allowed them to use the quickest routes up through the ville, many of which were kept hidden from the main walkways—which was something that worked to their advantage.

It was six in the morning, but even this early the place was bustling with activity, street vendors and food stalls plying their wares, others offering dubious services, of dubious legality.

Kane was used to moving through the busy streets, and he remained watchful, well aware that pickpockets operated at all hours of the day and night. He reminded Brigid to remain alert, though he knew she could handle herself.

They made their way toward one of the secure elevators that fed up into the towered structure of Cobaltville itself. As they crossed a street, Kane spotted the dark-clad figures of two magistrates on patrol. Even with their presence, the pits were a hive of illegal activity; people were just a little more subtle about it while they were around.

Kane brushed a hand through his hair, masking his face as the Mags turned toward him. He reached for Brigid and drew her close. "Kiss me," he whispered.

She fell into his arms and kissed him avidly as the magistrates strode past.

As they kissed, Kane watched the patrolmen through narrowed eyes, checked until he was certain they were far enough away that they weren't coming back.

"That was close," he said, unclenching from the embrace.

Brigid raised an eyebrow. "Don't get used to it, buster."

They hurried on, making their way past the street market towards the sealed elevator.

Brigid wrinkled her nose as they passed a food stall, the owners of which were busy cutting hunks of flesh from a cooked dog.

Kane saw her reaction and smiled. "Not hungry, Baptiste?" he teased.

She made a face. "Maybe not ever again," she replied.

Before long, they reached the pedway that led to one of the elevators that ascended up to the towers. The elevator was of robust construction, surrounded by a metal cage, its bars thick to prevent unauthorised access. A keypad and a card reader were located at the door to the cage, requiring a security pass to enter.

Two figures lurked in the shadows close to the cage, watching as they approached. Kane saw them, made a swift hand gesture to Brigid to warn her that there may be trouble. People wanted access to the upper levels, he knew, and they weren't above killing someone to gain that access, even if they could be certain that they would be met by magistrates at the other side.

Brigid pulled Phillips's security pass from her pocket while Kane waited on guard behind her. For added security, the card required a code to be entered into the touchpad once it had been swiped, and Phillips had divulged this information to Brigid before she and Kane had left the refuge.

In the shadows, the two figures shifted, coming alert as they watched Brigid feed the code to the card reader. Then they stepped out into the light, marching swiftly toward Kane and Brigid as the cage doors squeaked open.

Despite the presence of nearby mags, the two hoodlums were fearless as they approached. They were dressed in dirty clothes. The one on the left wore a hood that hid his face, while the one on the right had a kerchief over his mouth to disguise him. They both pulled knives from under their jackets as they strode purposefully, angrily, toward the Cerberus warriors.

"Trouble every day," Kane muttered as the two figures produced their weapons.

Chapter 27

"Company," Kane whispered to Brigid as the cage door slid back on automated runners.

The thug in the hood strode toward Kane, the knife blade thrust out before him, a sneer on his lips beneath the shadow of his head covering. "Give us the key, burger brain."

Kane remained calm. His immediate reaction should be to pull his sin eater, surprising these two would-be muggers and ending their short, unpleasant career right here. But he remembered the mag patrol they had passed just a street away, knew he couldn't draw attention. So shooting them was out.

The first thug waved the knife before Kane's face, while his partner reached for Brigid's elbow to pull her back from the opening door, his own knife ready in his other hand.

She flinched, swinging her elbow up and back as the mugger snagged it, pulling out of his grip and elbowing him high in the chest. The man grunted in pain and stumbled back, but recovered in a flash, reaching for her long, trailing hair and swinging the knife toward her.

Brigid dropped, letting all her muscles go loose and falling straight to the deck, surprising her attacker. Overbalanced, he stumbled, and then went down as she executed a leg sweep that kicked his feet out from under him.

KANE, MEANWHILE, WAS dealing with his own attacker with silent efficiency. He reached forward as the thug thrust the blade at him, blocking the attack with his forearm before stepping into the sweep of the knife arm and pulling himself close to his foe.

Now they were next to one another, and very near.

Kane rammed his hand into his attacker's throat, using the side of it like a blade. The thug gasped in pain, unable to make a sound.

Still holding the man's arm, Kane pulled hard, wrenching it from its socket. The knife clattered to the ground as the thug let go, sinking to his knees in silent agony.

Tears streamed down his face as he knelt there, reaching hopelessly for the knife where it had fallen. Kane could not have that; he swept his leg up and back, kicking the thug hard across his jaw before catching him in the back of his head with his heel as he fell. The man slumped face-first to the ground, disarmed and unconscious.

BRIGID'S ATTACKER HAD slammed hard against the ground, but he recovered quickly, scrambling toward his prey, the knife still clutched in his hand.

Now standing, Brigid glared at him as he pushed himself to his feet with the knife outstretched before him. "You sure you want to do this?" she asked, a grim expression on her face.

The thug seemed to think about it for a moment, then his eyes darted to where his partner had just been disarmed and rendered unconscious by Kane, and he clearly thought better of it.

Brigid laughed as the would-be mugger dropped his knife, turned and ran. "Hah, guess they weren't expecting victims who fought back," she said as Kane recovered from his own brief battle.

"Oh, they expect it, Baptiste," he told her. "That's why they come armed. There just ain't many other options down here in the pits."

"You're right," she agreed. "You forget how cruel life is down here."

"You weren't supposed to know," Kane said. "You were trained as an archivist for the Historical Division on Beta Level. No one thought to prepare you to deal with the low-level violence and corruption that was going on way beneath your feet, because nobody ever expected you to come down here."

Brigid looked sideways at him as they entered the cage that led to the elevator. "Are you...do you miss this, Kane?" she asked, as the security door closed and locked on its automated circuit.

"Who, me?" he asked innocently. Before him, the elevator door was pulling open on its runners. "What makes you think I'd miss somewhere like this?"

"I don't know," Brigid said, stepping into the elevator. "You just seem to revel in being here."

"A man finds what pleasure he can in his work," Kane told her as the door slid closed and the elevator began its ascent into the towers.

"Maybe that's the problem with our rogue magistrate," Brigid mused. "Maybe he enjoys it too much."

The strong preyed on the weak, and the magistrates could only scratch the surface of all that went on.

THE ELEVATOR DOOR opened on the lowest level of the Administrative Monolith. Epsilon Level was where all manufacturing took place. Kane exited first, wary for signs of trouble.

The elevator was located in a quiet corridor, which in turn opened into a wider passageway that ran the length of the tower they had entered. The passageway was something like a road, only it carried solely pedestrian traffic, with a wall of windows that looked out on the golden towers of Cobaltville, caught in the morning light as the rising sun nudged over the horizon. It was busy even at this hour, the regimented citizens trudging home from a night shift, the morning shift hurrying to work to keep the presses rolling, fulfill the product quotas for the barony.

There were at least a hundred of them, probably closer to double that, all trudging the long corridors to work.

The workers were dressed in uniforms of muted colors, mostly indigo, with a few dark green jumpsuits among the crowds. They looked uniform, too—men with the same haircut, short back and sides, all the same body type, all within the same window of ages, twenty-five to forty-five. There were women, too, each with the same body type, slim and underfed, stoop-shouldered from their labors, many with hair trimmed short like the men, while the others had pinned their long hair back in tight buns. Some workers carried small bags that contained their lunches, but they seemed, by and large, the same person over and over and over again.

Some chatted, some even laughed, but most simply trudged the long highway-like corridor to their destination, for another day laboring in the manufactories of Epsilon.

Kane watched them with pity, knowing full well that he had seen them before, had witnessed the shift change on Epsilon Level back when he had been a magistrate, patrolling the towers. He had remembered them differently, but they looked tired to him now, living lives beaten down by the baronial rule. Was this what he had been an instrument for, his fitting each individual into a role and a task that would overwhelm and ultimately destroy any individuality he or she had left?

Kane had not viewed it this way before, but now he understood what the ville system was all about: it trained every person for their role, not just magistrates, but all of them, each man, woman, child fulfilling a designated part of the plan, where losing their individuality was the price of a safer world.

Kane and Brigid watched the faces as they passed, alert for signs of sickness. It would not be hard to spot; the black tears and drool would mark any victim immediately.

They looked normal; tired, emotionally empty, but normal. Where they were pale it was from exhaustion, from never venturing out into the sun, away from the protective embrace of the ville. They were beaten-down people in a system that was designed to keep people down. Kane had seen the wider world beyond, but he knew that the system repeated again and again, from location to location, throughout history. It was the same pattern that the Annunaki had established when they had first come to Earth in prehistory, turning the indigenous humans into slaves who toiled for their adoration and glory. Kane hated it, that system, as he hurried with Brigid along the wide thoroughfare, checking faces, moving against the tide of people conditioned to follow the baron's rules.

They were normal, no black tears, no dark vomit or saliva. It had not hit here, not yet at least.

As the two of them reached another wide passage-way that led to a sky bridge connecting this tower to its neighbor, Brigid stopped.

A magistrate patrol was heading in their direction, two tall figures dressed in the familiar black armor of their office, sin eaters strapped to their wrists and ready for immediate access.

She turned to Kane. "What now?"

"We've made it this far," he said, stepping into whatever shadows he could find in the well-lit corridor. "Maybe they won't recognize us."

"Big maybe," Brigid said, following his lead.

Kane looked past her as the magistrates approached. They were coming this way—there was no question of that—and the Cerberus warriors had nowhere to hide.

"You there," called out the mag on the left. "Where's your ID?"

"Damn," Kane muttered.

It was 7:00 a.m.

The bodies in the living room looked glazed, the blood congealed in dark spots. The artificial heating of the apartment speeded up the process of decomposition.

DePaul had not slept, nor did he feel any need to.

He stalked through the room, eyeing the bodies for a moment. Was she beautiful, the woman? It was hard to tell, because a chunk of her face was missing where he had shot her.

He stopped, staring at her for a moment. She wore a short pink dress, better to show her legs. She looked like a lawbreaker, DePaul decided, and so did the man.

They both looked like dirty lawbreakers. Like everyone else in the ville. Like everyone else on the planet.

He passed through the room, moving to the open-plan kitchen. There was food there, a pot waiting on the stove, boiled dry now, with tiny clumps of chicken clinging to the bottom. He had turned off the heat when he'd arrived, after he had shot the two lawbreakers, but it had already cooked too long. He wouldn't eat it; there was no need—he survived on protein injections and nutrient feeds, linked directly into his armor by resealable tabs. He dared not touch the outside world directly, for fear of another infection laying him low, distracting him from his mission to save mankind from its base criminality.

DePaul reached the front door and pulled at it, stepping back into the shadows as he eyed the corridor beyond. He had been fortunate the night before—only a few people about, and no magistrates to challenge him. Today was different; today there was a two-mag patrol striding down the walkway as he opened the door, thirty feet from his position and marching in step. Were they looking for him? Had they been alerted, perhaps after the corpses had been discovered at the sentry gate? He didn't know.

He waited, pushing himself back against the wall of the apartment's entryway, leaving the door open slightly so that he could see out. The mags came, their footsteps echoing as they strode in time, shadows nearing the door beneath the overhead illumination.

DePaul ducked back, watching the shadows as they passed. Then they stopped, and he heard them discussing something: the open door.

"Hey, everything okay in there?" one of the mags asked, and DePaul heard his footsteps as he returned.

"It's fine," DePaul replied, his voice eerie through the filter of the mask.

The apartment door swung open, and the magistrate stood framed within it. "Sir?" he asked, then he balked at the sight of the dead bodies on the couch, and DePaul standing in the corridor wearing the terrifying mask and the pastiche of the magistrate uniform.

What happened next was a tribute to magistrate training and muscle memory. The mag jabbed out with his right arm, raising it and commanding the sin eater pistol into his hand.

DePaul witnessed the movement as if in slow motion, seeing not just the magistrate raise his gun hand, but also seeing ahead, knowing just what would happen next: the mag would fire, his bullet striking DePaul, and it would bring down an alert.

DePaul moved quickly, hoping to intercept the blast. The mag's sin eater fired the instant it touched his hand, index finger curled around the guardless trigger. DePaul was lunging forward at the same instant, snatching for the barrel of the weapon as it was thrust toward him.

The sin eater fired, the blast loud in the apartment, the acrid smell of cordite rich in the air. DePaul was faster, smacking the muzzle aside as it fired, and the bullet struck his sleeve with a loud report of metal on armor before ricocheting off and imbedding into the ceiling.

DePaul's other hand came up in the same quick movement, fist clenched and jabbing into the magistrate's unprotected jaw. The mag was knocked back by the blow, thudding against the door frame with a heavy clunk.

Outside in the corridor, just a few steps away, the second magistrate was staring in astonishment at the scene.

In the space of two seconds his partner had gone from peering into an open door, to a full-blown firefight with an unknown assailant. The patrolman activated the radio set inside his helmet, calling for backup.

Inside the entryway, DePaul yanked the sin eater from the first man's grip, pulling it free from the feeder that went into the sleeve holster. He yanked so hard that the mag was pulled into the apartment, too, stumbling a comical three steps forward.

DePaul drove his knee into the mag's gut, tossing the pistol aside. There was no use holding on to it; he had it by the barrel, and the time he took to turn it around would give his opponent time to recover.

The magistrate doubled over, exclaiming in pain as he was driven back.

DePaul backhanded him across the face, his knuckles slapping against the side of the helmet the man wore, and hurried to the door. The second magistrate was there, just calling in the incident over his helmet comm.

"Altercation at Sector 7-C, Beta Level," he said, before reeling off the apartment number and corridor identifier. "We're under attack. I repeat, we are under att—"

DePaul had reached him then, charging across the few steps that divided them, lifting his right arm forward and bringing his own sin eater into play. The compact automatic shouted angrily in the confines of the corridor, sending its deadly issue spiraling toward the mag. A second later his visor shattered, and he let out a shout of shock and pain as he staggered backward.

His left eye seemed to flash as the bullet struck, but despite the splintering of the visor, the helmet saved Magistrate Blythe from that first bullet. He turned and pulled his sin eater in one swift, slick movement, whipping himself out of the immediate field of the other man's blaster and sending a shot at him even as the gun met his hand. The bullet went wild, zipping over De-Paul's left shoulder and impacting with the wall.

DePaul raised his left arm as Blythe fired again, felt the 9 mm bullet graze his sleeve and rebound from the Kevlar-metal weave. A moment later he had his own weapon trained on Blythe, and fanned the trigger for a moment, sending a clutch of bullets at his opponent. They struck him in a line from sternum to solar plexus, and he went sailing back with their force, crashing against the far wall of the corridor.

DePaul stepped forward, standing over Magistrate Blythe as he struggled to regain his balance. The sin eater blasted again, delivering a bullet through the fractured visor of the mag's helmet, straight into his brain. Blythe twitched for a moment before sinking down the wall, dead.

DePaul looked around, left and right, checking the corridor. People were peering fearfully out from their apartments, a few more gathered at the far end of the hall, where a bank of elevators was located. They were archivists, he reminded himself, timid by nature and not inclined to get involved in a fight. But the report was already out on him, and in a minute or two magistrates would be filing down those corridors, boxing him in.

He needed to move quickly, up the agenda, get to his destination and cast his final judgment.

He stared down at the dead mag on the floor, turned to take in the other one who lay sprawled in the hallway of the apartment where he had killed the illicit lovers. What did it matter that he had killed them? They would all be dead soon. The purge was about to begin.

Ex-Magistrate DePaul stomped down the corridor toward the bank of elevators, stepping into the nearest and commanding it to Cappa Level, where his penultimate act was needed, before the final outbreak began. As the doors closed behind him, a second elevator arrived on Beta Level, Sector 7-C, its doors opening to reveal a squadron of heavily armed mags who had been scrambled together at the alert from Blythe.

"Freeze!" the squadron leader ordered.

But there was no one there to stop, only innocent citizens still reeling from the carnage that they had witnessed.

Chapter 28

"I said show me your ID," the magistrate barked as he stomped up to where Kane and Brigid were standing to one side of the window-lined corridor.

They weren't dressed for construction and manufacturing, Kane realized, which was why they'd been pulled up. But if the mags recognized them, Kane and Brigid would be in real trouble.

The magistrates had marched up to the Cerberus exiles, and the one who had spoken was waiting with his hand out.

Brigid stepped forward, plucking Colin Phillips's pass from the tight pocket of her pants. "ID. Of course," she said, flashing a confident smile as she handed it over. She was the more recognizable, of course, with her vibrant red hair, but Kane was a wanted man here, and his face was known to the magistrates from his time serving with them.

Kane held his breath as he watched the mag on the left take the pass and examine it.

The security pass was designed to unlock doors, and it featured no image, just a name and issue identification number. The magistrate looked it over for a moment and tilted his head with confusion. "Colin? That you?" he asked, turning to face Kane with the grim visage that his tinted visor lent him. He paused, checking Kane's face. "Do I know you?"

"It's pronounced 'Colleen'," Brigid announced, drawing the man's attention. "My parents had a pretty screwy sense of spelling. What can you do?"

"Colleen, huh?" the mag repeated, turning back to Brigid and holding the pass in such a way that she could not see it. "Can you give me the code number?"

"Of course," she said, before reeling off the twelve-digit identifier that was printed on the pass. Every Cobaltville citizen would memorize this number from birth, but Brigid had only glanced at it when she took the pass from Phillips. Her recital, however, was note perfect.

The magistrate nodded, then handed the pass back to her. "Checks out," he confirmed. "So what are you doing here on Epsilon?"

"Medical emergency," Brigid said smoothly. "Guy in the manufacturing hub got his hand caught in a packing machine."

"He okay?"

"Mangled," Brigid said, "but he'll live."

The magistrate turned back to Kane, clearly wondering about the familiarity of his face. Not all magistrates worked together; they had their own beats and partners. But it was entirely within the realm of possibility that Kane had passed this man in the mag ops center, back before he had been exiled from the ville. "You sure I don't know you?" the mag asked. "You look kind of—"

"We work all the levels," Kane said. "Maybe you were called to a 417 we attended."

The magistrate nodded. "Yeah, probably."

"Get on with you," the other mag told them. "And have a responsible day."

Kane resisted the urge to breathe a sigh of relief as the two patrolmen went on their way, leaving him and Brigid to continue down the corridor in the opposite direction.

"That was close," he said quietly. "Lucky you memorized the pass number."

"I didn't," Brigid admitted. "Score one for my eidetic memory!"

Then Kane really did breathe a sigh of relief. "Tricky, tricky," he said, as they hurried up the corridor and into a walkway that connected to the next tower. Outside, through the windows, the early rays of the sun were painting Cobaltville a fiery gold, but there was no time to stop to admire it.

THERE WERE PATHS between the levels that only the magistrates knew, ways to move between locations without being interfered with. These pathways existed even within the magistrates' hub itself on Cappa Level, and it was these secret paths that DePaul used now to make his way to the hangar area.

He stepped from the elevator and took a sharp left as a troop of magistrates marched up the far end of the corridor. A moment later, he had disappeared into a service stairwell located to the side of the bank of elevators.

The stairway was dimly lit, and was used primarily for repairs and transporting small pieces of equipment. DePaul hurried up the steps, making his way to the correct section of Cappa Level where the nearest hangar was located.

As he turned the bend in the stairwell, he saw a figure descending. The man had a magistrate's uniform on, but the maroon flash on his lapel marked him as a mag tech. The tech was carrying a heavy toolbox by its handle, and for a moment he didn't notice anything unusual about DePaul as he hurried toward him on the stairs. Then he stopped, staring through his tinted visor at the strange apparition before him.

"What the heck?" the tech spit. "I don't think you—"

DePaul raised his left arm and released the hidden catch there, and a cloud of dark liquid blasted from its reservoir beneath his bell sleeve.

The mag tech turned away, surprised more than hurt, shouting in shock. "That was a pretty dumb thing to do, perpetrator," he snarled, and he swung the toolbox that he was holding, before throwing it at DePaul.

As a rain of tools and heavy kit came hurtling toward him, DePaul sidestepped, grunting in pain as a flying wrench caught him in the flank. Then he stepped forward again, ascending the stairs and watching the technician, who was powering his sin eater into his hand.

DePaul met the man, slapping the weapon aside as it blasted its first shot in the echoing stairwell.

"Give up! You can't last five minutes on Cappa Level, you dumb punk," the magistrate shouted in a show of bravado.

DePaul batted the sin eater aside once more with his left forearm, then stepped in and kneed the technician in the crotch. The tech grunted in agony and slipped on his feet, losing his balance.

DePaul grabbed him by the lapels as he struggled to stay upright, punched him hard in the belly as the sin eater fired off another useless shot. The stray bullet shattered a light fitting and plunged that section of the staircase into sudden darkness.

As the technician dropped backward, DePaul thrust his arm out at the man's head and blasted a second jet of dark liquid into his face. The tech coughed, spluttering, as it struck his mouth and nostrils beneath his protective helmet.

The man shook for a moment, staring at DePaul through the tinted visor. The darkness seemed to flicker in front of his eyes and the nightmarish figure—already disturbing in his inhuman mask—seemed to become something more disturbing still. The face seemed to shift and mold, dark feelers emerging from the hard mask, hairy limbs reaching for him.

"No!" the tech cried. "No, leave me alone. Leave me...."

Satisfied, DePaul left him, striding past the magistrate where he was slumped on the stairs, ascending swiftly to the next level of the complex. Behind him, the insane screams of the mag tech could be heard echoing from the hard surfaces of the staircase.

Delta Level

KANE AND BRIGID could not help but be aware of the cooking smells the moment they emerged from the elevator onto Delta Level. They had checked all four towers of Epsilon Level, watched every face as it passed them, searching for hints of the awful virus that their unnamed enemy had brewed in the lab under the Sonoran Desert. So far, they had found nothing.

"Do you think we could be wrong about this?" Kane asked as they strode into the feeder corridor, toward the grand refrigeration plant where fresh food was flash-frozen shortly after acquisition.

"I hope we are," Brigid said. "But our guy's spent a long time preparing himself for this. He knows we're onto him—poisoning that tiny settlement to the west was bound to be noticed sooner or later."

"You think he did that?" Kane asked, as he slipped to one side of the thoroughfare and took in the faces of the food technicians who were passing.

A group of techs were herding escaped hens back to a cart, while eggs rolled across the corridor in all directions. For them, it was just another day.

Brigid nodded. "I've been thinking a lot about it. That was his test," she said. "A final chance to refine the properties of this weaponized virus before he unleashes it upon the world."

Kane looked at the steady flow of people passing. They wore hairnets and surgical masks. Some of them were moving large containers loaded with ingredients, shifting them from one section to another.

"We'd better keep moving," he said. "Maybe we'll get lucky…or unlucky, whichever it is."

Brigid glanced at him, worry plain on her pale features. "The clock's ticking, isn't it?"

"I feel that it is," Kane said.

THE NEXT MAG proved easier to quell. A knife in the ribs from in close, and DePaul let him slump to the floor.

His partner on the registrations desk leaped from his seat in astonishment, drawing his sin eater immediately. But it was already too late; DePaul was eating up the distance between them in the short reception space with his long-legged strides, leaping the low table that sat between them in the waiting area even as the first bullet was fired.

The round zipped past DePaul as his boots slammed down on the floor past the table. Then he kicked out, driving his right foot into the magistrate's gut and launching him backward. The man crashed into his desk in a jangle of limbs.

DePaul stepped closer, the black curves of his mask like some gigantic insect looming over the supine magistrate where he was lying on the desktop. DePaul held his outthrust hand before him, the drooping loop of the sleeve revealing the nozzle of the plague hose there. A moment later a blast of ice-cold liquid—the incubating plague mixed with the drug glist to add to its potency—blurted into the magistrate's face. Glist was a powerful hallucinogen refined from the perspiration of the sweatie subset of muties that roamed the Outlands. When it was suitably refined, its effects were almost instantaneous, triggering vivid hallucinations in the imbiber's brain.

The mag cried out, getting a mouthful and lungful of the noxious mixture. The glist in the mix worked feverishly quick, sending his brain into overdrive, warping his sense of reality until he saw only a shattered impression of what was really happening.

The magistrate began screaming as DePaul stepped away from him and hurried through the hangar bay doors located behind the desk.

The shots would draw someone, DePaul knew, but there was no time to worry about that now. He had a mission to complete, which meant getting into the hangar to distribute his wonderful gift of final judgment to every ville.

MEANWHILE ON DELTA Level, Kane and Brigid were working their slow, laborious way through the towers, using the skyways to make their way from one to the next. It was already eight-thirty. Time seemed to be hurrying away from them and no headway was being made.

Brigid halted on one of the skyways that linked towers three and four. The walkway was lined with windows, granting a fantastic view of the whole ville in all its magnificent manmade glory.

"This is crazy, Kane," she said, shaking her head.

He halted a few steps farther on and turned back. People were passing on the skyway, always someone going somewhere, keeping the ville functioning with their little designated roles.

"This was your idea, Baptiste," Kane reminded her. "You wanted to get moving so we could search for this thing."

"I know I did," she said, "but in my mind it was a case of walking straight to the scene of the crime and putting it in lockdown somehow."

"Doesn't work like that," Kane told her. "Take it from an old mag."

Brigid shook her head in frustration, biting at her lip.

"We can walk every corridor," Kane said. "We may get lucky."

"No, we've tried that. We need to be more methodical," she insisted. "Kane, you were a magistrate."

He looked suspiciously around the corridor, checking that no one had overheard. People passed by, ignoring the discussion. "Keep that quiet, yeah?"

"Sorry," Brigid muttered. "What would you do, if

you were a mag looking for revenge? Where would you go?"

"If I was this guy?" Kane asked. "Straight to the psych block to turn myself in."

"That's not helping," she began, "or maybe it is...."

"Huh?"

"A magistrate looking for revenge goes to the magistrates and poisons the system from within," Brigid said, realization finally dawning.

"Can't be done," said Kane. "Mag security is—"

"If we're right, then our man either is or was a magistrate," Brigid reminded Kane, cutting him off. "He knows his way around the mags' security. He could get inside. After all, we did."

Kane looked thoughtful. "But inside the mags..." he mused. "We'll need Cappa Level. You okay to slum it like that, librarian? I know you grew up expecting Beta things."

"I'll cope," Brigid assured him. "Which way?"

Kane pointed to another corridor, this one with glass on one side that looked out onto the Cobaltville landscape all the way down to the Tartarus Pits. "This way," he said.

They hurried on together, a new sense of purpose in their strides.

"You do realize that Cappa's full of magistrates, right? It's the level where we're most likely to be recognized," Kane said.

Brigid flashed him a tight smile. "You always love a challenge, don't you?" she teased.

"Yeah," Kane griped. "A challenge—not suicide."

Chapter 29

DePaul stepped into the hangar bay, an insectile, night-marish figure of terror in his long-beaked mask and the sweeping black wings of his coat.

Though located on Cappa Level, the magistrate hangar bay had roof access, thanks to the slant of the building, and an opening side door to grant passage for the Deathbird helicopters. These choppers were used on scouting missions beyond the ville walls, for surveillance and to take out rogue operators who strayed too close to Cobaltville's protective embrace. Eight Death-birds were lined up along both walls of the bay—sixteen in total—being serviced by magistrate technicians to ensure they were up to spec.

The personnel within the hangar had already gone to high alert, having heard the shots from the reception room. They watched the door warily as the sinister figure stepped through, seemingly unarmed and yet striding purposefully into the restricted space.

"Freeze where you are," a magistrate called Christopher ordered, raising his sin eater in his gloved fist.

Behind him, two other mags backed by seven technicians were poised with their own weapons, a tiny army against just one man.

DePaul slowly raised his arms, hands spread wide in surrender. "You have me, Magistrate," he said, his voice eerily filtered through the breath mask. "No need to shoot."

Magistrate Christopher remained where he was, holding his weapon steadily trained on the newcomer as he questioned him. "What happened out there? We heard shots, screaming."

"It's…difficult to explain," DePaul said. "Here, let me show you…." He lowered his hands slightly, ready to unleash the cleansing rush of vat-grown plague on these unsuspecting lawbreakers.

"Don't do that," Christopher warned. "If you move, I will be forced to shoot you."

DePaul halted, his arms a little lower than they had been before.

"Why is he dressed like that?" one of the techs asked, venturing out from cover.

"Is that a magistrate shield?" another asked, recognizing the red emblem emblazoned on DePaul's coat.

Christopher stepped forward, his sin eater poised before him. "Well? What is it?"

"I'm one of you," DePaul said, his filtered voice hollow, like something speaking from beyond the grave.

"That so?" Christopher asked, clearly unconvinced.

"How else do you explain my presence here, on Cappa Level?" DePaul asked him. "Now, may I lower my hands?"

"Keep those mitts where I can see them, buddy boy," the magistrate instructed. "Words don't prove nothing. Tennyson, Mallick, go check on what happened outside."

Two of the magistrates in the hangar went trotting toward the door and out into the reception area. As they drew level with him, DePaul calculated the distance and trajectory, working out how best to disable every person in this room. He would wait for them to return, then unleash the judgment upon them, passing the final sentence for their transgressions.

KANE AND BRIGID found an elevator and slipped inside, using the pass she had borrowed from Phillips to ascend to Cappa Level. As a roving medic, Phillips had access to all levels except Alpha, which meant he was on call to treat magistrates who had been wounded in the line of duty.

As the elevator ascended, Brigid's eyes met with Kane's uncomfortably, despite all the time they had spent together, and she began to shy away.

"You think Grant's going to be okay?" she asked over the quiet hum of the elevator motor.

Kane nodded firmly, as though convincing himself. "He better be," he said. "I don't think I have the energy to train up another partner like that."

Brigid looked solemn, shaking her head. "Don't you...don't you ever take anything seriously?" she asked him.

"I have a theory, Baptiste," Kane said. "You start making it serious and it becomes serious. Self-fulfilling prophecy."

She was flummoxed. "So even with your partner—our friend—lying on a...lying in the medical bay, you..."

"I'll tell you when it gets serious," Kane said grimly.

Just then, the elevator came to a halt and the doors began to slide open on the most dangerous level in Cobaltville.

MAGISTRATES TENNYSON AND Mallick marched from the hangar and into the reception area beyond. The room had a single desk, a bank of windows and a comfortable couch with a low table in front, handy for placing beverages while magistrates waited for their Death-birds to be prepped.

Right now, there was a magistrate lying on top of the desk, weeping quietly to himself, his sin eater held rigid in his hand before him and his helmet askew. Across the room, another was slumped behind the couch, a blood-soaked rip on the breast of his black uniform.

"Baron's blood!" Magistrate Tennyson exclaimed as he took in the scene.

Mallick looked up and around, spotting the familiar circular wound in the wall where a bullet had struck it. "Got a shot here and—" he began, pointing.

"Screw that shit," Tennyson shouted, cutting the man off and hurrying back toward the hangar. "We have to tell—"

As Magistrate Tennyson stepped into the hangar bay, DePaul triggered his nozzles and turned, sending a blast of infectious liquid at his face with one hose, while the second jet slammed against Magistrate Christopher, who had been questioning him. Both men went down in a splatter of dark, foul-smelling liquid, the force of the impact pushing them to the floor.

"What the—?" a tech screamed as he saw two of the three on-duty mags go down.

DePaul commanded his own sin eater into his hand and fired a shot, blasting the technician before he could comment further.

Swiftly, DePaul strode to the door that led to the reception area, hunting the last magistrate—and hence the greatest threat—as the other two struggled in the grip of the glist-laced virus.

Magistrate Mallick was on his way to the door when DePaul reappeared, and he was quick enough to leap for cover even as he commanded his own pistol into his hand and began blasting. His shots struck DePaul across the torso—one, two, three—then zipped away in a spray of sparks as the armored coat protected its wearer.

DePaul curled his index finger on the trigger of his sin eater, blasting a triple burst of shots at the retreating magistrate even as he dropped down behind the couch. The bullets struck the sofa, ripping chunks out of it and turning the stuffing to powder.

Mallick blasted back, activating his helmet comm as he returned fire. "Magistrate down. Repeat, magistrate down," he yelled, the sin eater bucking in his hand. "We are under attack, Cappa Level, hangar three. Request assistance."

As Mallick filed his report, DePaul came running across the room, advancing onto the couch as if it were a staircase, stepping from cushions to back in two quick strides.

Mallick glanced up as the shadow loomed over him, swinging his weapon to shoot. DePaul kicked out, the toe of his boot driving into the fourteen-inch barrel of the sin eater and kicking it out of the mag's hand. Mallick howled in shock as his wrist bent back, scrambled to reach the pistol as it slammed into the far wall. Still looming over him on the back of the couch, DePaul blasted, sending a burst of infected liquid into the exposed face beneath the helmet and visor. It was just like shooting that sniper at the mutie farm all those years ago.

Mallick sank to the deck and wrenched his helmet off as the liquid struck, hoping to keep the foul-smelling gunk from touching him.

DePaul lined up his shot and blasted, sending a single 9 mm slug toward the man's exposed face. The bullet buried itself in his forehead, drilling into his brain in an instant.

For a moment, Mallick's body twitched as he lay there, responding to the last signals from his dying brain.

DePaul turned back to the hangar, reloading his sin eater as he went to kill the technicians.

Cappa Level

KANE AND BRIGID were wondering which way to go when they heard the noise.

"A shot," he said, cocking his head to listen.

She looked alertly down the length of the corridor they were in, wary of magistrates finding them in a restricted area.

"No, make that shots," Kane said as more noises reverberated down the hall. "This way…" He started to run, that old point-man sense at work once more, tracking the specific source of danger in a level that was full of dangers.

INSIDE THE HANGAR, five technicians watched as the ominous figure stalked back through the doors, sin eater in his hand.

"He can't take all of us, lads," Greene whispered to the others.

One of his colleagues looked less certain. "I dunno. He killed all those mags," he muttered.

"We can take him down," Greene insisted, plucking up the pistol that waited in the armaments kit for the nearest chopper. Then he nudged out from behind the cover of the armored helicopter, the sin eater raised before him, its weight familiar from his days as a magistrate.

Greene's weapon blasted, but it was accompanied by a much louder roar as something came crashing through the wall of the hangar. "What th—?" Greene yelped as a battered SandCat mowed him down in a screech of straining brakes.

Greene's bullet cut through the air toward DePaul, but the aim was just wide. DePaul turned his head as the round whipped past, six inches from his hidden right ear. He had called the drone SandCat the moment he had left Beta Level, and it had followed its programming, using the service roads to ascend to the magistrate level, where the hangar was located. The SandCat looked battered, but DePaul had reinforced its front fender for just such an occasion, knowing precisely when and where he would require its appearance. Admittedly, he had not foreseen that it would run over an opponent who was in the process of shooting him, but sometimes, as the old saying went, the barons favored the brave.

The other engineers were looking at the scene in astonishment. The SandCat had plowed through one wall, hurtling in past two Deathbirds before running down their colleague.

"Greene couldn't have survived that," said Hirshey. "He was right—we can take this loon!" And with that, Hirshey was running out from safety, swinging a wrench over his head as he charged toward the dark-robed infiltrator.

DePaul shot him in the face with a blast of poison, the ice-cold liquid splashing across his head in an instant. Hirshey went down with a shriek of agony, and in a moment the potent mixture of glist was being metabolized by his system, turning the lights of the hangar bay into swirling rainbows of intense color and vibrancy.

DePaul stalked across the room, sending out another spurt from one of his hidden hoses, blasting two more engineers where they cowered behind the black shield plating of a helicopter. The guilty went down with yelps of surprise, drifting almost immediately into a semiconscious delirium as the hallucinogen took them.

The last engineer, a man called Bojeffries, was feeling either incredibly brave or incredibly desperate then. As DePaul made his way across to the drone SandCat, the tech ran at him, swinging a hammer above his head. DePaul saw the man's shadow as he stepped into the light, watched his reflection on the scratched ceramic finish of the SandCat, then brought his sin eater to bear, blasting him in the chest before Bojeffries could get close enough to strike.

The engineer went down with an agonized grunt, and the hammer went clattering across the deck. DePaul ignored him, his attention fixed on his mission now, accessing the rear of the SandCat, where the full canisters of his final judgment virus were held. He could not have entered the ville with them—too much risk, and besides, how would he have carried them while he made his way through the levels? Having them arrive twelve hours after he did at this designated point had meant he could move about freely, set in motion everything he needed to ensure success.

Beneath the front wheels of the SandCat, the engineer called Greene was drifting in and out of consciousness, his pain intense. His ribs had been crushed, his spine and both hips broken, and his left leg had been wrenched out of its socket as the three-ton vehicle came to a halt on top of him. "K-kill me," he muttered through bloody teeth.

DePaul looked pitifully down at him through the lenses of the eerie, inhuman mask. "I do not kill," he said. "I pass sentence on the guilty."

Greene sank into oblivion as his body started to shut down from loss of blood.

THERE WERE MAGISTRATES everywhere.

A squadron was marching in the direction of the shootings in the hangar bay, but there seemed to be some confusion. A second group of mags met the first in one of the broad corridors that characterised the magistrate level, and a discussion erupted.

"Beta Level—report just in, someone's killing magistrates," one of them explained, stopping the group that was hurrying toward the hangar. "We need all hands, right now."

"Beta?" the opposing leader asked. "I thought the report came from Mallick in the hangar bay."

"No, it's Blythe," the first mag insisted. "Sounds like a routine patrol just went sour on Beta."

Both groups seemed to have reached a momentary impasse. The sheer surprise of having a shooting inside the upper levels of the ville had unsettled them, and the fact that conflicting reports suggested it was the magistrates themselves who were the targets only added to the sense of unreality. Cobaltville was at peace—wasn't it?

KANE AND BRIGID sneaked through the shadows of the corridors, making careful progress to where the sounds of shooting had come from.

Kane ushered Brigid back as he spotted a patrol heading this way. There were mags everywhere. It was proving impossible to make any progress.

"This is your old haunt, Kane," she whispered. "Where are we headed?"

He thought for a moment, trying to work out where the shots had most likely come from. "Somewhere around the hangars, I think," he said, his steel-gray eyes fixed on the corridor as the mag patrol took a left turn and disappeared out of sight. "Come on— quickly."

Brigid jogged after him as he hurried along the next stretch of corridor, past two interview rooms with wide observation windows that showed what was occurring inside. One room had an occupant who was covered in tattoos, including a whole series of animal markings etched into his face.

Kane took a swift right turn and slipped into a storeroom as another magistrate came marching toward him and Baptiste. They waited there while the man passed, then stepped warily back out and hurried along the corridor, emerging outside the reception room that led into the hangar bay.

The area was littered with the dead and wounded, two magistrates sprawled in their own blood, two more weeping, bleary eyed, with drool smeared on their chins.

"Kane, look at their mucus," Brigid said, as the two of them hurried through the room.

Kane stopped, taking in the faces more closely. There

were specks in the drool—dark specks, like flecks of coal. "Is it—?" he began.

Brigid nodded. "I think so."

They kept moving then, hurrying into the hangar itself. What they saw when they entered made their hearts sink.

The main doors were open, exposing the room to the open ville beyond, and the Deathbird helicopters were powering up, their rotor blades whirring around as they prepared to take off. And there, in the middle of the room, amid the wreckage of a collision between a SandCat and a wall, the nightmarish form of DePaul stood, arms outstretched as he commanded the helicopters to take flight, like some insane conductor before his orchestra.

They were too late.

Chapter 30

Eight Deathbirds rose from the deck, their rotors blowing up a veritable gale in their wake.

DePaul had loaded each one with a deadly cargo—one single vial of the lab-created virus he called final judgment, taken from the refrigerated store of the drone SandCat. Each Deathbird had been programmed, each one destined to release its deadly payload in a different ville.

DePaul would handle Cobaltville personally.

The vials were small, roughly the size of a large flask, enough to hold three mugs of coffee. It would be enough, though; DePaul was certain of that. The virus spread easily, carried in spittle, and with the added ingredient of the hallucinogen glist, its carriers were impelled to kiss, to share the disease.

Mistrustful, the villes would hail the Deathbirds, and his automatic message would respond, promising a cure for a disease ravaging the Outlands—his disease—an inoculation that needed to be replicated and administered the moment the Deathbirds landed. After watching the accompanying video footage of the plague in action, local doctors would replicate the virus following his instructions—little realizing that they were replicating the plague itself. If they discovered their error it would already be too late; a single host would be enough to make the infection spread. DePaul had tested that in Freeville, was certain the final judgment would spread once it got a foothold. If one flask failed, that would not matter; he had stores enough to try again, to wipe out humankind from the planet and so cleanse the world of all crime. It was wonderful in its simplicity—no humans, no crime, the perfect solution for a magistrate overlooked by his superiors.

Crime was a disease, clinging to men like bacteria. DePaul's only regret was that he could not be there to pass the final sentence personally, could not oversee the final obliteration of the crime-sick human race.

He watched in glory as the Deathbird helicopters rose from the hangar bay.

KANE AND BRIGID stood in the doorway of the hangar, buffeted by the winds as the choppers began to rise.

"He's using A.I.—artificial intelligence—to pilot them. We have to stop them," Kane shouted over the cacophony of whirring rotors.

"What's he doing?" Brigid shouted in reply. "How can he—?"

"No time!" Kane spit, pulling himself forward by the door frame and hurrying into the room. He made it three steps before he began to tumble, but picked himself up and kept running, charging for something he knew was located on the far side of the hangar.

There, where the bay doors were drawing open, was an emergency override designed to seal the doors in case of an accident or a power leak. If Kane could only reach it, maybe he could slam the doors shut on those choppers before they left the hangar and took to the skies with their deadly cargo.

The man in the fright mask did not hear Kane—
not over the sound of the rotor blades. He was already
turning to leave the hangar, marching across the room
toward a separate exit, his long coattails whipping up
around him in the strong breeze.

Brigid saw the man move, and hurried into the hangar after him, hoping to cut him off before he could
escape. The moment she stepped into the room she almost fell, blown back by the tornado-force blast being
created by the rising choppers.

Behind her, the first squadron of magistrates on the
scene were just running into the reception area. The
lead mag called for Brigid to halt, but she didn't hear
him over the rising wail of helicopter rotors.

KANE COULD SEE the release button—actually, a red
lever, located behind a glass safety panel that needed
to be raised before it could be activated. The choppers
began to rise forward, moving at an angle of twenty degrees to the deck, rotors spinning as they sailed toward
the open hangar doors. Kane wouldn't make it; there
was no way to reach the cutoff switch in time.

The first of the Deathbirds launched through the
opening, picking up speed as it emerged and took to
the air in a whine of powerful motors.

Kane cursed between clenched teeth as he watched
it go, cursed again as a second 'bird passed through and
began to ascend outside the tower.

It was now or never, he realized. He couldn't reach
the switch, but he could blast it—though it would need
to be one hell of a good shot. Without conscious thought,
Kane powered the sin eater into his hand, steadied himself as two more Deathbirds passed him on their way

to the open hangar doors, and fired. The bullet left the pistol in a muted roar of propellant, rendered almost silent by the sea of noises all around it. Kane watched hopefully as the bullet raced to its destination, faster than the eye could track.

The next two Deathbirds were lining up to leave the hangar, nudging toward the open bay doors. Then the junction box on the wall holding the wiring leading up to the kill switch exploded, the glass panel blowing away and the wiring exposed as its fascia was destroyed by Kane's bullet.

Kane held his breath as the roll door began to rush down, almost a ton of sheet metal descending until it met the nose of the foremost Deathbird. It slammed against it, punching the aircaft to the floor like a prize-fighter, trapping it there in a shower of sparks and a screech of rending metal. The Deathbird continued to charge forward for a moment, the tail pulling up until the blades cut against the sealed door with a violent shriek of metal hitting metal.

The fourth Deathbird crashed into the back of its predecessor and an explosion erupted through the garage bay, painting the doors and everything about them with a burst of red-gold fire.

Kane was tossed to the deck in the cacaphony. He rolled under a workbench and held his arms over his head as more explosions began to erupt, fuel tanks meeting hot flames, running through the garage like some terrible game of telephone.

THE RESULTING EXPLOSION rocked Cobaltville. All four towers shook. Windows shattered and skywalks were torn from their housings, throwing horrified pedestrians out into the open air to tumble toward the distant ground.

Up in tower four, where the hangar was located, the exterior wall at Cappa Level glowed red with heat, the hangar doors buckling under the pressure as they tried to contain the explosion. At the bottom edge of one, tongues of fire blasted outward, sneaking through the tiny gap that remained where the Deathbird had become trapped by the closing door before it could seal.

The magistrates' hangar was located facing the Outlands, naturally, and not the ville itself, and it was this that saved Cobaltville from even worse damage. As it was, large cracks appeared almost instantaneously in the walls of the tower, and almost every window on Cappa Level, as well as levels Delta and Beta to either side, was shattered. The sound of breaking glass was so loud it could be heard five miles away.

BRIGID HAD BARELY made it to the exit door through which DePaul had left when the first chopper exploded. Suddenly, she found herself thrown against the far wall, striking it with a bone-jarring crash.

The next thing she knew was confusion, as the pain of the impact shocked her back from a momentary blackout. She rubbed her face, muttered, "Not dead."

Then a second explosion ripped through the hangar behind her, sending searing heat through the open doorway that led to this space where a freight elevator was located—the elevator DePaul had taken just seconds before.

Brigid curled herself into a ball, protecting her head as the fireball rushed through the next room, accompanied by the sound of more explosions and things being disrupted and destroyed.

THE SHADOW SUIT saved Kane—that and the work-bench—as the fires raged across the room, ripping through the hovering Deathbirds lined up to leave the hangar. The blast grounded them in one vicious slap, fuel tanks exploding as they reached optimum temperature. Around them, the fireball picked up the parked helicopters still waiting in their bays, roared over the ruined SandCat, and burned through the dead technicians and magistrates lying in the area.

Close to the back of the huge space, where it met with the reception area, the squadron of six magistrates was also caught up in the blast. It turned their skin a deep shade of red in an instant as it roared against them like the breath of a mythical dragon.

Twenty-five seconds and the whole thing had burned itself out, leaving only the charred evidence of grounded helicopters, blackened walls and a floor littered with tiny fires, not one of them wider than two feet across. Everything that could burn in the room had. Thick smoke hung in the air.

In the aftermath, Kane lay reeling, still crouched where he had rolled beneath the solid workbench. The bench's surface had been transformed from varnished beech wood to a mirrored black slab, and the metal vise secured to one end had been melted into what looked like a curving piece of surrealist art.

Kane pushed himself out from under, rose slowly to his feet and looked around. Fires were burning here and there, one wall flickered with flames as if it were a barbecue grill, and ruined helicopters lay about like the singed carcasses of giant insects caught in a forest fire.

Kane's ears ached from the blast and he choked on the smoke as he tried to breathe in.

"Kane!"

He turned at the shout, coughed again as soot shook from his hair. It was Brigid, of course, standing in the doorway that led back into the tower, looking dazed but otherwise as beautiful as ever, though her face and hair were smeared with soot.

"Baptiste? You okay?"

"Me?" she asked, striding over to him. "What the hell did you do?"

Kane glanced around him and shrugged. "Closed the door on those choppers. But two of them got out before I could."

Brigid looked thoughtful as she considered the implications.

"We have to stop them, Baptiste," Kane told her. "You know what's on them."

"Plague," she said. "But we're still speculating. We have no solid evidence that—"

"Guy launched them for a reason," Kane interrupted, "and he's only got one arrow in his bow, as far as we've seen. We could wait to see what happens, or we could chase them down. Question is, where are they headed?"

Brigid looked around at the scene of devastation, thinking on her feet. "Eight Deathbirds, eight packages of weaponized virus," she reasoned aloud. "Likely target would be nearby villes. And I'm guessing he'll target Cobaltville himself."

Kane shook his head, realizing things were suddenly

moving faster than he could keep up with. "You stop him?" he asked, stifling another cough.

"No, he was too fast," Brigid said. "Went in an elevator through there. I don't know where he's going."

Kane thought for a moment. "I do," he said. "Not many places left for the guy to visit now."

Brigid was still pondering the scene of carnage. "Fire destroys the virus," she concluded. "That's been true way back in history, too. We could use that."

"How? Burn down Cobaltville?" Kane challenged.

"No, but if we could blast the Deathbirds out of the sky before they reach their destinations..." she mused

Kane looked around in evident frustration. "We're all out of Deathbirds," he said.

"But Cerberus isn't," Brigid told him.

At that moment, there came a clattering of booted footsteps from the reception area, and twelve magistrates marched into the hangar bay, their sin eaters raised.

"Everybody freeze!" challenged the lead mag.

Chapter 31

The elevator ascended quietly through the tower. Inside, DePaul stood alone, his hands behind his back, watching the display panel as the cage moved from Cappa Level to Beta Level, and then began the final ascent to Alpha Level.

He remembered taking this journey once before, using this very elevator, back when Salvo and Hunt had taken him to see the baron when he was just eight years of age. It had been a traumatic experience.

Few elevators in Cobaltville could climb to Alpha Level, the place was so heavily restricted. It was an admin area, highly secure. And it was there that the baron lurked—Baron Cobalt, the master of all Cobaltville and the wellspring of the laws that governed mankind. Few ever met him, only the very best, the most trusted.

DePaul was smiling behind his hideous mask as the explosion hit in the hangar bay. The elevator cage rocked in its housings, and there was a terrible shriek of grinding gears from somewhere in the shaft as the mechanism tried to continue performing while the whole tower subtly shifted shape. DePaul staggered, taking two unplanned steps forward before recovering his composure.

The elevator continued to rise, passing through Beta Level, where the administrative records were held and monitored, and up into Alpha.

As the elevator reached Alpha Level, the lights changed, switching from a bright, cheerless white to a softer shade of dim yellow-orange, like the flesh of a mandarin.

DePaul stilled his mind, summoning the heads-up display inside his all-encompassing helmet. A blinked command, and the map overlay appeared before him, showing him the ideal route, sentry posts and ultimate location of the baron, tapping Cobaltville's main computer to do a pattern and heat analysis.

He was already in the mental zone when the elevator came to a smooth halt. The HUD map showed four sentries posted right in front of him, magistrates assigned to protect Alpha Level. DePaul shot even as the elevator doors began to slide open, his first bullet felling the closest of the mags on guard duty at the restricted elevator bank. The bullet drilled into the back of his neck, the tiny vulnerable section where helmet and armor did not quite overlap. The man went down like a wet rag, slumping to the floor before the elevator doors were even halfway open.

The second mag reacted swiftly, whipping his sin eater out and blasting a continuous burst of fire at the freight elevator. His colleagues joined him in seconds, adding their fire to his in a bullet storm.

However, DePaul had used the two seconds it took for the elevator doors to open to slip to one side, using the eight inches of corner where the control panel sat as cover while bullets peppered the elevator car. The stream of bullets went on for ten seconds before the mags outside finally eased off their triggers.

"Anyone in there?" DePaul heard one of them shout.

Then he swung his arm out, just over the protruding edge of the elevator wall, reeling off two shots, pinpointing the speaker's location by the sound of his voice. The man staggered backward as the bullet struck his chest, but his armor held.

The other mags responded in kind, blasting again, showering the interior of the elevator with 9 mm bullets. DePaul crouched in on himself as rounds flew all about the cramped space, and then the doors began to close on their automated circuit, bullets rebounding from their reinforced steel.

As the doors sealed, DePaul heard one of the mags shout, "He's getting away!"

But no, that was not the plan at all. He could guess what the magistrates would do next: they would wait a moment and then one of them would press the elevator call button, which would make the doors open again. DePaul had roughly five seconds to get his response in place. He leaped up, grabbing a ceiling tile and shoving it aside, using the wall to help him climb up through the roof access of the car, used when making repairs. Two seconds left.

IN THE HANGAR bay, Kane and Brigid turned as twelve riled-up magistrates came bounding through the flame-damaged doors from the reception area. The smoke was thick in the room, thick enough that it was hard to tell just who was who.

"Everybody freeze!" the lead mag yelled.

Kane stepped across to the doorway where Brigid had appeared, glancing at her hopefully. "There's no time for this, Baptiste," he whispered.

"Then go," she instructed. "I'll hold them."

"What about the 'birds?"

"Just go, dammit," Brigid hissed.

Kane bolted, darting from the hangar into the same side lobby that she had emerged from, the place where DePaul had disappeared five minutes before.

The magistrates paced warily into the room, six of them training their blasters on Brigid, while the others scanned the hangar for possible attack. She raised her hands in surrender.

"It's okay," she said. "I'm supposed to be here."

The leader stomped over to her, staring down at her through the tinted visor of his helmet. "Who are you? What happened here?"

"Medic," Brigid explained, waving her hands just a little in defeat.

"Medic?" the mag repeated, as his colleagues checked the room. It was littered with burning embers and ruined Deathbirds. "What kind of medic wears a blaster like that?"

Brigid winced. "I was bringing it in for checking when the explosion hit," she told him. "Found it in the Tartarus Pits. A Magistrate Lakesh has my report already, if you care to check."

She banked on the mag not bothering to verify her story right now, not in the middle of the chaos that had gripped the whole of Cappa Level.

One of the mag's colleagues disarmed Brigid, removing the TP-9 pistol and the hip holster where she wore it. "Nice piece of hardware," he commented as he checked the weapon's safety.

More mags were appearing in the hangar, trotting through the reception room to see what had happened. Several had blood on the exposed parts of their faces.

"So, you just happened to be here," the magistrate

interviewing Brigid said, clearly dubious, "when the explosions went off. And no doubt, you didn't see anyone or anything."

"Look, buddy," Brigid spit, adopting a more challenging attitude—which wasn't easy with her hands up in the surrender position. "I just arrived, and when I heard the explosions I figured maybe you and your people would appreciate the assistance of a medical professional. You want to check my story, contact Colin Phillips. He's a roaming doctor on call to this level."

"And you are?" the mag asked, still not certain of her story.

"His assistant, Lexa," she said, trying her best to sound convincing. She had to get out of here ASAP and get a message through to Cerberus about the escaped Deathbirds. Time was wasting. She only hoped Kane was having more success.

THE ELEVATOR HAD not been waiting for Kane, but it was too risky to wait, with all those mags poised to charge him with wanton destruction of property. So he had slipped into the emergency stairwell. Probably the smart thing to do, anyway, he reasoned—after all, the explosions that had ripped through the hangar had most likely caused structural damage to the tower.

He clambered up the steps, his footsteps echoing on their hard surfaces. Alpha Level—that's where his quarry would head, most probably. The guy had one hell of a grudge against Cobaltville, and anyone with that kind of drive, planning and—let's face it—lunacy, would have to go for the head honcho himself to really make his point.

So long as Brigid could handle the other stuff, Kane

thought, he might have a chance of stopping the big bad himself.

"Yeah, good luck with that," Kane muttered as he slipped from the stairwell into the level above the magistrate quarters.

On Alpha Level, three magistrates watched warily, ready for attack, as the doors to the restricted freight elevator opened once again. One of them was already wounded, having taken two shots to the chest. His armor had protected him from the full impact, but he had two cracked ribs and was now bent over, wheezing for breath.

The inside of the elevator was ruined, the walls pockmarked with bullets, a whole litter of shell casings strewn across the once immaculate floor. But there was no sign of the gunman.

"He's gone…?" the investigating mag said, peering into the car with his sin eater nosing before him. "He's not in here."

He took a wary step inside the empty elevator cage. As he did so, he noticed the missing tile in the ceiling above—but by then it was too late. A sin eater muzzle poked through and blasted off a single shot, shattering the man's visor as he looked up to check what he had seen. The visor split into shards, and the first bullet was followed by a second that shattered the magistrate's nose before burrowing into his face.

"He's in the roof hatch," one of the remaining mags cried out as his colleague sank to the ground in an explosion of broken visor and blood.

DePaul dropped through the hatch then, his pistol blasting again and again, shattering both kneecaps of the onrushing magistrate who struggled to return fire. Bullets flew, several striking DePaul's armored coat and mask.

Then he was out of the elevator and running toward the last mag standing, even as his colleague dropped to the floor, screaming from the agony of his ruined knees. DePaul blasted the man again, but this time sent a jet of ice-cold virus into him as he howled in pain.

Then DePaul was standing before the last remaining magistrate, the one who had already taken two bullets to the chest.

"Who…are you?" the mag asked between painful breaths. "What…are you…doing here?"

"I'm here to dispense judgment," DePaul told him as he raised his sin eater and pulled the trigger, sending a burst of bullets into his surprised face. The magistrate slunk to the floor in an eruption of blood.

DePaul bent down then, scanning the lobby area for any further threats. He reached forward, blasting the nearest two magistrates with a burst of final judgment, the liquid contained in the hoses hidden in his sleeves. His supply was coming to an end. As he stood up again, familiar black tears marked the faces of the magistrates—final judgment made on them at last.

Chapter 32

Brigid waited impatiently in the holding room on Cappa Level while a magistrate administrator called Albrecht contacted Colin Phillips to confirm her story. Showing outstanding quick-thinking, Phillips backed every word, and even added to "Lexa's" story, explaining that she was returning from a mercy mission for one of the most senior administrators.

Her gun had been removed and taken as evidence, along with its holster. There was no point arguing; she knew she had been lucky not to get shot then and there for carrying the thing.

Brigid spent the whole time watching the clock. Time was of the essence now. Cobaltville mags were still trying to piece things together, and they hadn't even begun to think to chase the rogue Deathbirds that were operating via artificial pilot.

Eventually—five minutes after Brigid had been escorted to the holding room—the administrator was satisfied enough to let her go on her way. "They're going to need all hands at the hangar," he reminded her. "They say someone planted a bomb there."

Not a bomb, Brigid thought bitterly, just Kane's usual subtle way of dealing with things. But to his credit it had worked—well, almost.

She marched from the holding room, past an open-plan office area where magistrates were trying to come to grips with what had happened. She overheard conversations about a massacre on Beta Level—her old level, where archivists operated. It made her wonder just how large scale the attack had been.

Brigid turned into an emergency stairwell the very moment she was sure she was unobserved, scampering down the stairs and triggering the commtact hidden beneath her skin.

"Mother, this is Lexa," she said. "Are you there?"

THE OPERATIONS ROOM in the Cerberus redoubt had been quiet for what seemed a long time. Once the liaising with Phillips had been completed and Kane and Brigid were away, there was nothing they could do but wait. Grant was still recovering from his first bout of radiation therapy, leaving everyone waiting on tenterhooks.

Brewster Philboyd was just having a spot of breakfast—one of the canteen's pastries with a smearing of fruit preserve—when the communications deck he was monitoring came to life with Brigid's voice.

"Mother, this is Lexa," she said. "Are you there?"

"I read you, loud and clear," he responded. "What's happening?"

"Target made it to Cappa Level," Brigid said, sounding breathless as she spoke. "Used A.I. to launch a squadron of Deathbird choppers that we suspect are transporting live virus. Kane managed to stop some, but two got away."

"Crap on a cracker," Philboyd spit, shaking his head. "Deathbirds, you said?"

"That's right. Two got away, Cerberus," Brigid stated

over the commtact frequency. "I can't do anything from my end. Can you track?"

"Tracking," Philboyd said, the hint of a quaver in his voice. As he spoke, he jabbed a button on his display and brought up a satellite feed. With a few keystrokes of manipulation, he brought up a distant overhead view of Cobaltville. He adjusted the gain, and on his screen, the display brought the outskirts of Cobaltville into sharp relief, showing where two Deathbirds were roaring through the skies.

"They're fast and armored," Brigid stated, "and we suspect they're heading for other villes."

"Which ones?" Brewster asked as he adjusted the image. Behind him, Lakesh and Edwards were hurrying over, aware that something significant was playing out at his desk.

"Don't know," Brigid admitted over the comm. "But you need to stop them before that junk hits another major ville."

Philboyd breathed a heavy sigh as he watched the drone Deathbirds peel away from one another. As they did, the image on the screen split, tracking each one separately, identifying it with a red circle. "We're going to need firepower," he said. "A lot of firepower."

GRANT WAS ALONE as he lay in the recovery suite. He had been drifting in and out of consciousness over the last thirty minutes or so, and had spoken briefly with Shizuka when he woke up, asking her to get him some breakfast. He was ravenous from the radiation treatment. While she was gone, he switched on his commtact and listened in on the general frequency, merely to keep the boredom and silence at bay. Thus he heard the hurried exchange between Brigid and Brewster Philboyd over his commtact. While the request had not been intended for him, he had little else to occupy his time while he lay in bed, hooked up to nutrient feeds. When he heard Brigid speak about the escaped Deathbirds, Grant muttered a curse under his breath. If those things were filled with the same crap that had poisoned his system, then the danger was very high.

"Someone's got to do something," he muttered, shaking his head. And he knew just who it needed to be.

In the Cerberus ops room, Lakesh was already putting together a plan.

"Two Deathbirds, top speed 180 mph," he explained to his gathered teammates. "We can track them via satellite and send out something to meet them."

"How long will that take?" asked Sela Sinclair.

Lakesh shook his head, clearly worried. "Too long," he admitted. "In situations like this, it's always too long. All we can do is pray we reach the helicopters before they reach their targets."

"That will take some fancy piloting," Edwards said, "and those pilots are going to need something fast if they're to catch up."

"Quite so, Mr. Edwards," Lakesh said, addressing the shaven-headed ex-mag. "We have two Mantas on site." Mantas were vehicles of ancient, alien design designed for transatmospheric flight. They were fast as lightning, but took a pilot of incredible skill to operate. "They are being prepped as we speak."

Edwards was shaking his head. "That's great, chief, but I can fly only one of them." For once, this was not bravado on Edwards's part; he really was one of a very select few who could actually pilot the incredible machines.

"We do have other options, but we must remain hopeful that Kane can return in time to take the other one into the air," Lakesh said. "Otherwise…" He trailed off, grim foreboding in his tone.

Cobaltville

BRIGID SLIPPED OUT of the staircase on Delta Level and made her way through the bustling crowds, trotting hurriedly to the nearest elevator and the fastest route out of there.

Magistrate presence was high here, no doubt in light of the attack on Cappa Level, and Brigid kept her head down, wishing there was something she could do to disguise her vividly colored hair.

"Next time, it's hair dye," she told herself as she turned into an adjacent corridor and checked the nearest wall map for the location of the elevators, searching for one that would take her down to the Tartarus Pits.

As she walked, she wondered how Kane was faring. But before she could hail him via her commtact, a magistrate appeared in front of her, blocking her path.

The man pointed to her face. "Hey!" he began. "You shouldn't be here!"

Damn, Brigid thought, he's recognized me.

Beta Level

EMERGENCY LIGHTING WAS in effect on Beta Level, and magistrates were marching in squadrons down the wide corridors, tending to the wounded and instructing people not to panic.

Kane slipped out of the stairwell and weaved between the crowds. Numerous archivists had come out from their desk jobs and were milling in the corridors, where there was less risk of falling debris. They hung about, awaiting instructions from the magistrates that it was safe to return to their desks. Almost all of them wore the small, square-framed glasses that marked their status as archivists.

Like sheep, Kane thought as he looked at the crowds. Not a single one of them smart enough to run away, even when the sky really was falling.

He had never planned this return to Cobaltville, and it surprised him now how disenchanted he had become with the place. The regimented living, caging people not with bars and walls but with rules and routine—but it all amounted to the same thing. They were all prisoners in the system, held in place where the baron—or whoever had claimed that role in the wake of the barons' collective desertion of their fiefdoms—wanted them, never to strive, never to know true freedom.

Your freedom is an illusion, Kane thought as he reached for the call button on the elevator bank. Your safety is only enslavement by another name. And even the magistrates were fooled by the system—all of them except for himself and Grant, who had broken the shackles and moved away from the rigid system of passing sentence and executing the guilty for meaningless crimes.

The elevator pinged a dull note as it arrived, the doors sliding back with an unpleasant squeak where the runners had become warped by the explosions below. Kane stepped inside.

Cerberus

GRANT WAS HALFWAY out of bed when Shizuka came striding back into his room. She was balancing two paper cups of herbal tea and a plate of plain toast in her hands, and her brows arched in almost comical shock when she saw Grant sitting up with the covers thrown back.

"Grant-san, what is it that you think you are doing?" she asked, her words coming out in a hurried tumble.

He looked at her, a grim expression on his face. "Problems at Cobaltville," he said. "Cerberus needs backup."

"Grant, no," Shizuka cried. "You're not well enough to—"

He held up a hand to stop her. "Shizuka, love, we need pilots to get out there and track some deadly virus. With Kane in the field, I'm the best pilot on site just now. I need to do this."

She looked thoughtful as she tried to recall the names of the Cerberus personnel. "What about Edwards? He's an ex-mag, he can—"

"From what I overheard, I think there are two targets, splitting up and heading in maybe opposite directions," Grant said. He was reaching for his clothes, which had been folded neatly in an unlocked cabinet beside the bed.

Shizuka nodded solemnly. "I understand, Grant-san," she said. "The clarion call of the warrior is powerful, drawing those who can to receive its benevolence. But I will help you, Grant-san. No arguments."

He smiled as he gave the petite samurai warrior an up-from-under look. "Me? Argue with you? Not in this lifetime."

Shizuka stroked his head as he reached for his pants and boots. "I'll be with you," she promised. "We'll do this together."

EDWARDS PACED THE ops room as Lakesh briefed him on the mission, along with two other pilots, including Sela Sinclair, who would handle Cerberus's slower contingent of Deathbird choppers.

Lakesh ran through a projected analysis of the targets for the two Deathbirds, bringing up the information on a large screen for all to see.

"The trajectory on target A brings it in line with Ragnarville, though fuel range may be a factor to consider," Lakesh said, pointing to the proposed location. "Best case is that we neutralize the threat before it reaches its target. Reba?"

Standing propped against a desk close by, Reba DeFore stood up straight and answered the chief's prompt. "This is a highly infectious virus," she said. "Having it released anywhere is cause for alarm. Our wisest precaution is to destroy it before it reaches any site of human habitation."

"Got it," Edwards acknowledged with a nod.

Sitting beside him, Sela Sinclair piped up. "So, what about the other hostile?"

"Now, that becomes more problematic," Lakesh admitted. "It is heading almost directly east just now. We're assuming that it is destined to deliver its deadly cargo to one of the major villes and not simply dump it at any site of human habitation. If we factor in those, the possibilities become mind-blowing."

"Distance between C-ville and the targets?" Edwards asked.

"Mandeville is the closest, at 215 miles. The others we're not so sure of," Philboyd calculated.

"We could get the Manta there for the Mandeville target," Edwards said, "then loop around and hopefully catch up to the one headed north. It'll take time, but I can't see many other options."

"The Manta is the fastest vehicle we have," Lakesh confirmed, "but we'll also send out two Deathbirds and hope they can track down the other target before it's too late."

"What we need is both Mantas up in the air," Sinclair said, confirming what everyone in the room was thinking.

Lakesh nodded. "That's precisely what we need, but until Kane returns we'll have to settle for—"

At that moment the door to the ops room swung open, knocking against the wall with a loud crash. Everyone turned, to see Grant standing framed within the open doorway. "I hear you need a pilot," he said.

Chapter 33

Everyone in the ops room turned, stunned to see Grant in the open doorway. He was leaning against the frame, dressed in a shadow suit. He looked exhausted, with dark circles under his eyes, and a kind of weight to his body language where he normally exuded confidence. Shizuka was standing behind him in the cavelike corridor of the redoubt, and she had an arm around his back to help him stand.

"Well?" he asked, eyeing the staring faces of his colleagues.

"Grant, I…" Lakesh began, at a loss for words.

"Close your mouth already, Lakesh. You look like you're trying to catch flies," Grant told him.

Reba recovered first, concern furrowing her brow as she rushed over to him. "Grant, you shouldn't be out of bed," she chastised. "You need rest to recover from—"

He held his hand up, staunching her words of concern. "Respectfully, shove it," he said. "You need a pilot. I'm the best you've got."

Lakesh was shaking his head, while Edwards turned away and muttered a single word: "Unreal."

"You need to heed Reba's advice," Lakesh insisted. "We can't have you out there in the field when your own health is at stake."

Grant paced wearily into the room, using a well-placed desk to help him balance. "I heard everything. Brigid says there ain't going to be much 'field' left unless you get the Mantas scrambled. Something about a virus being distributed."

Lakesh peered past Grant to scowl at the samurai woman. "And you agreed to this?" he queried.

"Grant is not one to sit out of a fight," Shizuka stated. "He is a warrior—he goes where he is needed, just as my ancestors did before me."

"If I sit this one out," Grant added, "it sounds like I may as well sit everything else out, and wait for the end of the human race."

Lakesh looked from Shizuka to Grant, trying to read their thoughts. "Are you certain that you can pilot a Manta in your current condition, friend?" he asked.

"Shizuka will take the backseat," Grant said. "She'll keep me on my toes. Besides, you do need me, don't you?"

Edwards rubbed a hand over his almost-bare scalp. "The Deathbird option is too slow," he said. "Two Mantas gives us at least a fighting chance of reaching everything in time. If the man says he's up to it."

Lakesh's gaze swept the room, taking in the concern on everyone's face for their brave colleague. "Reba, I want you to provide Grant with whatever suppressors and medication he needs to fight through this," he said. "No drowsiness, no side effects.

"Shizuka, are you capable of administering the drugs while Grant is in flight? If not, I will send Reba in your place."

"I am," Shizuka confirmed.

"Grant, get to the hangar bay now," Lakesh said. "I shall brief you on the way." He called across the room, "Brewster, send a message through to have Grant's Manta armed and fired up. I want it ready to launch in ten minutes."

"I'll aim for six," Philboyd stated, tapping his internal comms unit to life.

The personnel hurried to their tasks, with Shizuka scampering along beside DeFore as they made their way to the medical wing. DeFore was running through what they would need and explaining to Shizuka exactly how each drug was administered and in what proportions and what circumstances. She took a moment to ask why Dr. Kazuko had allowed Grant to leave his bed, and the silent look of fiery determination on Shizuka's face told her all she needed to know.

Grant and Lakesh split from them a few paces down the main corridor, hurrying to the bank of elevators that would speed them to the Cerberus hangar bay. Edwards trotted along beside them as Lakesh brought Grant up to speed.

"We'll provide more information while you're en route," Lakesh said, as he whipped through the task parameters.

"Just so long as you can find me the target," Grant told him, "let me worry about the details."

When the elevator arrived, Edwards placed a firm hand on Grant's shoulder. "Good to have you aboard, Grant. What you're doing—that's brave as hell."

Grant shrugged, offering up a resigned smile. "Yeah, well—Shizuka had that look in her eye. She can be pretty persuasive," he admitted as the elevator doors slid closed.

Cobaltville, Delta Level

BRIGID HALTED BEFORE the magistrate, wishing she still had her blaster within easy reach in the hip holster. The mag was pointing at her face as if in recognition, as a hygiene crew rushed past on the skyway, off to deep-clean an overburdened storage unit.

But then the mag seemed to think better of it and gestured instead to his own face, hidden as it was behind the stern helmet of his uniform. "Your face," he said. "It's covered in something. I think maybe you need to wash it. You can't be on this level looking like that—hygiene standards."

Brigid almost laughed with relief, but instead turned away and glanced at her reflection in the window of the skywalk. Though the reflection was not ideal, she could tell that her face was smeared with soot and her head was filthy. Little wonder no one had recognized her from her hair. Its vibrancy had been dulled almost to black with the soot she had been covered with in the smoky hangar.

"Whoever thought dirt would save my ass," she muttered as she hurried down the corridor, away from the patrolling mag. The words made her think of something else, too—something about their mystery foe and the mask he wore, the way his pillow was still sealed in a vacuum wrap.

Beta Level

KANE STEPPED INTO the waiting elevator the moment the metal doors slid open, urgent to get off the public street and out of sight before someone challenged him.

As he entered the car he stopped, utterly astonished by what he saw there. The interior of the freight elevator had been sprayed with bullets, the floor was covered in shell casings and a random pattern of pockmarks crossed the floor, walls and ceiling where someone had been using the elevator for target practice.

"Looks like they've been having a party without me," he muttered, pressing the coded keypad and requesting Alpha Level.

The doors closed and the elevator began its smooth ascent.

Cerberus

TWO IDENTICAL bronze-hued aircraft shot into the morning sky over the Bitterroot Mountains in Montana, streaking from the hidden hangar bay that served the Cerberus redoubt. The pair were fabled Mantas, aircraft designed in ancient prehistory by an alien race, and capable of phenomenal acceleration and other feats, including subspace travel.

They were constructed from a bronzy metal whose liquid sheen glimmered in the early morning sunlight. Their graceful design consisted of flattened wedges with swooping wings curving out to either side of the body, in mimicry of the seagoing manta, a look that had spawned their popularized name, Manta craft. Each one's wingspan was twenty yards, its body length was almost fifteen feet, but it was the beauty of the design that was breathtaking, an effortless combination of every principle of aerodynamics wrapped up in a gleaming, burnt-gold finish. The surface of each craft was decorated with curious geometric designs; elaborate cuneiform markings, swirling glyphs and cup-and-spiral symbols. Each vehicle featured an elongated hump in the center, the only indication of a cockpit.

Behind them, twin Deathbirds were only just launching from the Cerberus hangar. They were much slower than the Mantas, but would provide what backup they could if anything should go wrong.

Watching over the monitors in the redoubt ops room, the Cerberus staff let loose an impulsive cheer as the four craft rocketed from the base.

"And they're away!" Philboyd cried out.

INSIDE ONE OF those sleek Mantas, Grant sat in the pilot's seat, his head encased in an almost spherical flight helmet that matched the bronze hue of the craft's exterior. The helmet, attached to the seat and locked in place, not only masked his face, but fed a detailed heads-up data stream to him from the advanced scanning system that the Manta employed. Shizuka was seated behind him, and she watched carefully as his hands played over the rudimentary control board that operated the vessel. This was not the whole control system, she knew. Far more decisions were made by the pilot directly through the helmet, utilising the concentrated feed of the heads-up data.

"How are you feeling, Grant-san?" she asked, reaching forward to stroke one of his muscular arms.

"Still awake," he said. "You know, I actually feel pretty good, getting out here again after that crap laid me out. How long was I out for, anyway?"

"After the initial infection? Twenty-seven hours."

"Long enough, then," Grant said, goosing more power to the air pulse engines that drove the graceful, slope-winged Manta.

PILOTING THE COMPANION craft, Edwards checked his displays for a few seconds, watching Grant's Manta for any signs of trouble, such as erratic flying.

After a moment, Edwards activated his commtact and hailed him. "You okay in there, boss?" he asked.

"Metaphorical wind in my hair," Grant replied over the linked commtact. "I'm fine."

"Metaphorical hair…!" Edwards chided, before bringing his Manta around in a tight arc that would put it in line with the first of the two deadly Deathbirds. "You okay to handle Mandeville?"

"If I need help, I'll hail you," Grant promised.

The graceful Mantas turned east, two bronze lightning streaks rushing across the cerulean skies.

Alpha Level

DEPAUL STEPPED OVER the last corpse, making his way to the sealed doors that led into Baron Cobalt's suites. He would face him now, bring final judgment to this figure of law who had so failed the people he ruled.

The door needed a pass to enter and DePaul was momentarily stymied, until he grabbed a blood-smeared card from one of the magistrates. He swiped the pass through the reader, his sense of anticipation rising as the armaglass doors slid apart.

DePaul stepped inside, suddenly conscious of the weight of the final judgment ready to flow to his wrists, like blood flowing through his veins. A short flight of four steps led up into the baronial suite. The room was well appointed, with a panoramic window on three sides, floor-to-ceiling, looking out over the towers of Cobaltville. A figure leaped up from the couch as De-

Paul stepped through the armaglass doors—a middle-aged man with iron-gray hair running over his ears, his pate bald. The man wore a silk dressing gown and looked rather overfed.

"Who the hell do you think—" he began, but De-Paul stopped him with a wave of his gloved hand as he ascended the stairs.

"Where is Baron Cobalt?" he asked in his eerily filtered voice.

"What? I—"

The sin eater materialized in DePaul's hand and he fired immediately, sending a bullet straight into the man's gut. He tottered back to the couch, blood blossoming on his silk robe.

"Where is Cobalt?" DePaul pronounced again, holding the pistol trained on the figure on the couch.

"He—he's gone," the man said. "I'm DeSouza. I—I've been..."

DePaul shot him again, cutting him off in midflow. The man grunted, a second wound appearing high in his chest, two inches left of his heart.

"Where is Cobalt?" DePaul demanded again.

DeSouza was breathing heavily now and there was sweat on his forehead, terror in his wide-eyed gaze. "He left," he gasped. "They all left. All the...all the barons."

DePaul watched the man through the lenses. He could tell that he was not lying. And there was something more, too—did he recognize this man? DeSouza, DeSouza... The name was familiar from way back, when he had been a rookie here in Cobaltville.

"Psych Division," DePaul declared, making the word an accusation.

The man bleeding on the couch was drifting out of consciousness, but he looked up at the words. "What?"

"You were Psych Division," DePaul said. He remembered the man now. DeSouza had performed the psych evaluation that had got him dropped from active duty. Of course, he had been thinner then, with more hair— curly, thick and black. But the eyes—those penetrating little pig eyes were just the same.

DeSouza's head was lolling atop his shoulders and he seemed to be having trouble focusing. "Baron Cobalt changed," he said, his voice weakening, "...left us. The barons all changed...leaving the villes...in chaos. Reports...of anarchy taking hold, in Snakefishville... Thuliaville. We...couldn't let that...happen here. Not to Cobalt...ville."

Through the artificial barrier of his emotionless mask, DePaul watched the man speak, taking in his words.

"The loss of a baron," DeSouza continued, "is...crippling. It...would...have...destroyed us. So we made...a new baron...for the public."

"You?" DePaul asked.

DeSouza's head lolled as if it were adrift at sea. "Kept...pretense. Remained...unified."

DePaul shot him through the forehead, the bullet drilling at the spot just above where his untamed white eyebrows met. DeSouza slumped back, dead.

No baron to kill. DePaul had come all this way and there was no baron to kill. He was too late.

Chapter 34

Kane waited impatiently for the bullet-riddled elevator to complete its ascent to Alpha Level. He had been here before, years ago, back when he had been a magistrate. It still sent chills through him, recalling the way it had felt to meet Baron Cobalt back then. It was a mystical, semireligious experience, the hybrid baron partially hidden behind gossamer drapes, the better to hide his alienness, that he was something *other*. That was before Kane had discovered the true nature of the barons, and before all nine of them had evolved into the hateful Annunaki overlords, thanks to a genetic shunt from an orbiting spaceship called *Tiamat*.

Kane shook his head, piecing his strange life story together. "If I only knew then what I know now," he muttered.

He was prepared to be challenged by mags when the elevator doors opened, but instead was met by a scene of carnage. The corridor walls were splattered with blood. Two of the magistrates who stood guard over the entryway looked as if they had been gutted, and black tears smeared their cheeks. Kane marched past them, drawing his sin eater as he hurried along the corridor toward the baron's suites.

Kane stopped at a junction in the hallway and listened, stilling his thoughts, calming his breath, the old point-man sense searching for signs of danger. There was nothing, just silence. If he hadn't seen the abomination near the elevator, he would have thought he had been wrong to come here. But no—the lunatic in the fright mask was here; he felt certain of that.

Assured there was no one waiting around the corner of the corridor, Kane stepped out, sweeping the sin eater before him. Two more magistrates lay crumpled on the floor, dead. Behind them, the elaborate twin doors to the baron's chambers were open.

Kane paced toward them, looking left and right, wary of an ambush.

DePaul COULD NOT believe it.

Empty. It was impossible, and yet the baron's suite was empty. Just that fraud from Psych here, posing as the baron, living a lie to quell the public and apparently keep Cobaltville at peace.

DePaul had checked the complex of rooms that made up the suite, confirmed that there was no one here other than himself and DeSouza's corpse. No baron to receive sentence, no final judgment to dispense.

DePaul stopped his angry pacing, stood before the vast bank of windows with their panoramic view of Cobaltville, its golden towers a thing of wonder and of magic when seen from so far above.

The plague would still be unleashed. Even now, parcels were winging their way across the land to begin the final judgment of the human race, to purge all evil from this wicked world.

But it felt an empty gesture now, with no baron to pass sentence on, to share in his hideous victory.

HE HAD MET Baron Cobalt once, nineteen years ago, when DePaul was eight years old. Salvo and another magistrate, Hunt, who had lost a hand and worked now as a trainer in the magistrate school, had placed goggles over DePaul's eyes before accompanying him to a hidden elevator that needed two keys. The goggles blocked DePaul's sight, leaving him reliant on his other senses instead. The men did not tell him where they were going, only that he had shown remarkable potential in his classes.

Is this a reward? DePaul wanted to ask, but he knew better than to voice the question. Hunt could turn cruel at the drop of a hat, while Salvo was an unknown quantity to the child, but had a reputation for impatience.

The elevator rose, ascending far above Beta Level. It hissed to a pneumatic stop, and Salvo urged DePaul away from the wall, where he had been ordered to stand when they had entered.

The boy walked forward, feeling the slick floor beneath the soles of his standard-issue boots, footsteps echoing hollowly. He guessed they were in a large room with a high ceiling.

"From this point on," Salvo ordered in a harsh whisper, "no talking."

DePaul nodded, though he had not spoken for the whole of the elevator ride. One of his escorts took him by the elbow and steered him blindly forward. The echoes of his footfalls became muffled, and the pressure beneath them changed as he stepped onto thick carpet. At the same time, a scent caught his nostrils, tickling them. It was incense, DePaul guessed, heavy in the air, spicy and thick.

The man holding his elbow drew him to a halt, and

DePaul smelled the way the incense became more heady, almost overpowering.

Then came a noise, the steady beat of a gong. It chimed thirteen times, like a church bell cutting the night.

"Remove the goggles," Salvo ordered in a low voice, close to his ear.

DePaul reached for the goggles and slipped them up to his scalp, automatically narrowing his eyes against the expected brightness that must be waiting for him. But there was no brightness. Instead, the room he was standing in was gloomy, with incense trails thick in the air, a deep Persian carpet beneath his boots. Figures moved all around the room, and DePaul recognized the shapes as men, though he did not know who they were.

Suddenly, a spotlight of dazzling white light seared down from above, its brilliance almost blinding DePaul and forcing him to shy away, reaching to cover his eyes.

"Stand up straight, boy," Trainer Hunt ordered in his gruff voice.

DePaul's arms went back down to his sides and he stood, flinching in the brilliant white light. As he stood there, squinting through the dazzling haze, a voice spoke from somewhere in the room, one with a musical lilt that perfectly matched the pitch of the chimes he had heard a few moments before.

"You are DePaul, a servant of order, a soldier of the ville, a warrior of the baron."

DePaul gasped, felt a rising irrational fear well up within his chest. He could see a dim shape standing before him, but it was still partially hidden, seen through a semitranslucent curtain with shimmering flecks of gold in its weave, catching the light.

DePaul realized that the room had fallen into silence after the voice had spoken, and he suspected he was expected to say something in response. "I am Trainee De-Paul, sir," he said, failing to keep the scared tremor from his voice. Then he recited his magistrate induction number, which he knew by heart, even at eight years old.

The figure behind the curtain swayed, almost as if floating underwater. DePaul had the impression of pale golden skin, slim arms, a domed head and lean cheeks. Then he saw just a glimpse of the eyes, alien, indefatigable.

"You pledge allegiance to the ville," the figure behind the curtain trilled, "but remember—you belong solely to me. From the day of your birth, you have belonged to me, as did your father and grandfather."

DePaul bowed his head. "I am yours, my baron. I carry only your law in my heart."

The figure behind the gauze curtain swayed gently, watching the child through the golden weave until the dark goggles were replaced over DePaul's eyes and he was led away.

DePaul would dream of that moment every night for the next six months, replaying it over and over in his mind's eye. But he had never been able to speak of it to anyone, for while he was excited to have been chosen to meet the baron, he had never known such fear as he had that day. It was a fear he had been forced to bury deep in his soul. And a fear unresolved becomes ambition or hatred—or both.

DEPAUL'S THOUGHTS TURNED back to the present as he heard the noise behind him. He turned, commanding the sin eater automatically into his hand. The twin armaglass doors to the suite were open as he had lcft them, and there was a figure stepping through them. It was the man who had infiltrated his subterranean laboratory two days earlier—the ex-magistrate fugitive called Kane.

"Drop it!" Kane yelled as he ran into the room.

DePaul was already blasting, his finger squeezing the trigger and sending a stream of bullets at the charging figure.

Kane leaped over the couch with its corpse occupant, dived down behind a table as DePaul's blasts followed him. Bullets clipped furniture and drilled themselves into walls, shattering a vase and destroying the glass in two picture frames.

Kane blasted a shot from the floor, sending the bullet up toward the fright mask face of DePaul, where he stood framed by the massive windows. The bullet went wide, and DePaul ducked away with a swirl of flapping coattails.

Kane scrambled after him, springing out from under the table and blasting at the retreating figure. The bullet struck DePaul in the back, rebounding from his armored coat with a shower of sparks.

"You need to stop this now," Kane called after him. "It's over. Your virus is being eliminated before it can hurt anyone else."

The figure in the fright mask disappeared through an open door in the suite.

Kane took a moment to check his blaster, then weaved a zigzag path as he hurried toward the open door. Now it gets tricky, he thought as he halted there. Here was an ideal place for an ambush, and he had no choice but to walk straight into it. No choice except…

Kane plucked a flash-bang from a utility pouch at his belt, primed it and flung it ahead of him, into the next room.

A moment's pause and then the device went off, sending a blast of light and noise rocking through the baronial chamber.

There had been no time to use the earplugs, but even with the ringing in his ears, Kane heard an exclamation of pain from the next room, and he ran through to meet his foe.

DePaul was standing against the nearest wall, a gloved hand over his face, covering the circular lenses of his mask.

"Your war's over, bub," Kane told the nightmarish figure. "Whatever you think you're doing, it ends now."

"Never," DePaul spit back. "I shall cleanse crime from the world, Kane—a magistrate like never before, eradicating crime on a biological level."

Both men fired in that same instant.

Still dazzled as he was from the flash-bang, DePaul's shot went wild, whizzing over Kane's shoulder before impacting against the floor-to-ceiling panoramic windows that surrounded the room. The reinforced glass fractured into cobwebs.

Kane's shot was true. The bullet traveled the four feet between the nose of the sin eater and the beaklike nose of his adversary, splitting the appendage into a cluster of razor-sharp splinters. Several of those shards flew back into DePaul's suddenly revealed face, imbedding there with an immediate swell of blood. The other flecks peppered the wall behind the ex-magistrate like a shotgun burst.

After the shots, DePaul just stood there, reaching a

gloved hand up to his ruined mask and feeling his exposed face for the first time in an age. With the destruction of the beaklike protrusion, a whole chunk of the mask had fallen away, leaving most of the bottom half of his face and one eye exposed. The beak had filtered the air, and without it, the smells of incense and human life were oddly pungent. His skin was pale above the dark beard he had grown over his chin, his eyes a vibrant blue like sapphires. He looked haunted, the planes of his face cruelly angular, the skin washed out where it had not been touched by sunlight in a decade.

"It's over," Kane said, training his sin eater on the dark figure's chest.

DePaul's hand probed the ruined mask, moving more frantically by the second, smudging the blood that was leaking from his cuts. "No," he muttered. "No."

"Drop your weapon," Kane ordered.

DePaul pulled his hand away from his face, staring at the blood that stuck to his glove. His other hand drooped loosely at his side, still clutching the forgotten sin eater. "My blood," he said incredulously. "I'm…" He looked up at Kane then, horror on his face. "I can't be out like this. The germs. Don't you realize that?"

"Last chance," Kane sneered, still holding his blaster on the mysterious figure. "Drop your weapon or I'll be forced to drop you."

Sudden anger flashed across DePaul's face—anger and realization—and he rushed at Kane, bringing his own pistol up to blast the Cerberus man. "I'm exposed, you stupid fugitive scum," he howled.

Kane shot, sending a single bullet directly into DePaul's chest. It slammed against his armored jacket, knocking the wind out of him even as he blasted back.

DePaul's shot missed, striking the window behind Kane for the second time, drawing another instant cobweb there. DePaul was still running, charging at Kane even as the Cerberus warrior leaped back. With his eyes still reeling with the effects of the flash-bang, DePaul missed him entirely, and kept running for the dark figure he could see before him—the figure reflected in the fractured glass, his own dark reflection.

Kane shouted a warning as DePaul struck the window, still screaming insanely about being exposed, being dirty. He hit the pane at a dead run and, already weakened, the glass broke apart like wet tissue paper, disintegrating into a million tiny fragments as it rattled in its frame.

The window disappeared and so did DePaul, falling through the levels between the network of skywalks, past Beta, past Cappa, past Delta, past Epsilon.

Kane ran to the gaping hole and watched as DePaul's plummeting figure fell farther, dropping down through the gap where two service walkways met, disappearing at last into the shadowy districts of the Tartarus Pits, hundreds of feet below. Kane winced as the man disappeared from view. No one could survive a fall like that. No one.

Chapter 35

It had taken forty-five minutes to reach the rogue Death-bird. In all that time, Grant pushed his Manta's engine to its absolute limit, challenging the craft's specs as he determined to locate and disarm their prey. He knew he had to get it out of the sky. The alternative simply did not bear thinking about.

Sitting behind him, Shizuka watched as blue sky and clouds hurried past the portholes. She felt the swift passage as a weight against her body, the permanent sensation of being dragged backward where she was pressed against her seat. The Manta had internal gravity compensators, but even they could do only so much to alleviate the sensation—and besides, at least it reminded both her and Grant just how urgent this mission was.

"Grant-san, are you okay?" Shizuka asked. "You've been quiet a long time."

"Just concentrating," he assured her.

"Concentrate louder," Shizuka pleaded. "I need to know you haven't dropped off to sleep." She meant it. Before they had left Cerberus, physician Reba DeFore had entrusted Shizuka with a hypo of adrenaline, the kind that was used to combat anaphylactic shock in an extreme allergic reaction. If Grant's concentration should dip, Shizuka was tasked to administer the shot, keep him awake long enough to finish the mission.

A voice came over the commtact as they crossed what had once been the Colorado-Oklahoma border. It was Brewster Philboyd, tracking their progress via satellite. "You're two minutes out," he stated. "Clear skies."

Hidden inside the flight helmet, Grant's eyes narrowed. He was sensing the proximity of his target now, waiting to strike like a cobra. His index finger stroked against the grip of the joystick, where the trigger for the Manta's weapons was located.

Then he saw it down below, the familiar blocks of buildings, outlander strip farms located in the no-man's land between villes, the places where magistrates did not bother to look. The Deathbird was two hundred feet from the ground, hovering low, following its pre-programmed path to Mandeville.

Grant gritted his teeth in frustration as he watched the vehicle and its deadly cargo speed through the sky over the farmland. He couldn't take the shot yet, not until he could be certain that no one would get hurt—or worst still, infected.

He eased off the throttle and hung back, waiting for the chance to strike.

ROUGHLY SEVENTY MILES north, Edwards was closing in on his own target, his Deathbird escort many miles behind him, unable to keep pace.

The rogue Deathbird—the one operating via artificial intelligence—was following a straight line, five hundred feet above the surface. It took a few moments for Edwards to see it, its dark lines camouflaged against the shadows of the forest far below. Forest was good, he thought—forest meant no debris was going to wind up crashing through someone's dining table or land on their kid's lap.

He flipped the safety cover up on the joystick, primed the Manta's sidewinder missiles as he waited for the target to lock in place. One strike—that was all it would take.

"Let's call it a day and break for an early lunch," he muttered as he depressed the trigger and sent twin sidewinders hurtling from the missile bays located in the Manta's wings.

The missiles streaked through the air, rushing ahead of the bronze-hued craft in search of their deadly target. At the last moment, the Deathbird attempted some rudimentary evasive manoeuvres, the artificial intelligence that was piloting it acknowledging the threat. But by then it was too late. The first missile slipped by twenty feet from the target as the Deathbird helicopter jounced and rolled, but Edwards's follow-up snagged it right in the belly, obliterating the dark chopper in a burst of flame.

EVENTUALLY, KANE became conscious of the feel of the winds batting against him as he stood at the open window on Alpha Level. The wind tangled in his hair and threatened to send him over the side in pursuit of De-Paul, so he stepped away, commanding the sin eater back to its hidden holster.

"Baptiste, you have news?" he called, activating his commtact.

"I'm safe," Brigid responded a moment later. "Made my way back to the refuge. Got a little bit of soot all over, as well as a few scrapes. Colin's here patching me up now. You?"

"I'm finished. Just had a lesson in that old saw," Kane said, "of how it takes all kinds of crazy to make a world."

"The plague man?" Brigid asked.

"Fell out a window," Kane said. "Alpha Level."

"Ouch."

"Yeah," he agreed. "That's a lot of fall for one guy."

There was a momentary pause, and then Kane heard Brigid speak again over the commtact, only she suddenly sounded breathless. "Kane, I think we have your perp," she said.

"You what?" Kane asked, taken aback.

"Crowd gathering down here, couple of streets over," Brigid explained. "Someone just came in the refuge and told us that a guy fell from the high towers. I'm going to check it out."

"You do that," Kane replied, feeling a little sickened at what his partner would discover when she went looking. He couldn't envisage what a man who fell three hundred feet would look like, but he guessed it wasn't a lot like a man at the end.

Kane made his way to the baron's exclusive elevator and prepared to descend. He didn't belong here on Alpha Level. Just being here was making him feel... well, *dirty*.

"HELLFIRE," GRANT CURSED as he continued to track the Deathbird.

The aircraft was continuing its low-flying passage across what should be empty terrain. Should be, but wasn't. A convoy of vehicles streaked by below, following a winding road across the hilly ground. The Deathbird and its deadly cargo hovered over them at not inconsiderable speed, its shadow crossing theirs as it passed by.

Grant did a quick mental calculation, figured how far the debris would fall when he blasted it, held his nerve and waited.

Ten seconds. Twenty. Fifty. It all took so long before he could be certain that the fallout wouldn't brain someone or dunk them in the path of that dreadful virus, a strain of which was still running through his own system, forced into remission by the radiation therapy.

AFTER PHILLIPS HAD finished patching her up, Brigid Baptiste made her way through the winding alleyways of the Tartarus Pits until she stood with the massed crowd staring at DePaul's dead body. Calling it a body was charitable; the man had fallen so far and landed so hard that all he really was was a smear in ragged armor. But Brigid recognized that armor, and she knew now why he had worn it.

It hadn't been for protection from bullets—that had been a happy bonus when he had come up against Cerberus and later the magistrates in Cobaltville. No, he wore that suit out of fear—sealed armor, a mask with its filter system purifying the air he breathed. Brigid knew, maybe not for certain but certain enough, that the man had been a germaphobe, terrified of touching the outside world with all its impurities and bacteria and germs.

It all made a kind of deranged sense.

THE DEATHBIRD WAS over open ground now, flying low over a patch of scrubland where plants grew wild and the grass was higher than a magistrate's eye. Grant watched through the heads-up display, waiting for the targeting reticles to line up and hold on the unmanned Deathbird.

It took an instant—a very long instant, the kind that seemed to last almost an eternity—and then the reticles went green as the target locked in place.

Grant stroked the fire button, ejected a single sidewinder missile that streaked away from his Manta in a burst of white-hot propellant. He held his breath as the bomb raced toward its target, watched as the Deathbird tried to evade it, all too late to do any good.

Then the chopper exploded as the missile struck, its dragonfly-shaped chassis transformed into a cloud of metal splinters in less time than it takes to tell.

"Did it," Grant said, his tone laced with disbelief. "Blew up that sucker good."

Congratulations came immediately over his commtact, and at the same moment, Shizuka leaned forward and stroked his shoulder. "Well done, Grant-san," she said. "Now let's go home."

He nodded in agreement. "I could sleep for a week," he admitted.

The Manta streaked past the cloud of metal before rising and turning away, heading back toward the Cerberus redoubt many miles to the north and west. The threat was over.

Chapter 36

The Cerberus warriors disappeared into the shadows after that, making their way back to the redoubt via various means, keeping clear of the authorities and avoiding too many difficult questions.

Cobaltville would recover. Colin Phillips, under instruction from Brigid—who passed it on from Reba DeFore—led the treatment of those who had been infected by DePaul's final judgment virus. It was deadly, yes, but only if it went untreated. With medical know-how, radiation therapy and a staunch supply of antibiotics, the plague could be held at its early stages, so long as the doctors moved quickly enough. Phillips made sure that they did. In all, sixteen people died from contracting the virus, and another two dozen—mostly magistrates—had been killed during DePaul's brief reign of terror. It could have been so much worse.

Kane was glad to get away from Cobaltville. He had been born there and had lived there for the first thirty-two years of his life, but the place felt like a trap now, a prison. Working with Cerberus had taught him a lot, but he realized now that the most important lessons were the ones he had happened upon by himself. Maybe it was true what they said—that you could never go home again.

Brigid had returned to the interphaser and jumped

home without waiting for Kane, taking the jump-board with her. Kane had assured her over the commtact that he would make his own way there, and would call for a lift when he needed one. Two days passed before he made the call, and when he did it was Edwards who came to pick him up in a Deathbird helicopter.

Grant had returned to base straightaway, where he was treated to more radiation therapy and a course of antibiotics to clear all infection from his system, and confined to bed for the rest of the month under strict doctor's orders. The orders were not anywhere near as strict as Shizuka's, who told him in no uncertain terms that stopping a potential plague outbreak was only once a valid excuse for endangering your own life.

"Next time I'll come up with something better," Grant promised her, and he was rewarded with a reluctant smile.

Thus, it wasn't until seventy-two hours later that all of CAT Alpha were back at Cerberus to compare notes. They met in Grant's recovery room, where the big man was lying in bed reading a book of ancient Japanese philosophy.

"Hey there, hero," Kane cheered as he entered the room. "How's life, lying on your back doing nothing?"

Grant looked up from the book of philosophical musings and smiled. "To be honest, I've reread this page eight times over and it's still not going in. Shizuka laps this stuff up, though, so I think it must be me."

Kane looked over his shoulder before striding over to the bed. "I'm guessing from that comment that Shizuka isn't around, then?"

"Ah, your point-man sense never fails, does it?" Grant teased. "And no, she had business at New Edo.

She'll be back before they let me out of bed. If they ever do."

Brigid joined the two of them a few minutes later, a sheaf of notes clutched under her arm and her square-framed archivist glasses perched on her nose. "Kane, I heard you were back," she said. "Thought I might find you here."

"Gotta check you've all been treating my partner right in my absence, don't I?" Kane teased by way of acknowledgment.

Brigid made a show of smelling the air around Kane and pulling a face. "You need to wash," she said, "or you'll set his recovery back two weeks."

"Hey, he's only been laid up three days!" Kane objected.

"Exactly," Brigid retorted with a brief but genuine smile.

"So, what do we have on the plague man?" Kane asked.

"A case isn't over until you have the name, is it?" Brigid said. "Well, I have bad news—we don't know who he was, only that he was probably a magistrate, like you said."

"And that's it?"

"That's it. I think he was probably suffering from mysophobia," she stated.

"Myso-what-now?" Kane and Grant asked in unison.

"Mysophobia," Brigid said. "He was germaphobe. That explains the suit and protective mask."

"And I thought he was just a nut," Kane opined.

"Well," Brigid said, rolling her eyes. "I think his mysophobia became psychologically muddled with his magistrate training, so that his obsession with crime became twisted with his fear of infection. So he wasn't stopping crime," she told Kane. "He was cleansing the world of a disease called crime. Subtle difference, but an important one."

Kane shrugged. "You say potato," he said in a sing-song voice.

Grant interjected before the two of them could continue to bait each other. "So what did you guys get up to while I was stuck here?" he asked.

"We cleaned up," Kane said.

Brigid shot him a wicked look.

* * * * *

JAMES AXLER

DEATH LANDS®

HIVE INVASION

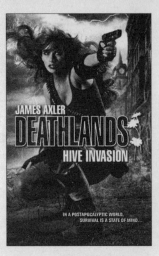

HARNESSED MINDS

Desperate to find water and shelter on the barren plains of former Oklahoma, Ryan and his team come upon a community that appears, at first, to be peaceful. Then the ville is attacked by a group of its own inhabitants— people infected with a parasite that has turned them into slave warriors for an unknown overlord. The companions try to help fend off the enemy and protect the remaining population, but when Ryan is captured during a second ambush, all hope seems lost. Especially when he launches an assault against his own crew.

Available January 2015 wherever books and ebooks are sold.

GDL120